LAST PORT OF CALL

THE QUEENSTOWN SERIES - BOOK 1

JEAN GRAINGER

GOLD HARP MEDIA

To my mother, Hilda. My closest ally, biggest fan and dearest friend.

CHAPTER 1

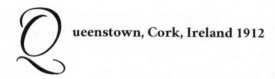ueenstown, Cork, Ireland 1912

'YOU SAID we could go down. You promised, Mammy.' Harp Delaney thought she might have sensed a crack in her mother's normally stern exterior. Rose was peeling potatoes at the large sink in the basement kitchen. The room was warm and welcoming and smelled of baking and soda crystals.

'I did not indeed promise any such thing. You see it fine from the top window, don't you? What business have we down there, with all sorts coming and going? Now it's more in our line to take down the net curtains on the top floor – they're as grey as smoke, so they are. Go on with you now, and I won't tell you again.'

Harp knew better than to contradict her mother; she would get nowhere. She trudged upstairs to get the curtains, deep in thought. She could try Mr Devereaux, see if he'd take her, but he never went anywhere. In all of her twelve years, she'd never once seen him leave the huge house on the cliff overlooking the port of Queenstown. She thought he would understand, though, why she wanted to actually be there, to see it in person. She could watch from the window, of course she could. The Cliff House was the best house in the whole town. It commanded the best view of the entire harbour of Cork, the islands of Spike and Haulbowline, the headlands of Roches Point on one side and Crosshaven on the other, jutting out, keeping guard over the entrance to the second biggest natural harbour in the whole world. But to be down at the quay, to see that magnificent unsinkable ship looming up out of the water, that would be really something. Millions of people left Ireland from Queenstown; it was the biggest and busiest port in the country, and for centuries people had set sail from it to the New World, some as prisoners in chains, some as free men and women.

They say it's unsinkable, the biggest ship in the world. It's so big it has to stay out in the bay and the people have to be brought on and off by tender. It was built up in Belfast, and already it has been to France and England and now it is coming here and then going all the way across the Atlantic to America. She wanted to feel the excitement. Imagine *Titanic*, the pride of the White Star Line, being there, in their home town, today.

Queenstown had spoken of little else since the arrival was announced. Every child in her class knew. The ship would leave Southampton, then go on to Cherbourg in France and then Queenstown. She smiled. The teacher said Cherbourg wrong – with a hard 'ch' at the start, like 'chair', instead of the correct 'sh' sound, and 'bourg' pronounced like 'berg' – but she didn't correct him; she never did. To do so would earn her nothing but slaps for impertinence. And anyway, the others didn't like it – they thought she was showing off – so she kept her own counsel most of the time. They thought her strange enough as it was.

She knew the correct pronunciation and could have explained it in English or in French had she been asked, but Master John McTernan never asked and she never volunteered. Her teacher was nice enough, and he was a good teacher considering most of the class barely opened a book once they left the schoolyard, but Harp wasn't like that. She wasn't like anyone, she thought ruefully. She'd tried so often, more when she was younger, to blend in with the other children, but she never managed to become one of them. She said the wrong things and she looked odd too, and so eventually she stopped trying to make them like or accept her. She sat in class each day and did the work assigned. She got top marks on her tests, and her homework was always completed perfectly and in full.

But the only real learning she did was in Mr Devereaux's sitting room overlooking the bay. There, she was in heaven, reading Dickens or Austen or Proust. Mr Devereaux was like her; he didn't say much. But he didn't seem to mind her being in his room, reading quietly, while he pored over his pages of prime numbers or chemistry tables. She wasn't sure what he did exactly, but it seemed by the look of concentration on his face to be very important. He didn't work at anything, though. He'd been born at the Cliff House, then the family went to Japan, where old Mr Devereaux had a posting with the British government, and from there he went to boarding school in England and then back here. That's what rich Protestants did, not that Mr Devereaux was religious – he had hardly been inside the door of the little church on the hill since she'd been born.

Old Mrs Devereaux died last year, and though it wasn't nice to say it, Harp was relieved. The woman had a way of looking at Harp as if she were trying to memorise her face or something. She stared but never spoke. It was very disconcerting. She was a crosspatch anyway, forever barking at Mammy and behaving like there was a whole household of staff downstairs like in the olden days, when in fact there was just Mammy now.

She should be more use, Harp supposed – some of the girls in primary school were used to doing all sorts of work around the house, lighting fires, cleaning windows – but she preferred to read. At the moment she was reading a lot of philosophy, some Greeks but mainly Immanuel Kant and Jean-Jacques Rousseau. She went through phases. Last year she'd been fascinated by medieval languages and thought she might go on to teach herself another language next. Already she could converse easily in French, English, Irish and German, so perhaps Spanish or Italian. She liked studying languages. She'd

3

learned Latin when she was eight, and it made other languages so much easier when she could understand the root word.

Sometimes, after dinner she discussed the points she discovered with her mother, and she loved how Mammy never made her feel silly. Mammy respected and listened to her opinions as if they carried as much weight as her own. Though she wasn't much use around the house, Harp knew her mammy was proud of her, and it made her warm inside.

Sometimes they talked about music. There was an old harp in the study, and Harp was teaching herself some Irish tunes. Mr Devereaux seemed to enjoy listening to her play as he read.

At night, tucked up in her little room under the eaves of the house, she would read by candlelight. She liked to read interesting things during the day, non-fiction, but before she slept, she always got lost in a novel. At the moment she was reading a story about an archaeologist who had uncovered a plot to kill an Egyptian nobleman when he read the hieroglyphics in a previously unopened tomb in the Valley of the Kings. They revealed a curse on the nobleman's family through time, all the way back to Ramesses. She'd had a marvellous time reading up about the tombs across the Nile from Luxor in Egypt and saw some truly graphic pictures of people who were now blind because of the river blindness caused by the blackfly there.

She wished Mr Devereaux spoke more. He knew so much but was very quiet. He always answered her gently when she asked him a question, but his answers were short. However, he spoke more to her and her mother than to anyone else in the world. Harp noticed he changed when her mother came in the room, seemed to straighten himself up and made eye contact with her, something he avoided doing with everyone else. Not that there were many visitors to the Cliff House, just Mr Cotter, the solicitor; Mr Byrne, the accountant who administered the Devereaux Trust; and sometimes the vicar. But if they had five visits a year from anyone, it was a lot.

Mr Devereaux had learned much as a young man in Tokyo, or Edo as it was called up until 1868. His father had been stationed there from the late 1850s up until 1875 and negotiated a series of trade and diplomatic treaties between the Japanese and the British. On the wall of the dining room was a picture of Mr Devereaux Sr aboard a British iron paddle schooner called the *Enpiroru*, presented to the Emperor of Japan from Queen Victoria.

When Mr Devereaux spoke about Japan, he became quite animated, and he would tell her of the Meiji Restoration and the subsequent move to more Western ideas that followed.

Her mother tutted that she shouldn't be bothering him, but she didn't think he minded; she didn't chatter on and on. He never mentioned the weather or other trivialities – he said something about a specific topic and then went back to his books. She found him restful and never felt pressure to speak as she did when she was out in the world. They were alike in so many ways. Each day at some point, she slipped into the library attached to his room and read quietly, often hours going by with no communication between them whatsoever.

Harp was unclear about how long her mother had been the Devereauxes' housekeeper. Since before Harp was born for sure, but the whole matter of the past was something Rose never wanted to discuss.

When Harp had asked where her daddy was after first going to school at age four – the other children demanded to know – her mother told her that he was dead and up in heaven. They had no relatives; her mother's parents were long dead too, and Harp had never met them. She didn't know why she didn't have lots of aunties and uncles and cousins like all of the boys and girls in school, but her mother shut the conversation down abruptly whenever Harp tried to raise it.

Rose answered Harp honestly on most things but sometimes said that Harp would discover whatever it was she asked about when she was older, which infuriated Harp. Sometimes her mother mentioned that she had worked in the house since she was a girl. Harp assumed she left to get married and then came back again when her husband, Harp's father, died, but the details were scant.

Harp didn't mind too much not having a father, but she wished she could have something to tell the other children at school when they asked. She felt the red-hot spotlight of their inquisition and blushed and mumbled under their gaze. If she just knew the story, she could say it for once and for all and be done with it. It was one of the many reasons they thought her odd. She knew she was. She wished she could converse easily with the others, talk about the local news or even flirt with the boys, but she couldn't. She never knew what to say, and whenever she did speak, everyone looked at her like she was mad.

It didn't help that her eyes were a strange grey colour or that her hair was a kind of reddish blond but neither straight nor curly or that she was too short or too skinny. At twelve, she noticed that most of the other girls had a burgeoning bustline, something the boys sniggered about constantly, but Harp's narrow chest remained depressingly flat. Some of the others were always going on about liking boys or liking girls, but none of that remotely interested her. Even if it did, she was no beauty, she knew that, but she wished she looked a bit more like the other girls. She was too small and thin to look remotely womanly.

In the books she read, the heroines were dark-haired sultry beauties or blond beguilers; none of them ever had that not-quite-blond, not-quite-red hair that she had. And her grey eyes were unsettling; it was never a colour you read about except on a criminal with murderous intent – not ideal on a small twelve-year-old girl. When she explained this to her mother, Mammy had kissed her head and hugged her, weeping with mirth, clearly her predicament causing nothing but hilarity.

She was never invited to the birthday teas of the other children, and she knew her mother was hurt on her behalf, but it was difficult to say why she was excluded except that she was odd.

She'd never had a friend.

Sometimes, when she was little and the other children were arranging to play together, never inviting her, she cried, asking her mother if she knew of any way she could fit in. Rose had looked so sad then, so utterly heartbroken, that Harp stopped telling her how much she minded, and after years she found she didn't really care any more. She had her home and the library and her mother, and that was all she needed.

Mixing with others was so difficult. She didn't even talk like the other children. She couldn't help using words like 'vicariously' or the hypothetical imperative. She tried to speak as they did, but it was hard and unwittingly a word would slip out and she would feel their gaze of mistrustful bewilderment once more.

'Ah, Harp,' her mother would say, smiling benignly, 'it is a fruitless quest to try to blend in when you are created to stand out. You will do great things, go to interesting places, meet fascinating people. You are destined for something other than this.' She would wave her hand to indicate either the house or the town of Queenstown; Harp was never sure.

When the time had come to go to secondary school the previous year, Rose had explained that it really wasn't for servants' children but more for the offspring of the professional classes or even the bigger shopkeepers in the town. But Harp had pleaded and her mother relented, paying the fee from her wages. Harp had hoped there might be someone there like her, someone she could befriend, but alas, no; it was more of the same. The children who attended didn't do so out of a love of learning but because they were sent there. It was disappointing.

She stood in the main upstairs bedroom, which overlooked the harbour – it had been Mrs Devereaux's room – and gazed out. Her mother had sent her up there to do something, but she'd forgotten what. She went to the small bookcase under the window. It was one she rarely visited, being full of Mrs Devereaux's choice of literature – romances – but it would do. She took a book and sat on the window seat, but even the first paragraph bored her. Simpering heroines and grumpy handsome earls dancing around each other until one or another cracked and declared passionate love – it was all so drearily monotonous. It was as if they only had one plot and swapped silly titled men and women and fancy houses in England in and out to make each book seem different. She snapped it closed and replaced it.

Mr Devereaux wouldn't allow such ridiculous books in his

personal library. He really only liked non-fiction, though he did have some old fairy story collections she'd enjoyed when she was younger. Of course, Mr Devereaux didn't collect all of the books himself. The Cliff House had been built in the 1700s, so there were some lovely antiquarian books as well. He never minded if she read them, even if the pages were delicate and yellowed with age. She treated them with the reverence they deserved.

He was her friend, she realised. He wasn't like anyone in any other way either. He was old – Mammy said he was fifty-two years old – and he wore his silver hair long and sometimes even tied back with an elastic. His skin was pale, though that was from hardly ever venturing outside, she supposed. He was small and slight and not a physically robust man.

He did look unusual, with his wide cheekbones and almond-shaped eyes. He dressed strangely too, in colourful shirts and loose trousers, and often he wore nothing on his feet, preferring to be bare-foot. 'Eccentric' was the word her mother used, though always affec-tionately. She'd taken care of him and his mother for so many years, an easy affection had grown between them. She chided him for working too late in dim light, or not wearing an extra jumper in the winter when the house was stone cold despite the fires.

It might be old and draughty, but Harp loved the Cliff House. It was by far the most imposing building in the town, a double-fronted Gothic mansion with ten bedrooms, four sitting rooms and several other rooms – libraries, salons and drawing rooms – the vast majority of which were closed and filled with furniture covered in white sheets.

It had been in the Devereaux family for generations. Mr Devereaux's great-great-grandfather built it, having made a fortune in the colonies, and those who'd once lived there were now resting in the Protestant graveyard beside the church at the top of the town. The Devereauxes were French Normans who came to Ireland after the Norman invasion of 1169, establishing themselves first in Dublin and Wexford but eventually moving to Cork. They were traders and merchants, and one notable ancestor was knighted, thus elevating the family in society and allowing the construction of such a house as the Cliff House. Where all the money went was another of the unexplained mysteries of Harp's life, since these days they lived like poor church mice. The roof leaked, the windows were rotten, and there wasn't a spare penny for repairs.

Her mother explained that Mrs Devereaux left a trust fund for the upkeep of the house and the care of Mr Devereaux, but it was a paltry sum and the remainder of her money had gone to Mr Devereaux's brother, Ralph, who was in India. Harp had never met Ralph; he'd left years before she was born and had never returned. There was a portrait on the stairs of Mr Devereaux and his brother when they were younger. Mr Devereaux looked very much like he did now, just younger, but Ralph was dashing and handsome. Harp had pointed out how attractive he was to her mother one day, but Rose had dismissed it as foolish talk and told her that it was not appropriate for her to speak of their employers in that manner.

As Harp wandered back downstairs, having forgotten to do whatever her mother had instructed her, she saw Mr Devereaux's door open. His rooms were made up of a bedroom, a sitting room and a library, all connected by double doors that he never closed. The sitting room and library had floor-to-ceiling bookshelves, and the books were arranged first by subject, then alphabetically. There were a pair of huge red leather chesterfield sofas either side of the enormous fireplace, the leather cracked on the arms, as well as three Queen Anne chairs, each upholstered in dark-green velvet, all worn now on the seat. The fireplace was red Cork marble, and the polished walnut floorboards were covered with oriental rugs Mr Devereaux's father had brought back from Japan when he retired in 1880.

Her favourite piece in that room, apart from the harp that some previous Devereaux had played years ago, was the maroon Edison Gem gramophone. It was new, and both she and Mr Devereaux loved it with its huge red horn, beautiful mahogany casing and brass handle. It featured both two- and four-minute gearing as well as a combination reproducer, which meant it could play all cylinder records.

He loved the modern jazz music coming out of America and

ordered records, which he played over and over. But the music they returned to each night was O'Carolan – sometimes a phonograph recording, and increasingly, his playing.

Harp music had soothed her to sleep since she was a baby, and one of her earliest memories was her mother lifting her upstairs to bed with the recording of 'Eleanor Plunkett' ringing peacefully in her ears.

'That's why I called you Harp,' Rose said once, in a rare moment of introspective nostalgia. 'Because I knew you would love that sound. When you were in my belly, the moment that music played, you settled.'

When she was younger, it hadn't occurred to Harp to question how her mother could listen to harp music when she was pregnant far away in another house with her husband, Harp's father, but now it did. However, like all other questions pertaining to her mother's life before coming to the Cliff House, it was shut down.

Her mother was right, though. Nothing could soothe her like the pluck of the strings, but it didn't make for an easy life. Harp was not a name, as the children at school were apt to point out; it was a thing, like a table or a chair or a bucket. And the fact that she played the very instrument she was named after was even sillier, not that anyone at school knew she could play. But it *was* her name and yet another thing about her that was unlike everyone else. She sometimes wished her mother had not been given to such a flight of fancy and just called her Kate or Hannah or Mary...anything normal.

And it wasn't as if her mother was one for mad notions – quite the opposite. If Mr Devereaux was eccentric, her mother was every inch a perfect lady. She dressed in sombre colours, every garment pressed and stitched to perfection. She never showed any flesh, except her face, which was unlined and porcelain white and framed by her perfectly set dark hair. Harp thought her mother was beautiful. Her lips formed a natural cupid's bow and were never tinted but were naturally red, her long dark eyelashes framed her brown eyes, striking-looking with her dark colouring, her cheekbones were high, and the hollows of her cheeks and her jawline were as contoured as if Michelangelo himself had sculpted her.

'Harp, come in here. I want to show you something,' Mr Devereaux called as she passed. He so rarely spoke, his voice startled her.

She stepped into his room that smelled of pipe smoke and woody cologne. Her seat by the large bay window was as it always was, ready for her, her current books in a pile on the small table beside it. His desk was pushed into the bay of the other window, piled high with papers and drawings and books open to various pages. Rose knew never to tidy it; it might look chaotic but it was perfectly ordered to him.

His needs were few. He ate whatever Rose brought up to him, and Harp sometimes wondered, if Rose didn't bring his three meals a day up to his study, would he ever stop to eat?

Because he'd been sent to school in England, as was the norm for people from his class, he spoke with a British accent, but he held that country and all it represented in disdain. Harp knew he was fiercely pro-Irish independence. He read the writings of Wolfe Tone, Robert Emmet, Charles Stewart Parnell and Daniel O'Connell, gently directing Harp to read them too. He'd not left the house since 1873, except for one reluctant visit to a doctor in London last year.

He beckoned her closer and opened a parcel that had been delivered earlier that morning as she was eating her porridge in the kitchen. It was a velvet box, the size of two decks of playing cards side by side but thicker. He handed it to her. 'It's for you. Open it.'

Should she refuse it? Her mother was anxious to always remind Harp of their position within the house, how they relied on the Devereauxes' good graces for all they had – a roof over their heads, food in their bellies – and hammered home how they should be grateful, but Harp had a different relationship with Mr Devereaux. They understood each other in a way that nobody else could. He didn't talk down to her, or make her feel like an oddity. She could be herself with him. He was an important part of her life. She could never say it, of course not, but he was. She didn't have a father, or a grandad or even an uncle, but she had Mr Devereaux and he was worth more than all of those rolled into one.

CHAPTER 2

*H*arp heard her mother's light tread on the stairs and silently prayed she wouldn't enter the room. She wouldn't approve. Sometimes she thought her mother wished Harp would spend more time downstairs and not up here filling her head.

But Harp thought all she learned in this room would prove enormously useful once she finally got out into the world. She often dreamed about where she would go – to America, Japan, Australia, China even. She longed to see the poles, north and south, and she was following the adventures of explorers making bids to reach the poles avidly. She had followed in the newspaper the story of Peary and his efforts to reach the North Pole in 1909, and the excitement when she finally heard that Amundsen had beaten Scott to the South Pole last December was still as fresh in her mind as if it were yesterday.

She gazed in wonder at the velvet box. The dark navy-blue of the velvet made the pale skin of her hands look almost translucent. Gingerly she took it from his hand, and the weight of it surprised her. There were two tiny hinges on the long side of the box, so she gripped it and opened it. Her eyes were drawn immediately to the contents. She barely registered the pale-blue silk lining, or the name 'Keane's Jewellers' written in gold inside the lid. There, nestled beautifully in the silk, a navy-blue swivel clasp ensuring it didn't budge, was the most exquisite fountain pen she'd ever seen. It was gold, with a silver nib.

'Take it out,' Mr Devereaux said softly.

She did as he asked and felt the cool weight of the pen between her fingers. And then she saw it, the engraving, the letters 'H' and 'D' fashioned to look like a harp. She was speechless. This had been tooled specially for her? She opened her mouth but no sound came out.

'Do you like it?' he asked gently.

'I...I've never seen anything as beautiful in all of my life, but it's too much, for someone like me, to have something so fine as this... H. D., for Harp Delaney. They're my initials.'

He looked solemn and shook his head. 'Harp Devereaux,' he said quietly.

'My name is Delaney...' she began. 'But it is the same initial as Devereaux, so...' She didn't want to cause offence. Perhaps he was mistaken, or maybe he wanted her to feel like she was more to him than a servant's child; that thought made her glow inside.

'I don't make mistakes,' he said quietly, guessing her thoughts. 'You're Harp Devereaux, and though your life has only had twelve short years so far, you will see many things finer than this as you fulfil your destiny.'

'But I can't take this! My mother would –' she began, and then she saw her mother, standing in the doorway. She sent up a fervent silent prayer that Rose would not take away the magic of the moment by saying something dismissive.

'What is it, Harp?' she asked, but her voice lacked its usual brusqueness.

'It's a fountain pen, a beautiful one, the most beautiful I've ever seen. And it's engraved.' She held the pen out for her mother's inspection.

Rose took it and examined it, running her index finger over the engraving. 'It is beautiful all right.' She returned it to Harp. 'See you don't lose it, and say thank you to Mr Devereaux for such an extravagant gift.'

13

'Thank you, Mr Devereaux. I will treasure it all of my life,' she said quietly, meaning every word.

'You're welcome, Harp. I'm so happy you like it. Use it to write your essays, your memoirs, whatever you want to do. You will travel far and do a great many adventurous things. I hope you'll remember me.' There was a note of regret in his voice and she longed to hug him, but her mother would most certainly not regard that as proper behaviour.

'I won't need to remember you because you'll be here, won't you?' she asked, fearful it was a going-away present of some kind.

Did she imagine it? The briefest of looks between her mother and Mr Devereaux? She was probably being fanciful.

'I will, Harp, but you won't.' He smiled slowly. 'You have a bright future far beyond the borders of Queenstown, County Cork.'

'Yes, well' – Rose began gathering the cups from his morning tea – 'if you want to see this infernal big ship, though it's just another one and we see plenty of them every day so I don't understand what all the fuss is about, you'd better get yourself downstairs and this lot washed and put away.'

'You'll take me down to see it?' Harp was incredulous. Could this day get any better?

'I will, but we're not hanging about all day, do you hear me?' She looked sternly at her daughter, a smile playing around her lips. 'Mr Devereaux thinks this is a momentous day and you should be part of the spectacle, so I'm going to take you down.'

'Thank you, Rose,' Mr Devereaux said warmly.

Harp noticed how Henry Devereaux always spoke so gently and kindly to her mother, catching her gaze as he did so, not at all as she had read about how masters addressed their servants. But it was just another aspect of her life that was out of the ordinary.

'Won't you come, Mr Devereaux? Please?' Harp asked as she stood with a tray of dirty dishes. He was the one who could truly appreciate the majesty and magnificence of the vessel. Her mother would just moan about the crowds and complain about getting coal smuts on her dress from the chimneys of the tugs that brought smaller ships in and out of the port.

'I'll see it from here, Harp. I don't think I could make it back up the hill if I went down.' She heard the sadness in his voice. 'And when you come back, you must describe it all to me in glorious colour – the sights, the sounds, the smells, everything.'

She knew why Mr Devereaux never went out – he wasn't strong enough – and she didn't press him on the subject as he was such a gentle person. But she was disappointed. Today of all days. Her class-mates would surely be around the town, watching everything, and she would have loved to have shared it with him.

Her mother left the room, taking the tray from Harp, instructing as she left, 'Run upstairs and get your outdoor boots and your coat. It's bright but chilly.'

Harp was alone with Mr Devereaux and she stood there, watching his back as he gazed out over the harbour.

'I really love the pen,' she said quietly.

He turned and his eyes were bright. His smile lit up the room. 'You are special, Harp Devereaux, and I'm very proud of you. Never forget that.'

Then he turned and faced the window once more.

CHAPTER 3

$\mathcal{B}$y the time Harp and her mother had walked down the ancient steep steps – worn in the middle from centuries of feet and several sets of which crisscrossed the steep town – to the quayside, the passengers boarding the ship had been processed through the White Star Line ticket office at the water's edge. There was a carnival atmosphere, and everyone was decked out in their Sunday best. Tinker women sold paper flowers, and their men set up stalls on street corners to repair pots and pans. Ponies and donkeys as well as horses were tethered to the railing outside the Imperial Hotel, and Harp and her mother skirted around a steaming pile of dung. Harp knew Mr O'Donovan, the manager, would have a fit if he saw it, as it was positioned at an ideal location for a guest to tread on. Draymen cursed as people walked directly in front of them as they tried to make their deliveries to the various businesses that dotted the main street. The public gardens gleamed emerald green, and the bandstand had recently been painted.

There was a brass band playing, and the sea glinted azure in the spring sunshine. The weather had been unseasonably warm and the sunshine added to the sense of gaiety. Donal Collins had opened the front window of his sweetshop and was serving ices and cones of sweets, and the smell of molten toffee made Harp's mouth water. She resisted asking, though; her mother would definitely say that eating as she walked along the street was far too unladylike.

Though her mother was a servant – and she reminded Harp often how they had nothing to their names – Rose Delaney walked with the carriage and poise of a woman of much more elevated social standing. She never drew attention to herself, but she certainly never fraternised with the other women in the town who worked in the other big houses. She cautioned Harp constantly on the perils of having notions above her station but nonetheless seemed to embody those very notions herself.

As they stepped out from the stone staircase with its high walls onto the street, they saw her. There she was, *Titanic*, the huge hull, the four black chimneys. From their vantage point at sea level, the ship looked even bigger than from the house. It was moored two miles away at Roches Point, but even at that distance, it was easy to see how it was the most celebrated ship in the world. Harp thought about the many facts she knew. The number of rivets, how many tonnes of coal it would take to make the crossing, the length from stern to bow, – she found it all fascinating.

As they walked up the street, past the hotel and into the main square where the shops bustled with business, she soaked it all up. It felt nice to be part of something, to feel connected to the town on this most auspicious of days. People were everywhere, from the roughest to the finest.

She was thinking about the three different classes of ticket, and how even the third-class passengers had napkins and menus for mealtimes, when she spotted him. Emmet Kelly. And beside him his henchmen, Jimmy Mullane and Donal Deasy. They were in her class at school and made a pastime of trying to torment her. Her mother went into the draper's for some new shoelaces as Harp stood outside.

The boys were sitting on the railing above Blackie Nolan's black-smith's forge, their legs dangling low enough that they could knock a man's hat off with their feet should they want to. The smithy was busy today, with horses throwing shoes, and the hammering and heat could be heard and felt even out on the street.

The boys looked over at her, nudging each other and giggling, caffling and fooling as always, and Harp's cheeks burned. She never told her mother about the boys at school, or the names they called her, or how they teased her for being clever.

'Hello, Harp Delaney,' Emmet called.

She looked sharply upwards, trying to intimidate them. It was not seemly for boys to be shouting at young ladies in the street.

'Are you going to America, Harp?' he sneered. 'Sure wouldn't the Yanks love you with your lovely Irish name?' He laughed as he mimicked playing the harp.

'They'd deport her for being a know-it-all,' Jimmy Mullane yelled. 'Nobody likes a show-off.'

Harp knew he was referring to the test they'd had in school the day before on the history of the harbour in front of them. She'd got one hundred percent as always, and the master had given her a gold star for her exercise book. Jimmy got five hard slaps with the switch because he got almost every question wrong, despite the master spending the whole week teaching them about the many events of Irish history associated with the port.

Donal Deasy did have the grace to look embarrassed and urged the other two to shut up, but they were on a roll.

'Oh, she's a right brainbox, *Miss* Delaney,' Emmet said, putting on a silly voice, 'but brains won't get her a husband. She's going to need something else for that.' Emmet winked and gestured with his hands that he was referring to a bosom. 'Which is, I'm afraid to say, sadly lacking.'

Harp normally did not respond to their jibes as it only encouraged them, but something about the ship sitting in all her glory in the middle of the harbour, the endless possibility it afforded those fortunate enough to have a ticket, made her brave. One day she would board such a ship, and she would travel and learn and write all about it. She might go to university, that was her dream, but whatever her future held, it did not involve staying there and seeking the approval of idiots such as these boys were.

She mustered her strength, thinking of Lady Macbeth telling her husband to screw his courage to the sticking place. She could do this; she could stand up to them. In a clear voice that she was sure they could hear, she spoke. She made no eye contact but seemed to address the air around her. '"When a true genius appears in the world, you may know him"' – she paused and allowed herself a small smile – 'or her, "by this sign, that the dunces are all in confederacy against him", *or her.*'

She looked up and shielded her eyes from the bright light. 'Dean Jonathan Swift said that,' she explained, speaking slowly so they would understand. 'I don't suppose you've heard of him?'

Before she had a chance to turn, Jimmy hooked her parasol from her hand with his foot, throwing it to Emmet, who opened it and twirled it around.

'God, you are such a weird girl. D'ya hear her, lads?' Emmet hooted and Harp felt her cheeks burn.

'Give that back,' she demanded. But her outrage only fuelled their foolishness. She should not have riled them; she knew that now. If that parasol got ruined, her mother would be furious.

Emmet threw it to Donal, who threw it to Jimmy, now perched on the pillar of the smithy's gates.

'Or what? You'll get your da after us?' Emmet jeered.

'Oh, she can't, her da is dead, *supposedly.*' Jimmy Mullane placed heavy emphasis on the last word. 'Or what about that quare hawk, Mr Devereaux?' He said the name in a poor approximation of an English accent. 'Maybe he'll come to your rescue? Maybe he's the daddy? You look just like him, Harp, all thin and creepy. Maybe your high-and-mighty ma isn't so posh after all, offering *all* the services to the master of the house, eh?' Emmet guffawed, pulling a grotesque face and wiggling his fingers menacingly. 'Is the quare hawk your papa, Harp? Is he?'

None of the boys saw Mrs Delaney emerge from the draper's, and all three were once again sitting on the bar between the pillars. Harp watched in fascinated horror as her mother came out of the shop, quick as a flash walked behind them and in rapid succession hooked each boy's trousers with the cane of her parasol, pulling them clean off the bar and landing them in the muddy puddles below. They howled as they each landed painfully on their bottoms, and Harp could scarcely believe what she'd seen.

'Come along, Harp,' her mother said briskly, picking her daughter's parasol up from the ground, making no reference whatsoever to the events of the previous two minutes. 'Don't dawdle.'

Harp had to skip along to keep up with her mother, who, though she was wearing her lovely brown suede kid boots, walked at the speed most people ran. The only sign that the exchange with the boys had meant anything were the two points of colour on her mother's high cheekbones.

Rose Delaney didn't adorn herself with powder or jewellery, and if anything, Harp had to admit she looked stern, but when she smiled, her face transformed. Harp could make her smile and so could Mr Devereaux, but almost everyone else was terrified rigid of her. Sister Alphonsus had slapped Harp when she was in high baby infants for wetting her underwear by mistake, and when Harp came home, wet and miserable, still in the same clothes but with two reddened palms from the stick to add to her woes, the nun had had a visit from Mrs Delaney she wouldn't forget in a hurry. Likewise, the butcher might have a reputation for leaving other housewives a little short if he could get away with it, but not Harp's mammy. He and all others who supplied the house knew it was wisest not to cross her. Now Emmet Kelly knew it too.

Harp hurried along the main street, taking care to keep her petticoats and skirts out of the dirt underfoot. Her mother's face was set in that way it always was when they went out, as if only the most audacious person would dare to interrupt her.

The ship dominated the skyline as the crowds milled about. One hundred twenty-three mainly third-class passengers were embarking and only eight were getting off. Of course it was the last port at which the vessel could take on mail for the United States, so the post workers had been working since the dawn to get it all ready for delivery to the ship.

Lots of people had come down from Cork for the day on the train just to see *Titanic*, and Harp realised how lucky she was to live in the most beautiful town in Ireland, maybe even the whole world, where she could see her and all the other ocean liners from her bedroom window.

St Colmans's Cathedral stood proud and majestic high over the town, daily Mass almost filling the huge church as people from all over Ireland knelt and prayed for a safe passage, a better life, and prosperity and peace for those they'd left behind. For most liner passengers, particularly those in third class, the sight of the coloured, stacked, terraced houses of Queenstown, the imposing cathedral, the green park, the bandstand and the handsome main streets were the last images of their native land they would ever have. Only a tiny percentage ever returned to Ireland again, and Harp was proud that their last view was of Queenstown. She imagined old people telling their American grandchildren about this place, pride in their voices.

Ireland was heartbreakingly beautiful, but centuries of occupation by the British had brought it to its knees economically. Harp didn't remember the famine, of course, as it was seventy years ago, but there were people who did, and the scenes at Queenstown then were inscribed indelibly on the memories of the old people. The ones who made it to Queenstown were the lucky ones. They got the price of a steerage ticket to the New World, and they boarded, half-starved and in rags, while the remains of their family either died or went to the workhouse. Harp had read about the ships that left during those years, laden down with oats, grain, livestock, whiskey, beer, as the population died of hunger.

Nobody would guess, speaking as he did with an English accent, how appalled Mr Devereaux was at how the Irish were treated. Even now he felt that Mr Redmond wasn't going far enough in looking for Home Rule for Ireland while remaining part of the Empire; he advocated for total and complete independence. When she'd asked him

21

how that could be achieved, he'd replied quietly but with a gleam of triumph in his eye, 'By revolution, Harp, all-out rebellion.'

Such talk was seditious and dangerous and people were arrested for less, but she didn't worry about him; he didn't see anyone so there was nobody to tell on him to the police. But even hearing him say the words gave her a chill of fear fused with a thrill of excitement.

They learned nothing of the Irish struggle against oppression in school. But she read privately all about the O'Neills and O'Donnells fighting the British in 1601 in Kinsale with the help of the Spanish; then Wolfe Tone and the French at Bantry Bay in 1798, trying to follow in the footsteps of the *sans-culottes* who cut the head off their king; then poor Robert Emmet, who led the United Irishmen in 1803. Throughout the centuries the Irish had fought and died for their sovereignty and had failed every time. But it did not daunt them. Harp believed in her heart that one day Ireland would be free, that the glorious green island would come out from under the thumb of British oppression for once and for all.

Those hungry days felt lost in the mists of time that day as peace and prosperity abounded. Those leaving were of course seeking a new life, an adventure perhaps, but they were not leaving with empty bellies and no shoes.

Her mother too recalled people being evicted for not paying the rent, battering rams taken to their homes, leaving them destitute. Mammy told a story of how a widow woman she knew was accused of stealing a gold brooch from the Protestant family she cleaned for. She was dismissed, her reputation in tatters. Nobody believed her capable of theft but that didn't matter; the Protestant landlord's wife said she did it, so therefore she did. She had to send her children to the workhouse because she had no money, and she threw herself in the river. The mistress of the house later found the brooch on a cape she seldom wore, but by then the woman was dead and her children forced into a life of drudgery.

There were no repercussions for the accusers. That was just part and parcel of being British ascendency – one law for them, another for the Irish people. Her mother wouldn't like to hear such talk, though, not because she didn't agree but because such sentiment drew the authorities down on one's head and that never ended well.

The people there that day didn't look oppressed, Harp had to admit. Business in the town was booming, and she got the impression that people were happy enough to give their allegiance to the British king, but perhaps that was because they knew no other way.

Thoughts of revolution, Home Rule or anything else political was far away that day. People licked ices and children sucked sweets. Men, some in working clothes, more in their Sunday best, stood and took it all in as the women pulled little ones by the hand or pushed them in prams. The excitement in the air was tangible.

'Let's go to the railing, Mammy. It'll be going again soon,' Harp urged as the tugs sounded their horns. *Titanic* was only in port for enough time to get the disembarking passengers off and the new ones on and to take on enough supplies and mail before setting sail once more.

Her mother allowed herself to be pulled across the road, into the park and to the railings, where they could see all of the activity on the quayside below. Seemingly thousands of bags of mail were being thrown from the shore to the tender, as well as boxes and crates of supplies for the ship. Harp gazed as boxes of bright-yellow lemons and ruby-red strawberries were handed from one docker to the other, forming a human chain of produce.

'Imagine eating strawberries on the ship, Mammy?' she said, her eyes bright with the sheer bliss of it all.

'Strawberries in April? They must have come out of glasshouses. But yes, it would be very glamorous, I suppose,' Rose conceded. 'Harp, if you get smuts on that white dress, I won't be able to get them out, so don't lean forward so much. Those railings have never seen a cloth, you may be sure.'

The breeze was brisk and not altogether warm as Harp reluctantly took a step back. Her bonnet was tied with a ribbon, but it didn't feel that secure, not that she cared. The tender was arriving from *Titanic* to the shore, and the people who were disembarking there in Queenstown were aboard. She and her mother, along with the entire town it seemed, watched as people came ashore, waving to the gathered crowds. A priest came as part of the group. He had a camera and was taking lots of snaps of the ship at anchor, the crowds gathered at the dock, the people waiting to take their place on the tender, embarking on the most exciting trip of their lives on what must be the world's most magnificent ship.

'I'm going to sail to America on *Titanic* one day, Mammy,' Harp said.

'Are you really?' Rose asked with an indulgent smile. 'And where are you going to get fifteen pounds and ten shillings for your fare, would you mind telling me that? Do you plan on finding yourself a rich husband?'

'I'll earn it,' Harp replied indignantly. 'I'm going to be a writer and I'll discover something amazing and write a book about it and then I'll have loads of money. And you and Mr Devereaux can come too, and we'll get a suite of rooms, not just a cabin. The chef in first class is from a famous restaurant in Paris, you know. We'll eat like royalty.'

Rose chuckled – Harp loved how she could make her do it. 'Well, since Mr Devereaux isn't able to come down to the town here, I can't see him wandering around Broadway in New York City, can you?'

All around them the people bustled and inched forward to see the spectacle. Harp put her hand to her bonnet, fearing a gust of wind might take it away. She didn't know why she said it, but the words tumbled out. 'Before you came in this morning, Mr Devereaux gave me that pen and said that it was for me, but he called me Harp Devereaux. At first I thought he made a mistake, but he said he never did, and he doesn't. The boys at school say he's my father.' Her eyes never left her mother's. 'They're always saying I look like him and that my real father didn't die...'

Despite hearing this rumour since she was five years old, it was the first time she'd ever raised the possibility with her mother. It never felt right, not that it did now, but being there, beside the ship with all its infinite potential and her complete certainty that one day she would sail on it, the small-minded gossip of a port town seemed less important.

Her mother's face was inscrutable, but she looked taken aback. She even opened her mouth to speak and closed it again. 'Let's walk,' was all she said, leading Harp away from all of the crowds.

They walked in silence with their backs to the ship, up the quayside where the people thinned out to where the railway line ended. Carriages sat on sidings, waiting to transport the day trippers back to Cork once *Titanic* sailed away.

There was a bench at the very end of the quay, and Rose Delaney stopped and sat, an action that surprised Harp. Such public amenities had never been part of their lives; it was as if Rose didn't think such places were quite seemly.

Harp sat beside her mother, knowing something momentous was coming. She didn't believe what the boys said, of course she didn't. Mammy and Mr Devereaux would never lie to her, and anyway she knew how babies were made and there was no way Mr Devereaux and her mother ever did that – the whole thing was ridiculous.

'Harp, I need to tell you something, and it might come as a shock.'

For the first time ever, Harp saw her mother as something less than sure and confident.

'I should have said something before, I suppose, but there was never the right time. I didn't know people had said things like that to you. I would have been more honest if I'd had any idea...' She seemed to struggle to find the right words.

'More honest about what?' Harp asked, feeling very unnerved by this turn of events.

'Those boys, what they said...' Her mother exhaled. 'It's not... Well, the thing is... Oh, Harp, I...'

'Are they right? Is Mr Devereaux really my father?' Harp asked, trying to process the information.

Her mother looked pained. 'Look, Harp. It's complicated, but yes, you are a Devereaux. But it is Ralph, not Henry Devereaux, who is your father.'

Harp swallowed. 'But you said my father was killed and that you were pregnant when he died and you came to work for the

Devereauxes after I was born.' She couldn't understand what her mother was saying to her, not really.

'That was a lie.' The words fell like heavy stones.

'So what is the truth?' Harp asked gently.

Her mother shot her a sideways glance, her face contorted in pain and something else – was it shame?

'Please, Mammy, tell me,' Harp urged.

Rose inhaled and focused on a point on Haulbowline Island, directly in front of them in the harbour. 'I began working as a house-maid in the Cliff House when I was fourteen. There were two footmen and a butler as well as a cook and a housekeeper in those days. I came from a poor background, so it was a good position to get.' She swallowed. 'Old Mr Devereaux was dead by then and Mrs Devereaux lived there with her two sons. Mr Henry, he'd always been a bit...well, a bit like himself really, I suppose. He'd gone off to school and everything, but he was in his mid-thirties, I believe, when I came and he was unusual. He didn't like to go out or meet people – he wanted to be on his own. But his brother, Ralph, was different. He was handsome and charming and loved socialising. He was twenty-five when I came and well...' Her mother's cheeks flamed with the embarrassment of telling the tale. 'He seduced me. I...I wasn't forced, nothing like that, but he promised he'd marry me and I foolishly believed him. Of course someone like him would never marry a servant, but I was naïve and silly and so I...he and I...' – she swallowed again – 'began a relationship.

'I would never have allowed him if I thought he was lying, but as it turned out, I wasn't the only one. Some wife of a banker in Cork had also caught his eye, and so his mother found out. He had some debts built up as well, and so it was decided to send him away to India, to a cousin there who would find him some work. I never saw him again.'

'Go on,' Harp said, trying to take it all in.

'Well, he was gone, I don't know, maybe two months or so, and I realised I was pregnant. I handed in my notice and went home to my parents, but they wanted nothing to do with me – they threw me out. I lived on the streets in Dublin until you were born. The night you arrived, the nurses in the place they brought me to wanted to keep you, have you adopted, but I couldn't allow that, so I slipped out with you in my arms in the dead of night.'

'And did you not tell Ralph? Write to him even?' Harp asked.

'No. I had no address for him, and besides, he'd gone without even saying goodbye so I knew I meant nothing to him. If it had just been me, I would never have darkened her door again, but I had you to consider now and I needed help. So putting my pride in my pocket, I came back here and told old Lady Devereaux of my predicament.'

'Did she believe you?' Harp found she wasn't appalled but fascinated.

Rose nodded. 'Funnily enough she did. She knew what Ralph was like. But she chided me for being so foolish as to give in to him. She agreed that I could stay so long as I concocted a dead husband from somewhere, and she would let me work and raise you here, provided I never told anyone who your father really was. She made me sign a legal paper to say I would never reveal the truth.'

'Did Ralph know?' Harp wondered.

Rose shook her head. 'He has no idea, unless Mrs Devereaux told him, which I doubt. You look nothing like him, so nobody ever suspected.'

'The boys at school say I look like Mr Devereaux.'

Rose smiled. 'And you do, very like him. And believe me, Harp, Henry Devereaux is fifty times the man his brother is, so be glad you take after your uncle.'

Her uncle. Mr Devereaux was her uncle and she was a Devereaux, not a Delaney.

'But why did you never tell me?' Harp found that she was delighted with the news. Of course if it ever got out, people would sneer and say things, but she was used to that anyway.

'I wanted to, but I'm a respectable person now, Harp, and I've raised you to be the same. For so long I had to keep quiet for fear of eviction and destitution, and now, well, what would be the point? We don't want gossip and we don't need anyone else, so it's best to keep it to ourselves. I fell so far, but through the, if not kindness, then at least pragmatism of Mrs Devereaux, we had a home and you had a future. It seemed a small price to pay.'

Harp stood up and offered her mother her hand. 'I'm glad you told me.'

She felt very grown up all of a sudden. She tried hard to imagine her mother and the handsome Ralph Devereaux from the portrait doing the marriage act and failed. But they must have because she was there. She found the whole revelation exhilarating. The best person in the world after her mammy was Mr Devereaux, and now she'd discovered he was her uncle and that was wonderful.

He was right – he never made mistakes and she was a Devereaux.

'Let's go home,' she said, her eyes bright, all thoughts of the magnificent ship forgotten. Something far more exciting was happening. She couldn't wait to see him.

CHAPTER 4

*H*arp saw the scene in her mind every time she closed her eyes.

She'd scampered up the steps to get home, to tell Mr Devereaux the news that she knew he was her uncle and that it was the best news ever. All thoughts of *Titanic* had dissipated in the wake of the extraordinary revelation.

Her mother had been puffing and her face was red with exertion from trying to keep up with her daughter. Harp had gone in through the gate in the wall of the steps as usual, into the garden. Everything looked just as they'd left it: weeds pushing cheekily up through the gravel, the gnarly old apple tree that gave an abundance of the most delicious Cox's Orange Pippins each autumn leaning precariously on the garden wall, the tree like a corner boy up to no good, her mother used to joke.

Harp ran around the back – the front door hadn't been opened in years at that stage – and let herself in. The kitchen was just the same, the delph from breakfast drying on the rack beside the big, deep Belfast sink, the large black flags on the floor, the table cleared and scrubbed, ready for dinner preparations, the big black enamel range that never went out heating the room, winter and summer, the tea cloths hanging on the line over it. Everything neat and tidy.

She scurried out the door of the kitchen into the wide bright hall- way, almost skidding on the silk carpet runner as she rounded the ornate bannister to bound up the stairs, taking two at a time. The landing overlooked the hallway and was home to a huge walnut side- board on which sat all the china dolls Mrs Devereaux had loved. Harp thought they were a bit creepy with their glass eyes, real hair and fancy handmade clothes, and thankfully she'd never felt the urge to play with them as Mrs Devereaux would have had a fit if she did.

She ran along the corridor and went into his study; she had never knocked on his door in her life, secure in the knowledge that she was always welcome, regardless of the hour. If he slept, he always closed the door into his sleeping quarters so she would never catch him in a state of undress.

She found him, sitting in his chair, the brown leather wingback, same as always. It was positioned to the right of the bay window, facing Roche's Point, the last spit of land before leaving the safety of Cork Harbour and setting sail on the high seas. He told her once he liked to sit there and imagine the thoughts running through the heads of the people leaving, or the first impressions of those arriving. His small side table had the cup of tea her mother had delivered before they left, a cheese-and-tomato sandwich untouched on the plate beside it. The rosewood and brass inlaid octagonal clock ticked loudly on the wall. It was four thirty in the afternoon.

At first she thought he was sleeping. His head rested on the back of the chair and his eyes were closed. He didn't keep usual hours; some- times he read all night and slept most of the day. He was known to eat a big meal of meat and potatoes as she was having her porridge before school. His circadian rhythm, just like every single other thing about him, was so different to everyone else.

A book was open on his chest, as if he'd been reading and just dropped it. She could see it clearly – *Contemplation* by Franz Kafka. On the side table beside him was a D. H. Lawrence book, under that *Marriage* by H. G. Wells. The only thing that made the scene look anything but tranquil was the glass of water at his feet, toppled over but not broken, a small puddle of water just beside his foot.

'Mr Devereaux!' She'd rushed towards him, knowing he wouldn't mind her waking him; his quiet happiness at seeing her was always evident. But he didn't move. He was always a light sleeper. When he dozed in his chair normally, even the turning of the door handle would be enough to wake him.

She still didn't worry at that stage. It wasn't until she touched his hand that she began to think all might not be as it should be. He wasn't cold exactly, and she knew from a phase she went through reading about autopsies that it took around twelve hours for a human body to be cool to the touch and twenty-four hours to cool to the core. Rigor mortis commenced after three hours and lasted until thirty-six hours after death. She knew that police and detectives used clues such as those for estimating the time of death. But what immediately struck her was that he was unresponsive.

In the future, she would recall with piercing agony the next few minutes. She shook him. His mouth dropped open ever so slightly, but his eyes remained closed.

Her mother arrived, took in the scene and did as Harp did, calling him, then opening one of his unseeing eyes with her thumb. His pupil was slightly dilated.

Harp had stood to the side in horror. This could not be happening. He could not be dead. It wasn't fair. She needed to speak to him, tell him she knew why he called her Harp Devereaux, see the smile on his face. They had so much to do, so much to share. This was not right. But however wrong it was, however incomprehensible or unfair or cruel, the truth was, he was dead.

If time slowed down during those few minutes, it sped up in the following days. The doctor came, then Mr Quinn, the local undertaker. He took Mr Devereaux's body away. She had read about times like these in books; usually there was a lot of activity, food being prepared, guests coming to pay their respects, but not in their case.

When Mr Quinn took him away to prepare him for burial, the house was eerily quiet. There was nothing to be done. Rose had written a telegram to Mr Devereaux's solicitor in Cork, who would probably contact his brother, Ralph. She and Harp walked to the post office to send it, and that process had, of course, announced his death to the town. Mrs O'Boyle in the post office was known as 'News of the World' behind her back. Nothing was a secret once Madge O'Boyle was in on it.

Together they'd walked back up the steps. Nobody said anything, no condolences were offered, though they were observed surreptitiously by several people who might have seen or heard about the doctor or Mr Quinn arriving at the house. There could only be one reason for their visits. But why would they commiserate with them? Rose was just the widowed housekeeper and Harp her fatherless child. The neighbours would speculate that Rose and Harp would be out of a job but that Henry Devereaux's death was nothing more than an inconvenience to them.

Harp remained stoic, as her mother had trained her to be, but inside she screamed. 'You didn't know what he meant to us!' she wanted to shout, but she couldn't speak, let alone raise her voice. It was as if a ball had lodged in her throat and no sound could come out.

Mr Quinn called again that evening to say he'd been in touch with the vicar and the funeral had been arranged. Ralph Devereaux was informed of his brother's death but there was no question of him returning. India was so far and travelling would take too long. There was no further impediment to the ceremony going ahead.

Henry Devereaux had been baptised in the small Protestant church in Queenstown before the family moved to Japan, but his adult foot had hardly ever been inside the door. He'd presumably attended his father's funeral a few years before Harp was born, then his mother's the previous year, but apart from that, Harp didn't think he'd ever gone to church.

He told her once when she was questioning the point of learning an entire catechism for her first Holy Communion, 'It's all just an elaborate fairy story, Harp, dreamed up by mortal men years ago and designed to keep the masses in line, to ensure everyone knew their place and did as they were told for fear of the fiery pit.'

Her mother had shot him a fierce warning glance that day, and he'd been quiet for days after that.

Rose took Harp to Mass every Sunday, and while Mr Devereaux never again commented on their practice, Harp knew he thought it a load of old nonsense. Perhaps he was right, but then could they all be wrong, all the priests and bishops and the pope and all of the other religious people? Were they all being fooled into believing a lie? When she asked her mother about the subject, as usual she was more pragmatic, less radical.

'Well, Harp,' Rose explained, 'I'm not completely sure. Nobody can be. Nobody's ever come back to say heaven is real. But the way I look at it is I would like it to be true, I think it might be, and even if it isn't, what harm does it do to spend an hour a week in the church, thinking about our lives, being grateful for what we have and trying to be good people? The rules of the Church are generally good ones – be kind, don't tell lies, don't kill or steal or be disrespectful. Those are good rules to live by, aren't they?'

Harp had to agree. But while Mr Devereaux didn't dismiss faith as such, he did give her a book by Friedrich Engels, Karl Marx's collaborator, that explained atheism. Harp had read a lot of philosophy and believed that people have a barometer inside them that knows right from wrong. She felt that living a good life and not hurting people could be achieved by non-believers as easily as by those with faith in the spiritual world.

He would have probably objected to the church funeral if he could, but in the absence of a family member to make a decision or any other method of burying the dead, they went ahead.

The vicar came out onto the altar and began the ceremony. Harp did exactly as her mother asked, and they both sat, dressed in black, not fidgeting, not crying, completely impassive.

Reverend Simcox, a tall slim man with an English accent, was not acquainted at all with the deceased, having only moved to the Queenstown parish five years ago. Harp recalled him calling to the house one day, presumably a courtesy visit to introduce himself to a member of his flock. She was much younger then but remembered it vividly, as Mr Devereaux refused point-blank to see him and her mother was mortified as she had to make some excuse.

Nonetheless, the vicar did his duty admirably that day, making all the right noises about eternal salvation. Harp could hear Mr Devereaux's voice in her head as the vicar quoted John 11:25–26.

"'I am the resurrection and the life," says the Lord. "Those who believe in me, even though they die, yet shall they live, and everyone who lives and believes in me shall never die.'"

'Ah, but I did die, Harp. You see, I told you – fairy stories.' Remembering his lopsided grin comforted her.

Harp had never been inside the Protestant church in Queenstown in her entire life. It wasn't allowed. And if Canon Long knew she and her mother were sitting there now, he'd probably take a dim view of it, but Harp didn't care, and in this instance, neither did her mother.

The mahogany box was almost level with her head as she knelt on the hard kneeler. It had come as a surprise that the Protestants didn't have long pews like the Catholic church had; instead each person had their own chair and kneeler, with a little shelf for a hymnal and a prayerbook. A few other people she didn't know dotted the church, but the only mourners were her and her mother.

It wasn't hard not to cry. She couldn't even if she wanted to. All of her emotions were churning sickeningly inside her, pressure building like seltzer water, but she couldn't let them out. He was gone. It felt so wrong to even say it. Mr Devereaux was gone.

Mr Cotter, the solicitor, was at the funeral, as was the long-suffering accountant, Mr Byrne. A few of the older Protestant families of the area had sent a representative, and Mr Quinn stood respectfully at a distance, his hat in his hands. But the truth was, nobody had seen Henry Devereaux for years and years. His parents had been sociable when they were younger and Ralph was well known in society as a young man, but Henry had always eschewed social contact and so knew almost nobody.

The service was interminable and Harp tried to block it all out, all the talk of death and the kingdom of heaven and all of it. She used a trick Mr Devereaux had taught her in one of his more animated moments for when things got too boring. He showed her how to make a face that looked like she was completely engaged, but then mentally escape. He told her to picture her imagination as a bluebird, flying out of her head, leaving her face and body at the boring event and soaring out of the windows, over the town, over the ocean, crossing deserts, forests, cities, flying through sun and rain and wind and finally coming to rest wherever she wanted, on a white-sand beach, at a theatre or a concert, in a library, in a restaurant, on a yacht – wherever she wanted to be at that given moment.

Harp focused her eyes on the ancient-looking vicar, cocked her head slightly to the left, one ear ever so slightly inclined to the speaker. She tried not to smile at that bit; he'd said the ear was vital to the look of complete concentration. And then she let the bright blue-bird fly, out through the stained-glass windows, over the harbour. She knew exactly where to go: to the island. When she was little, her mother had invented an island called Bolloping. It had palm trees and warm azure water, but it also had caves, and in each cave was a library. The books were arranged by colour, not by title, so one could get a surprise. Each night as Harp lay in bed, her mother inventing the tale as she went, Rose would ask her what colour they should choose. She might pick orange, and then they would go to the orange cave and select four orange books. One might be about primates, another a cookbook, another a romance featuring a dashing pirate who really had a heart of gold, and the fourth could be a book about a talking rabbit. They would make up the contents of each book, and soon Michael the talking rabbit would be making a sumptuous cream cake to invite a chimpanzee called Bingo and Blackie the pirate to tea.

She let her imagination rest on Bolloping. She was probably much too old for such childish fantasies, but today she needed to be anywhere but there in that dank, musty-smelling church, with Mr Devereaux lying still in a box before she ever got to tell him she knew who she really was.

Mr Quinn had several large black umbrellas that were necessary, because as they walked to the churchyard and the Devereaux plot, the heavens opened. It was a cold day for the time of year, and a stiff breeze blew the rain off the sea. Harp didn't care if she got wet; in fact, she wanted to. She would have loved to stand out in it, allow the cold drops to trickle down the back of her starched collar, to soak the horrid black dress, to drench her hair, just so she could feel. Anything was better than this dull nothingness, this sense that she would never again be happy. But her mother accepted the umbrella and pulled Harp under it with her. They picked their way across the uneven ground, around old gravestones sticking out here and there without rhyme or reason to the formation. Eventually they reached the Devereaux plot. It was one of the more imposing ones, a double grave with a black marble edge. There was a marble plinth, atop which was a large stone angel the size of a tall man, one wing outstretched, the other curled in, and the angel's finger rested on her lips to quiet the living.

The freshly opened grave emitted an earthy aroma, like the smell one got when it rained for the first time in weeks on hard ground, only amplified. Harp inhaled; it wasn't an unpleasant smell. Somehow she knew that whenever she smelled that for the rest of her life, she would be brought back here, to the little churchyard beside the Protestant chapel on this, the worst day of her life.

More droning words from the vicar. She allowed them to wash over her. The Protestant prayers were different anyhow, so she didn't know them. Then the undertaker and his son, a boy she recognised as being a few classes ahead of her, lowered the coffin with ropes into the hole.

The handful of gathered men each took the shovel and threw a shovelful of earth down, the dirt landing with a thud on the coffin. She and her mother just stood there, the rain drumming on the black umbrella. The gravestone would be inscribed in due course to add him to the list.

The stone bore the name Devereaux, carved in solid letters and inlaid with gold against the black marble, without embellishment.

Harp read from the top down:

George Ralph 1732–1801

Emily 1750–1820

Henry Joseph 1770–1834
Emily 1781–1844
Ralph James 1800–1802
Evangeline 1808–1876
George Joseph 1809–1884
Henry Davis 1833–1896
Matilda 1840–1911

The last two were her grandparents. Mr Devereaux's father had died before Harp was born, but Matilda Devereaux, her grandmother, let her be raised in the Cliff House knowing she had Devereaux blood in her veins but never allowed her to be acknowledged.

Mr Devereaux – Harp could never think of him as anything but that – never spoke about his family at all, and they'd never been to this graveyard before.

Henry George Devereaux 1860–1912

That's all there would be to remember him. Nothing to indicate what kind of man he was, how clever and kind and interesting. Just the words and the dates. Nothing more.

His would probably be the last name ever carved on the stone, she realised. Ralph was younger but settled in India, nobody had seen him for years, and surely he would die and be buried over there.

She tried to imagine her own name there.

Harp Mary Devereaux 1900–

She shook the morbid thought from her mind. The Devereaux family had not acknowledged her in life; they certainly wouldn't now.

The rain fell relentlessly and the skies darkened.

Normally people would sympathise with the family at that point, but there was nobody to sympathise with – Harp and her mother were just the staff – so the crowd dispersed the moment the vicar finished.

Matt Quinn removed the ropes and put them in the back of the hearse, then he approached them and said kindly, 'Can I take you back to the house, Mrs Delaney?'

He was a gentleman in every sense of the word and everyone liked him. At five foot ten and fairly slight, he wasn't a powerful man. But he commanded the respect and affection of everyone in Queenstown, as he dealt so kindly with them when the time came to bury a loved one. He had sandy hair and blue eyes, and something about him made one feel that it was all going to be all right. He had been married to a terrible harridan who was never done carping about this one or that, and they had only one child, a son. Bessie Quinn died in 1910 of TB, and Matt and the boy had lived alone ever since. Matt Quinn was one of the few people with whom Mr Devereaux had exchanged a few words now and again, when Mr Quinn came to the house with deliveries and they talked about matters political. They were aligned in their thinking about Irish independence. He was a well-read man, Mr Devereaux always said.

Harp watched her mother shake her head, and in a voice Harp didn't recognise, she replied, 'Thank you, Mr Quinn, but my daughter and I will walk.' She took the umbrella down and went to fold it up to return it to him though it was still raining.

'Not at all, not at all. Keep the umbrella. You'll need it on the way home. I'll call for it someday – there's no rush.' He turned and then paused. 'Are you sure you won't take a lift back? You'll get drowned walking up the hill, and I can go that way as easy as not?'

Her mother seemed to relent and nodded sadly. 'Thank you then, Mr Quinn. A lift in your carriage would be most welcome.' She smiled but it didn't reach her eyes. She handed him back his umbrella.

He opened the back door of his carriage, pulled by four black horses with plumes on their heads. His son was on the front seat holding the reins, dressed in long black oilskins for protection against the pouring rain. Harp slid in beside her mother as Mr Quinn closed the door and jumped up beside his son. The carriage was lined in black button-down satin, and the seats were upholstered in dark-grey velvet. She'd hardly ever been in a carriage before and never one as fancy as this.

A thought popped into her head – *Wait until I tell Mr Devereaux about it* – and the realisation that she would never tell him anything again felt like acid in her stomach.

Mr Quinn drove slowly up the winding hill to the Cliff House, pulling up on the gravel outside that was in danger of being taken over by weeds. Harp remembered a time when they had a gardener, a jolly man called Mr Finch, but the money for such luxuries had dried up and her mother ran the house on a shoestring.

The undertaker got out and came around to open the door to let her mother out. His son did the same on the other side. He smiled and said, 'I'm really sorry for your troubles, Harp.'

Nobody else had acknowledged that Mr Devereaux's passing had any impact on her whatsoever. That small kindness seemed to unblock the tears that had refused to flow earlier. 'Thank you,' she managed, blinking them back.

She walked around the back of the carriage, the house looming over them all, and glanced at her mother. Rose looked just like the alabaster statues in the Catholic cathedral – cold, set in stone. Her face had not one touch of colour; even her lips seemed to blend into the paleness.

'If there's anything I can do...' Mr Quinn said quietly, and her mother just nodded.

They stood on the gravel, looking out to the harbour, as the carriage pulled away.

'Let's go inside, Mammy.' Harp tugged on her mother's sleeve and took the key of the house from her handbag. She opened the front door, and it scraped as it always did across the black and white diagonal tiles. It seemed fitting to go in that way that day for some reason. It all looked and smelled so familiar, the scent of beeswax polish and sunlight soap, the polished hallstand with the umbrellas in the polished shell casing. There was a five-foot-tall china urn that Mrs Devereaux had received from the wife of the British Ambassador to Japan as a parting gift standing beside the hallstand. Harp had always hated its grotesque faces and gaudy design, but Mrs Devereaux loved it. Mr Devereaux suggested to his mother once that it had been such an ugly thing that the ambassador's wife had only given it away to get rid of it, and Mrs Devereaux was so offended that she didn't speak to her son for months. Best time of his life, Mr Devereaux had remarked wryly. Harp found herself smiling at the memory.

The stairs on the left of the hallway curved gracefully up to the first floor where Mr Devereaux lived, and then to the second, and finally to the attic bedrooms where Harp and her mother slept. Straight ahead was the kitchen, pantry and scullery, and to the right the salon and the drawing room, neither used in years and years. Under the stairs on the left were the mahogany double doors to the dining room that spanned the entire east wing, with perfect views over the harbour. Nobody had eaten a dinner in there in Harp's lifetime.

She led her mother to the kitchen and stoked the range, setting the kettle on top. On the table were a tray of sandwiches and a cake, cut neatly into slices. Harp felt such a pang of, what was it? She didn't know. Pity? Maybe. Her mother had prepared the food this morning in case anyone came back after the funeral. Of course nobody did.

She helped her mother off with her coat and hung it on the nail behind the door, then did the same with her own. Rose then busied herself with preparations to make tea. The only sounds in the room were the clatter of cups and saucers and the kettle coming to boil.

'Go up and change out of that wet dress, Harp. You'll catch your death,' Rose instructed.

Harp did as she was told, and by the time she returned, dressed in her normal day dress over which she'd put on her woollen cardigan, her mother had made the tea and set it on the table.

Rose took the waxed paper off the sandwiches, saying they'd might as well eat them. Harp found she was hungry, which surprised her to no end as she was so very sad, but she remembered reading the letters Jane Austen wrote to her sister Cassandra in which she stated, 'Composition seems to me impossible, with a head full of joints of mutton and doses of rhubarb.'

She supposed that bodies needed food to function normally, and therefore it stood to reason that when one was in a time of difficulty, one needed to function to a higher degree and should therefore eat more.

She noticed her mother was mindlessly stirring her tea but had yet to take a sip or eat anything. Harp placed an egg-and-cress sandwich and another of cheese and tomato on her mother's plate and put a napkin alongside it. But both the tea and the food remained untouched.

'Mammy, please eat. Mr Devereaux would not want you to go hungry.'

Her mother looked at her again. This time tears brimmed in her green eyes, making them look like the sea on a stormy but blue-skied day. 'You never got to tell him,' she said, her voice hoarse with emotion.

'He knew, Mammy. Remember I told you? Just before we left to go and see the ship, when you were gone downstairs, he called me Harp Devereaux again and said he was proud of me and that I was special.'

'Really?' Her mother gave a sad smile, one that held years of regret.

Harp nodded.

Rose placed her hand on Harp's. 'I know it is hard, but nobody must ever know who your father is, Harp. It wouldn't be right. And when they come and put us out of here, we'll just have to go and not say a word because we have no proof. And anyway, I would just look like a greedy housekeeper making up a story to get something out of it. I won't have that, do you understand me, Harp?'

Harp had no idea what her mother was going on about. 'Who will come to put us out of here? Why would anyone do that, Mammy? Sure this is our home. We live here...' Harp suddenly felt panic. She would have to learn to live without him. She had no choice but to accept it; she knew he was gone and was in heaven. But why was her mother talking about leaving the Cliff House?

'Harp, my love.' Her mother turned and took both Harp's hands in hers; they felt cold as marble. 'This isn't our house, you know that. It belonged to Mr Devereaux for the duration of his life, left to him by his mother, but now it will belong to Ralph, I suppose. It will stay in the Devereaux family anyway, like it has done for generations. There will be no more need of us, so we'll just have to move on, go some-where else.'

Harp wanted to withdraw her hands from her mother's cold ones. That was ridiculous. 'But where would we go? Would I have to go to a new school?' Harp hated change; even the slightest décor changes in the house upset her. She liked familiarity – it made her feel safe.

'No, you won't. You won't be going back to school.' Rose could hardly form the words, and Harp could see her sadness as she watched the dawning realisation of what she was saying register with her daughter.

'You mean never go back to school at all?' Harp was incredulous.

'Well, I suppose I do,' Rose answered. 'I don't know how much longer we'll be allowed to stay here, so we'll be moving on somewhere else anyway, and the term is almost over, just another few weeks. Most girls in your position would have left at twelve anyway...'

'But...' Harp could see the conflict on Rose's face. 'But if I leave school, how will I go to university? I need to matriculate, and take my exams and...'

'Harp.' Rose paused. 'I don't know how to say this. Going to university was always just a pipe dream – I should never have allowed the fantasy to go ahead. The belief that you were destined for an education, for travel, for financial and social success was a silly dream that could never come true. It's my fault, but I never wanted you to have to face the reality of our lives, that you were the illegitimate child of a housekeeper who had no money or name behind her, the things necessary to realise such lofty ambitions.' Harp heard her mother's voice crack. 'I took the easy way out and let you believe that this was a possibility when it just is not. None of that is going to happen.'

To Harp, the words sounded so hard, so cruel. She had lost Mr Devereaux, was about to lose her home and now was about to have her dreams crushed too. 'What? Why not? Mr Devereaux told me I could go to Queen's College in Cork, or Trinity in Dublin, or even to the Sorbonne in Paris, and I would study and –'

'Harp.' Rose stopped her. 'Don't be silly. You know why not. I can't afford it. School costs money and I could just about manage the fees for the Star of the Sea here from my wages, but university costs a lot more and we are destitute. Now that he is gone, the trust fund that kept this house and paid me will revert to Ralph, such as it is. I doubt there is much because as you know we were just barely making ends meet, but now that Henry's gone and we are facing, well, whatever we are facing, it's time to give up on that fantasy because it just will not happen.'

'But Mr Devereaux said –'

'Harp!' Rose raised her voice and Harp jumped. 'You're not listening. You cannot stay at school because I can't pay the fees, do you understand? I need to find a job, a live-in position, and so do you. Hopefully we can work in the same house, but I…'

'You…what? I don't understand. I have to get a job in a house, as what?' Harp was confused. Other girls her age, and from the social class to which she really belonged, were raised in the knowledge that they would be expected to leave education and work, but not her.

'I don't know, a scullery maid, a dairy maid, something like that…' Harp could see that the words hurt her mother to say. 'Every day since he died, I've looked at the situations advertised in the newspapers, but none of them were for a woman and a girl. I hoped that maybe we could get work together, at least we could stay close…' Her mother's voice trailed off.

'I don't know anything about dairy cows or washing clothes. How could I do that?' Harp was incredulous. 'You know how I'm no good at that stuff.'

'You'd have to learn, and I'll teach you, in whatever time we have left here. I should have done this a long time ago.'

'Teach me about housekeeping?' Harp was horrified.

'Yes, because that is your future. I'm sorry. I should never have allowed you to think it was going to be anything different. That's just not how the world works. Mr Devereaux and Ralph got an education because the Devereaux family were wealthy. Look at this house! It is magnificent, and back when he was a child and his parents were alive, there were no leaks or cracks or rattling windows. They had money, Harp, and they educated their children with that money. But we don't have it, and we never will.'

'I always thought this was my home…' Harp said quietly.

'It was, in the sense that I worked here and you were allowed to stay because of, well, because of the circumstances. But my parents were poor – they had nothing.'

'And now I'm the same,' Harp said slowly.

It didn't require an answer.

'If there was a way, I would take it, Harp, I swear I would, but I've been awake every night since he died and I can't see a way out. I will do my best to find us a position together, in a house where we can both work, but those are few and far between. If we had a house, a room even, I would get a job and at least we could stay together, but most domestic positions are live-in. And besides, we don't have a place of our own, so...' Rose swallowed. Harp could see she was barely able to form the words in her mouth. 'We may have to separate.'

'Separate?' Harp asked, aghast.

'I hope not. I pray we won't have to. I'm trying my very best to find something. But any day now they will come and say we need to leave, Harp, and we have nowhere to go.'

'And we have no money at all?'

Rose shook her head. 'Very little.'

'So what will happen now?' Harp asked. 'I know you think they will send someone to evict us, but if Ralph is in India, then they throw us out and the house just lies empty?'

Rose shrugged and sighed. 'I don't know, Harp. He might sell it, or even come back here, but whatever happens to this old place, it won't be anything to do with us.'

The reality slowly dawned on Harp. Of course her mother was right. She'd just assumed they could stay, but of course they couldn't. Unless... 'Maybe if we told Ralph the truth, maybe then he wouldn't make us. Mr Devereaux wouldn't want us to have nowhere to go,' Harp suggested.

Rose shook her head. 'Ralph was nothing like his brother, Harp. He was...' She inhaled. 'He was cruel and greedy and brash. He wouldn't care that you are his child even if we did tell him, I just know it, and telling him would make everything a hundred times worse.'

'But he won't even want this house!' Harp exploded. This really was too much to take. 'He hasn't set foot in it for years! He couldn't even be bothered to come to visit his only brother or his mother even, so he's hardly going to turn up here and want to live here now, is he?' Harp knew she shouldn't shout at her mother, but she was so upset and this was just nonsense.

'It won't matter, Harp. None of that matters. He would have been Henry's heir and so his estate would go to him. It's how things work. I know...' Her mother's voice cracked under the strain of it all. 'I know how much this place means to you, how you thought of it as home all of your life, how he wanted us to feel that way, but it's over, Harp. He's gone and we will have to leave.'

CHAPTER 5

'*M*aster McTernan.' Emmet Kelly raised his hand. 'Why is the road to the workhouse in Midleton called *cosán na marbh?*' He smirked at Harp as he asked the question. The teacher had his back to them while he wrote the homework on the blackboard.

The master loved Irish; it was his favourite subject. He became so animated when teaching the language of their forefathers that any child who displayed interest in it was immediately in his good graces. It wasn't officially on the curriculum – being part of the British Empire meant children spoke English only – but the master taught it on the quiet. Harp was already fluent, having read all of the Irish mythology in the original Irish language the summer she was ten, so the master often looked to her for support with his endeavours.

Harp knew why Emmet was asking, to humiliate her, but she would have to endure it.

The master turned around, his long face a beam of delight. He was shiny-faced and bald, except for a straggly greasy bit of hair that he combed across his head, and his tweed suit was covered in chalk dust. He had long fingers and a gentle disposition, and Harp liked him. He only slapped them very rarely and even then not too hard, unlike their previous teacher, Sister Regina, who was a savage with the switch.

'What do we think, class, *cosán na marbh?*' The master looked around, and Harp deliberately stared at a knot of wood on her desk.

'*Cosán?*' He asked. 'Where does that word come from?'

'Pathway?' Donal Deasy suggested.

'*Maith an feár*, good man yourself, Donal. Indeed it is a pathway. And *na marbh?*' He waited for a moment before turning to Harp, easily the best in the class at Irish.

'I don't know, sir,' Harp mumbled.

'Ah, Harp, you do, I'm sure. *Na marbh...*' He made a grotesque face and the class giggled.

'The dead, sir.' Kit Lehane piped up. '*Cosán na marbh* is "pathway of the dead".'

'*Sin é*, that's it.' The master clapped his hands, delighted with his students.

'So we have *cosán na marbh* on the way to the workhouse because of all the poor misfortunes that lost their lives inside there, who were evicted with no place else to go. But thanks be to God, that's not a fate awaiting any of us today.' He grinned as the bell rang for morning break.

Harp slowly gathered her books and pen. Two weeks had passed since the death of Mr Devereaux, but she still felt terrible; the pain in her chest and tummy was constant. The tragic news of the sinking of *Titanic* had barely registered with her, though it had shaken the town to its foundations. Prayers were said, Masses offered up. It was all anyone could think or talk about, and no doubt if the unthinkable had not happened in her own life, she too would have felt the loss of the magnificent ship. But she couldn't feel anything but heartbreak and fear for the future.

All of those people, so full of hopes and dreams, sliding to the bottom of the sea – she envied them. At least they felt no more pain. All she felt was empty and alone and worried. She couldn't go into service. She would be terrible at it, and to be separated from her mother, so soon after losing Mr Devereaux and her home... It was a fate she couldn't begin to contemplate. The image of her as an inept and hopeless scullery maid crying herself to sleep in a strange house night after night, a cruel housekeeper or cook berating her for her uselessness, went round in her head constantly.

She thought of the line in *David Copperfield*, when he admonishes Dora for the manner in which she dealt with a servant. 'Unless we learn to do our duty to those whom we employ, they will never learn to do their duty to us.' But Dickens was wrong. The rich had no duty where the servant class were concerned; they owed them nothing. Her mother had served the Devereaux family for years, and now it was over and she was to be cast aside. It had never occurred to any member of that family what would become of the servants once the last Devereaux died. Try as she might to channel her anger at Mr Devereaux, as surely he would have known this would happen, she couldn't find it in her heart to blame him. He would never have meant for this to happen, but such matters would not have entered his head.

She had brought her pen to school that day, just once, to let people see how beautiful it was. Master McTernan remarked upon it, held it up reverentially and showed everyone the exquisite craftsmanship. She'd told him and the entire class that it had been a gift from Mr Devereaux, but she knew as she did that it was a mistake.

Emmet had teased and tormented her all through the day, still bitter from her mother's pulling him off the railing. In the schoolyard at breaktime, he followed her, his cronies behind him. 'Oh, the quare hawk gave it to ya, did he? A parting gift for his darling girl?' He laughed that horrible laugh of his, the one that made everyone look. ''Tis a pity your dear old daddy didn't leave you something better than an old bit of a pen, isn't it, considering yourself and your strumpet of a mother are heading for the workhouse now?'

Harp hated to listen to him, hated even more that everyone was paying attention. She couldn't bear to hear him talk of her mammy and Mr Devereaux that way, but she had no answer for him.

She tried to walk away but he stood in front of her, so close she could smell his foul breath.

'Maybe your mammy can find another quare hawk with a load of money and a big auld creepy house, and maybe she can warm another man's bed to keep a roof over your clever little head? And not leave you high and dry now without tuppence to your names.' He ruffled Harp's hair roughly, and she could feel her heart thumping in sheer terror.

'Mr Devereaux didn't leave us nothing. He left me this pen because I'm a Devereaux and...' she began, but the words wouldn't come. She couldn't defend him, her mother, herself. It was all so hard. Her heart felt like it was actually broken – she had a pain in her chest – and the worst was that nobody could know. She had to pretend like she was fine, but more than that, she had to try to look like she didn't care that the most important man in her life was gone.

'Shut up, Emmet. You're nothing but a gob on a stick – nothing to say, but the loudest voice.'

Harp swung around. Nobody had ever stuck up for her before. Was it a trick?

It was the undertaker's son, and he was with three older boys; they must have been sixteen or seventeen, almost done with school. The Quinns lived on the beautiful curved terrace at the top of the hill with large three-storied houses, so while they weren't gentry in the way the Devereaux family were, they were well off.

The gathered crowd laughed and Emmet fumed. He opened his mouth to say something cutting to his cousin but shut it again upon seeing the school principal, Master Barry, ringing the bell.

Harp turned and felt her face burn. She knew she should say something to him, to thank him, but she feared that she might cry so she mumbled something, her head down as she passed him.

He put a hand out to stop her and she looked up. 'Are you all right, Harp?' he asked as the other children all made their way noisily back to the classrooms.

She nodded and swallowed.

'Don't mind that eejit Emmet,' he said kindly. 'He's just jealous because you live in a lovely house and you're miles brainier than him.' He smiled and it crinkled his china-blue eyes, the same kind eyes she remembered from the day of Mr Devereaux's funeral. He was very tall and thin and had freckles and close-cut red hair.

'Thanks.' She felt embarrassed that she didn't know his name when he knew hers.

'Brian,' he volunteered.

'Thank you, Brian.'

Mr O'Flynn, who taught the older class, had emerged from the teachers' tea room and was bearing down on them across the schoolyard.

'I better go. Mind yourself, Harp,' Brian said as he sprinted back to the senior section of the school.

Feeling a little better, she returned to her classroom.

It was hard to concentrate and the master had to call her three times to hand up her work, she was so lost in thought.

Harp knew that every day the postman passed without a letter, her mother sighed with relief at another day's reprieve. Then by afternoon she would be worried again, thinking the solicitor handling the estate would call in person and be horrified to find them still there.

She'd packed up their things so that should they need to make a speedy departure, they could, but where would they go? Mammy had a little money in the post office, but she told Harp that it would only last a week or so. After that, well, she had no idea what would become of them.

Harp felt the sting as the spitball of wet paper hit her cheek. The master had his back to the class and Emmet was grinning again. She wiped it off her face and then from her desk to the floor. A second later another one landed, this time on her blotter. There was more sniggering from behind. She brushed it off with her sleeve, keeping her head down so they couldn't see the tears.

Normally if they were being particularly mean, she would go home and sit in the library and read a story in which the villains got their comeuppance, but she couldn't bring herself to go in there now. Mammy was too worried about their future to bother her with this, and anyway she would just tell Harp to ignore them.

'Is Brian the giant your boyfriend, Harp?' she heard someone hiss.

'Brian the giant and Harpy the smarty – what a pair.'

A few of the others giggled.

'Would the babies be huge or tiny? Or would they be mousy or foxy?' Emmet was warming to his theme.

Harp couldn't take it any more. 'Leave me alone, Emmet Kelly! Please just stop it and leave me alone!' Her words ended in a sob as she shoved her pen in her pocket and stormed out of the classroom. She heard the master call her from the door but she ran on, ignoring him.

She ran all the way towards the Cliff House, blinded by tears. Her books and lunch bag and everything were still at school and she would probably get slapped the next day for running away, but she couldn't bear it; she couldn't listen to Emmet and the others for another second. But she couldn't go home. Her mammy would be so cross, and besides she couldn't explain – it was too hard to find the words. She ran all the way to the Protestant church on the top of the hill. The gate was too heavy to open, but she'd noticed a gap in the wall the day of the burial, so she went round and climbed in that way. She made her way across the uneven ground of the churchyard. In contrast to the day of the funeral, the sun was warm, and she sat beside the grave, the earth still dark and loamy where the gravediggers had replaced it.

Everything was terrible. Emmet Kelly was always mean, but it never hurt this much before. She had not one friend, and now she and her mother were going to lose the only home she'd ever known. She had not even been able to play her harp since he died as the pain of the music he loved so much was too difficult to bear.

'Mr Devereaux,' she began, 'I...I can't... Please...p-please come back... Don't leave...' The words would not come. They stuck in her throat, and hot burning tears coursed down her cheeks. She sat there, hugging her knees, sobbing.

CHAPTER 6

'And you are only telling me this now?' Rose Delaney used her most imperious tone on the Reverend Mother and principal of the school.

'Mrs Delaney.'

Did Rose imagine it or was there a slight emphasis on the 'Mrs'?

'Your daughter left the school without permission from her teacher, just stormed out. Do you expect the teacher to abandon the other children and go in search of what is proving to be a very highly strung and difficult girl?'

'Harp is not difficult. And if by highly strung you mean intelligent and sensitive, then yes she is. And of course she is not like other children, but to dismiss your duty of care to her in this fashion is frankly unacceptable.'

The nun's face tightened, but Rose did not break contact with her cold blue eyes.

'Well, perhaps Star of the Sea is not the right environment for your daughter, Mrs Delaney, if we are so far beneath her intellectual ability.' The words dripped like acid. 'Harp has delusions of superiority. She's been that way since she walked in the door as a junior infant, and it has done her no good whatsoever. Your rearing of her to be aloof has meant she has no friends. You would do well, Mrs Delaney, to consider your circumstances, and both you and your daughter should behave accordingly. Frankly the girl is deluded. She claims now that she is a member of the Devereaux family for whom you worked, so clearly she is not right in the head. Now, I must get on. Good day to you.'

The nun swished past her, her habit rustling as she walked, and Rose grabbed her sleeve. 'My daughter is perfectly fine in the head, and she is not a liar. She *is* a Devereaux.' Rose fought the urge to pull the veil from the nun's head. Her rage at being treated like that far exceeded offence on her own behalf, but how could someone be so cruel to poor little Harp, especially now. Could the Reverend Mother not see the child's heart was broken?

'Well, in that case, she's no better than she should be.' Sarcastic disdain dripped from every word. 'Remove yourself from my school at once, and I'll thank you to keep your sordid and tawdry past away from here in the future.'

Rose maintained her composure, on the outside at least, and walked out of the school. Where would Harp go? Harp had run away two hours ago, and it was only when she didn't come home from school that Rose had walked down to meet her. Discovering Harp left the school hours earlier and nobody saw fit to inform her or go looking for a grieving child astounded her.

She hurried away from the school. Harp hadn't come home. She had no friends – the nun was right about that – so there was only one place she could be. Rose trudged up the hill, past the Cliff House, further up and to the other side of the town. April would soon be giving way to May, and the sun was weak but persistent. She was overdressed for the climb up the 400 steps that were the spine of the town. She passed St Colman's Catholic Cathedral, which dominated the skyline, taking full advantage of its place, overseeing the town and the harbour, representing the supremacy of the Roman Church. Beautiful, yes, certainly, and to hear the carillon of bells ring out over the harbour would gladden the hardest of hearts, but it left no ambiguity about who was in charge.

No doubt it would be just a matter of hours before the canon would be informed of her revelation, and she doubted she would get much of a welcome in that church once the truth was out. For the first time since she discovered she was pregnant with her daughter, she didn't care who knew her secret. She was at the bottom; there was nowhere to go from here.

The nun didn't have to tell her she needed to consider her position; she was well aware of the gossip. But they'd never had proof until now. The irony that her daughter didn't look so much like Ralph but like her Uncle Henry was not lost on her. She might have got away with it, but there was no denying it now even if she wanted to. If people thought Harp was Henry's, then at least that was something. His fine strawberry-blond hair was hers, as were his delicate features and his long fingers, and most of all his grey eyes that could on occasion look almost blue but not quite. Harp was beautiful, though not in the conventional sense, but Rose could see even now how she would capture a man's heart in the future.

Henry loved her and she him in their own peculiar way. They looked alike, and in so many ways they were. Neither of them fitted easily into society, and they both found interactions awkward. They were both bookish and quiet. She loved them both, and the need to protect them was overwhelming. Henry didn't need her protection any longer, but Harp did. What could she do? Harp was right when she said she would be awful in service, but what else was there?

Rose paused and turned, gazing out over the port. The islands of Haulbowline and Spike were hives of activity, pleasure boats, fishing trawlers and military ships all going about their business as if this were a normal day, as if her world weren't crumbling to ash in her hands. The shock of the sinking of *Titanic* was still felt, leading to speculation that people would be too nervous to travel, something that would devastate a town so reliant on the transatlantic trade, but it went over her head mostly. She had bigger problems.

She even considered writing to Ralph, begging him to help them, if not for her sake, then for their child's, but no matter how desperate she was, she wouldn't do that. It would be pointless anyway. Ralph was feckless and selfish; he wouldn't help.

She'd even thought about using the last of their savings to buy third-class tickets to America – maybe there was more opportunity there – but she knew nobody there. She didn't know anyone here either, but she might get a job, and maybe one that supplied board... But with Harp it all seemed so hopeless.

She berated herself for not making plans. She should have considered this prospect. That day the *Titanic* came, she was carefree, the future not costing her a single thought, when she had no right to be so blithe. What a fool she'd been, breezing along as if nothing could interrupt her life, when she knew Henry wasn't well. He'd never been robust – even as a younger man he'd been delicate – and so he was allowed to live as he did, away from everyone. It suited the older Devereauxes too; a son as odd as Henry wasn't to be displayed. They had Ralph, the handsome, charming, devilish Ralph, to fulfil that role. His mother had spoiled him and told everyone who would listen how he'd been his father's pride and joy. Ralph was the polar opposite of Henry in every way. Henry was slight and pale and one got the impression that he trod lightly on the earth. Ralph, on the other hand, was powerfully built and strong, an expert horseman, an accomplished hunter and cricketer. He liked fine food and wine and the company of his class, and to her knowledge, had never read a book in his life.

And even now, all these years later, she hated the pang in her heart she felt at the mention of his name. Old Mrs Devereaux might have been an insufferable snob, but she was right about one thing: Rose had made a monumental fool of herself with Ralph, thinking even for one second that someone like him would ever have settled for a servant. Her face flushed at the memory of how easily he'd taken her in, by him promising the sun, the moon and the stars. How she made herself believe when she was in his arms that their fumbled love-making was more than what it was – an arrogant young man taking advantage of an inconsequential girl whose name he could barely remember. He gave her Harp, and despite the terror of those early months of her child's life, she could never regret that. She loved her daughter with all of her heart. Quirky and bright, if a little dreamy, she was the best of Rose, and now Rose was going to let her down.

THE LAST HAPPY day of Harp's childhood was that day, the day *Titanic* sat in the harbour, a ship with a future full of promise and hope. And like that unsinkable ship, their lives too had struck disaster.

There was no way Harp would survive in service. She'd not been reared to it for one thing, not like Rose herself who had never been under any illusion from childhood that anything but a life of skivvying awaited her. But also Harp was special. She was an intellectual, she preferred books to people, and Rose had never insisted she learn how to keep house. Rose had been short-sighted, like an ostrich with her head in the sand.

A heart attack, the coroner had said. Doctor Lane told her it was an ongoing problem, that Henry would have been aware that his heart wasn't in perfect condition. Doctors would have explained that it was unlikely he would live into old age. Rose knew Henry went to London in the past year to visit a specialist, but she'd assumed he'd just go on as he'd always done.

If only he'd have said something, given her some indication that their little world was about to come crashing down. They did talk occasionally, when Harp was in bed, but he never mentioned his health. He took his medication, didn't exert himself physically and lived a quiet life. She'd had no reason to think that wouldn't be the situation for years to come.

Old Mrs Devereaux had made sure he was provided for; the trust fund for the upkeep of the house and the care of Henry saw to that, just about. But now there was nothing. No income, no security and no home. The thought of Ralph coming to claim his inheritance, seeing Harp, filled her with dread. Would he recognise Harp as his daughter? Would he even recognise Rose? She looked nothing like the girl she was then, silly and flirtatious, setting her cap at a jaunty angle, even risking a little rouge on her cheeks and lips. Now she wore conservative clothes, dark, buttoned up, old-fashioned if anything. Her hair was always pinned in a style more suited to an older woman. Never again would she allow a man to take advantage of her, that was certain.

She finally reached the top of the steps and began the descent down the hill to the Protestant church. It was teatime now, and men were coming home from work, mostly on the quayside or in the shops and businesses of the town. She envied them their simple lives. The small terraced houses they lived in were not commodious by any means but they were secure, and they had their wives and children around them. They had enough – a roof over their heads, food on the table – and they knew where they fit in the world. She was neither one thing nor the other, and as for Harp, she was the squarest of pegs in the roundest of holes.

She passed poor children without shoes playing on the street. They had filled a tobacco tin with sand and drawn a hopscotch pattern on the ground with a stone. They laughed, jumped and played together. She wondered if she'd have been better off to accept that life, courted John Colman, the footman at the Cliff House, when he'd asked her to go for a walk with him on a Sunday afternoon. But back then she'd been young and foolish and only had eyes for the young master of the house.

John had married Betty, the scullery maid, a few years later, and they lived somewhere around there with their large family. She saw him now and again down in town – he worked in the post office now – and he always greeted her with a smile. Perhaps if she'd not had such notions of her own importance, she would have married a decent man from her own class and been happy. But as her mother was fond of saying, if wishes were horses, beggars would ride.

She held her head high as she passed the women on their steps watching their children play, barely acknowledging them with a slight incline of her head. She knew they found her stuck-up and aloof, thought she had ideas above her station, and they were right, but it was how one survived. Being among the ordinary people, her own kind, meant questions, and she had no answers.

The Protestant church was picture-perfect with its limestone walls and beautiful Gothic stained-glass windows. It stood on a high bluff with the churchyard all around it, where the generations of dead members of the gentry rested peacefully. Headstones stood at odd angles, tipped over slightly with time. Several of the more prominent families had large tombs. Even though the whole layout was higgledy-piggledy, there was an odd symmetry to the disorder. Rose preferred it to the more angular Catholic cemetery, with the dead-straight lines of evenly spaced graves.

She grasped the heavy wrought-iron gate and pushed hard against it. Years of wind and rain, combined with the salt from the sea air, had rusted the hinges, and moss and lichen clung to the granite pillars either side of the gate. With one hard shove, the gate opened, creaking and scraping as it moved over the uneven stone.

Suddenly a thought struck her. Would Harp have been able to open that gate all by herself? She doubted it. Harp was small for her age and certainly not physically strong. But if she wasn't there, then where was she? Rose didn't allow the panic to rise in her chest. Harp had to be there.

She exhaled in relief as she came around the corner of the church. There Harp was, sitting beside the grave, her arms around her knees, her head resting on them. She looked tiny and so much younger than twelve. Rose walked to her and sat beside her on the grass.

'I'm sorry I ran away from school, Mammy,' Harp said, looking up at her, her hand shielding her eyes from the sun.

Rose's heart broke at her daughter's tear-stained face.

'They were throwing things at me and then they said things about...about Mr Devereaux and you, and I just... And I said I was a Devereaux...' The tears welled in her eyes again.

'It's all right, Harp. It's all right, my love.' She put her arm around her daughter and pulled her thin frame towards her.

'What are we going to do, Mammy?' she heard Harp whisper, and there was no mistaking the despair there.

'I don't know yet, but don't you worry, my love. I'll think of something.'

CHAPTER 7

*H*arp and her mother sat down to a meal of boiled eggs and toast. A hot pot of tea and a jug of milk sat on the table beside them. They'd walked back from the graveyard together, and Harp had shown her mother the gap in the churchyard wall where she'd got in.

They let themselves into the house and began preparing, neither commenting on how there was now no need for a tray. Every meal they'd ever made together, they set the table for two in the kitchen and prepared a tray for Mr Devereaux.

'Why did he always eat alone?' Harp asked in the silence.

Rose looked at her. It broke her heart how like Henry she was; it was funny how she'd never really noticed before. She used to think that she wasn't like Ralph and that was all that mattered. She remembered the relief seeing her hair fine and fair, not thick and dark like his was, her delicate features nothing like his strong, handsome face.

'Years ago, when his mother and father were alive, they were served in the dining room. Then as she got older and less able, Mrs Devereaux ate in her room, remember? And Henry did the same.'

'Do you think he might have wanted to come down here, to have the company?' Harp persisted.

Rose shook her head. 'No, he was happy in his rooms, you know that. He didn't like to leave them.'

'Why did he never go out, Mammy?'

'I think he just preferred his own company. I also suppose his heart was never strong and Queenstown is all hills no matter which way you go, so walking probably wasn't an option for him.'

A frown appeared on her daughter's face. 'Was he frightened to go out, do you think?'

Rose considered the question and tried to answer as she always did, taking her seriously, weighing up the answer, never dismissing her as childish. She wanted her to remember Henry as he was to her, to remain forever in her heart as her friend, but the truth was that Henry was a complicated man. And she owed her daughter the truth now, at long last. 'I'm not sure frightened is the word. But he was unique. He was very clever, as you know, and he liked to work on complicated mathematical problems or translating old languages – he could do things nobody else could. But then things that we can do easily, like having a normal conversation, doing a job, even shaking someone's hand, he found that incredibly hard and so he didn't do it.'

'The boys at school call him the quare hawk,' Harp said sadly.

'I know they do, and you know what, Harp? Mr Devereaux *was* strange to other people. He was different – his dress, his long hair, his way of being – and so he was a quare hawk as those children say. That's what the outside world saw on the rare occasions they did see him. But what nobody knows is that he was also kind and interesting and he trusted us and we were very fond of him. And that you and he were friends. We had a nice life here, the three of us, and we must remember him with love.'

'Sometimes he used to tell me where he was while I was at school.'

'I remember.' Rose smiled.

'Every day he would go somewhere different, like to Machu Picchu, or the Andes, or to Prince Edward Island. He went there through his books and he let me read them and I would feel like I'd been there too.'

The faraway grief-filled voice of her child tore at Rose's heart.

Henry Devereaux and Harp had a connection that nobody else in the world knew about or could understand. It was as if they saw a kindred spirit in each other, and the fact that she was a twelve-year-old girl and he was a fifty-two-year-old man had nothing to do with it.

This house was her connection to him, to her life, her childhood, but they would have to close the door on it and say goodbye – not just to their home, but to him. She'd assured Harp she would solve it, but she had no idea how. Each day was one step closer to eviction, destitution.

They tidied up and went to bed early, ending another worry-filled day. Rose kissed Harp's forehead, reassuring her once more that she would think of something. She hoped the words didn't sound as hollow to Harp as they rang in her own ears.

She tossed and turned. The bed seemed hard and lumpy, something she'd never noticed before. Why did she not insist Mrs Devereaux make provision for Harp before she died? She might have done it to avoid scandal. If she had, Rose would at least be able to keep a roof over their heads. Why did she never speak to Henry about what would happen if he died? Why did she not save every penny she earned instead of spending it on school fees and shoes and clothes for her daughter and herself, making them up to look better than the poor people they were? Round and round in her head every night since Henry died, the same admonishment, the same relentless regrets, tied up with pain and loss and frustration and fear.

Her thoughts were interrupted by the sound of her bedroom door opening, and there stood Harp, in her long white nightie, her hair falling around her heart-shaped face, her dark-grey eyes failing to mask the pain in her heart.

'Harp, are you all right?' Rose asked, sitting up.

'I'm scared.' Her voice was barely audible. 'Can...can I come in with you?'

'Of course you can.' Rose threw the cover back and moved over, making way for her child. Together they curled up and managed to give each other wordless comfort.

* * *

THE NEXT MORNING Harp was up and dressed for school before Rose woke. It was the first of May, and there was to be a procession and the decorating of the May altar. They would sing 'Queen of the May', and each day of the month, one child had to bring flowers for the special table with the statue of the Virgin Mary. Harp hoped she would be picked soon, before the daffodils that grew all around the Cliff House were gone. It was the only bright spot in an otherwise dull and pain-filled day. She'd learned over time to try to find one nice thing in each day to focus on; it made not having any friends and being bullied by Emmet bearable.

Before Mr Devereaux's death it had been easy. She would picture what activity she would do in his study that afternoon. She could research something, or read a story, or look at a picture of a famous painting, or play the harp... The possibilities were endless, and being in that room made her feel like school was a necessary interruption to her real life, the one that happened at the Cliff House. His books, the gramophone, the harp – they were all still there, but without him, she just couldn't go in there. She had not been in the study since the day he gave her the pen, the day he died.

* * *

HARP WAS SITTING at the table eating a bowl of porridge, and her heart ached when she saw her mother come into the kitchen. Her mother's hair was neatly brushed and pinned, but her face was pale. The skin beneath her eyes looked almost translucent.

'It's a nice day today, Harp,' Rose said as she boiled the kettle to make herself a cup of tea.

'It is.'

'How about you take a day off? We could cut the lawn and maybe weed the flowerbed in the side garden, and perhaps if the rain stays off, we could have our tea out there in the pergola.'

Harp's eyes brightened at the prospect. 'But what about school?'

she asked. Her mother never let her take a day off, even if she was
sick.

'I think you've learned all you can learn in Star of the Sea, don't
you?'

'What do you mean?' Harp's brow furrowed.

'Remember, I explained – I can't afford the fees. The term is almost
over now anyway and you won't be going back in September, so
maybe it's best to just stop going now. Besides, myself and Sister
Regina had words yesterday, so I'm not sure you'd be particularly
welcome.'

Rose tried to inject confidence in her voice, tried to make her feel
like this was all part of the master plan, but it wasn't and Harp knew
it. There was no plan, just a dark abyss of a future. The depth of pain
in her mother's eyes seemed unfathomable.

'Will I change into my old dress then?' Harp asked, looking down
at her yellow cotton school dress, lovingly handstitched by Rose.

Rose nodded. 'We don't want to get that one all dirty in the
garden.' She tried to smile, but it died on her lips as Harp trudged
back upstairs.

CHAPTER 8

*L*ater that morning, dressed in an old smock and pinafore, Harp turned as she heard the crunch of motor car wheels on the gravel behind her. A motor car was a rarity in Queenstown. The priest had one and Doctor Lane, and of course the Protestants all had one, but they still attracted attention.

She'd been half-heartedly weeding the side bed. Her mother had filled it with French marigolds back in the spring, and their cheery orange heads were being obscured by the dock leaves and nettles growing in between the plants.

Thomas Jefferson was wrong, she thought irritably, *when he said no occupation is as delightful 'as the culture of the earth, and no culture comparable to that of the garden'. Give me a book any day.* All weeds did was come right back again after they were pulled, whereas knowledge stayed in one's head forever. Besides, if they were going to have to leave, Harp had no idea why they were bothering. *Let Ralph Devereaux weed his own flower beds.*

She still couldn't believe what her mother said, that they would have to leave. The logical part of her knew she was right, of course. A servant and her child would never be allowed to stay in such a grand house, or any house, but she'd never felt like the servant's child here.

To her, the Cliff House was home, her home, and her mother and Mr Devereaux's home. She knew every nook and cranny, and nowhere was off limits to her. She knew it needed repair. They regularly had to empty buckets in the winter when the leaks were more like little streams, but Mammy would just laugh and say, 'Summer will come soon enough and dry everything out.' Mr Devereaux never even noticed. Then they'd toast bread in front of the fire for their supper, smearing home-made blackberry jam all over it, and forget all about the leaky roof or the rotten window frames. Was life not cruel enough to take Mr Devereaux from them without throwing them to the four winds as well?

Her mother had gone inside for a glass of water. Her pile of weeds was about ten times higher than Harp's because Harp kept drifting off into her thoughts and forgetting to pull them.

The motor car was very fancy – open-topped and coloured dark brown with gold trim and shiny spoked wheels – but it wasn't driven by a driver, as was the norm, but rather by the man inside himself. The door opened and a youngish man stepped out, dressed in a navy-blue suit and sparkling-white shirt. Around his neck he wore a splendid blue and white polka-dot silk bow tie, and from his breast pocket, a handkerchief in the same fabric spilled. His hair was oiled in a very fashionable style, a curl falling entirely intentionally over his forehead. Harp thought he was very handsome, though he looked like a dandy and she suppressed a smile.

'Good morning, Miss. I'm looking for a Miss Harp Delaney and a Mrs Rose Delaney?'

'I'm Harp and Mrs Delaney is my mother,' she answered, intrigued.

The man gave her that look she was used to getting from adults who could not decide if her manner of speaking, making eye contact and annunciating clearly was impertinent or not. He smiled, so he must have decided it wasn't.

'It is very nice to meet you, Miss Delaney. My name is Algernon Smythe, from Carling, Ellison and Smythe Solicitors, London.' He extended his hand and Harp took it, shaking it.

'And how may we be of assistance?' she asked.

'Well, the purpose of my visit is to bring to your attention a matter in which we acted for a Mr Henry Devereaux. Unfortunately we were unaware of his passing until a few days ago. I came as soon as I heard. My condolences. I understand your mother was in his employ?'

Harp nodded. 'Yes, my mother is the housekeeper here.'

The man nodded and grinned; he seemed pleased that all was as it should be. 'Indeed. So I understand that Mr Devereaux had legal counsel here in Ireland pertaining to other matters, but he sought our advice and service earlier this year on a very particular matter, and that is the reason for my visit.' His accent was clipped and very upper-class English. Nobody from around Queenstown, even the landed gentry, spoke like he did.

'You'll want to speak to my mother then,' Harp responded, enjoying the novelty of someone other than her mother or Mr Devereaux speaking to her as an equal. 'Please, follow me.'

'Lead on, Miss Delaney,' he said with a flourish, and Harp was sure she had never in her life encountered anyone like Algernon Smythe.

'Mammy!' she called as she entered. She felt like she should be calling her 'Mother' or 'Mama' or some such affectation.

Normally yelling like that would have Rose frowning in disapproval, but these were different times and she knew that to bring a stranger into the house without forewarning her mother of his presence would be a more grievous crime. 'There's a gentleman here who wishes to speak to you,' she called again, hoping her mother would appear soon.

'As a matter of fact, Miss Delaney, it is to both of you I wish to speak. The matter concerns both your mother and you.' He smiled and his eyes twinkled.

He looked like someone holding a delicious secret, and Harp knew the news could not be the dreaded eviction. Whatever it was, something told her it was good.

Harp was fascinated with him. He wore a gold and navy brocade waistcoat inside his jacket, and his shoes shone a gleaming tan leather. In his hand was a leather briefcase, with his initials engraved on the gold clasp. It was the exact same colour as his shoes – no coincidence, Harp was sure.

She was spared answering him by the arrival of her mother, who looked flustered.

'Mrs Delaney, a pleasure to meet you.' Mr Smythe offered his hand and Rose took it, glancing briefly at Harp, the unspoken question of who this was and what he wanted passing between them.

'My sincere condolences on the recent passing of Mr Devereaux. Is there somewhere we could converse?'

'Yes…yes, of course.'

Harp could see the vein pulsing at her mother's temple, always a sign she was stressed.

Rose led him to the drawing room; they had recently aired the downstairs rooms in anticipation of a visit from someone official.

'P-please, have a seat,' Rose said. 'Might I offer you some tea?'

Harp hated to see the terror in her mother's eyes. She was reminded of the man in the Goya painting *The Third of May 1808*, who is facing a firing squad with a mixture of appeal and defiance. She had studied the painting at Mr Devereaux's suggestion.

'Certainly afterwards,' Algernon Smythe said with a smile, 'tea would be most welcome. I drove from the port at Wexford, and the roads, while undoubtedly scenic, are somewhat haphazardly surfaced in the rural areas, are they not?' He grinned.

'I…I would imagine so…'

Harp watched as her mother struggled to regain her composure. She was clearly convinced that this was the meeting she'd been dreading for weeks, the day they were going to be told to leave the Cliff House. Harp wasn't so sure.

'So let me get on now.' He opened his briefcase and extracted a manila folder tied with a dark-green treasury tag. 'I explained to Miss Delaney outside that I am here on behalf of my firm, Carling, Ellison and Smythe Solicitors, of Highgate, London, and we are the representatives for Mr Henry Devereaux –'

'I'm sorry,' Rose interrupted. 'Mr Devereaux's solicitor was a Mr Cotter in Cork. I –'

'Yes, that is, I believe, the case pertaining to some aspects of his legal needs. He appraised us of that fact when we spoke last year. But this legal matter was of a particular kind and he sought advice and legal services with us with regard to this.' He looked down at the folder again.

'But I don't understand... I... Mr Cotter dealt with...'

Algernon Smythe raised a hand gently. 'Please, Mrs Delaney, all will be made clear very shortly, I promise, if you can just be patient.'

Harp reached over and took her mother's hand. The returning grip she got would have made her wince were matters not so critical.

'Now then, I understand this is a little unconventional, but the late Mr Devereaux was nothing if not that.' He grinned, and Rose nodded, uncertain. He went on. 'Mr Devereaux came to see me and explained the situation regarding the ownership of this house, how upon his death, it would revert to his brother.' He smiled. 'The reason he chose our firm is because my late father acted for the late Mr and Mrs Devereaux.'

Harp felt her mother stiffen.

Rose responded, 'I did know some of the details, yes.'

'Indeed. And to that end he wished to ensure that in the event of his death, matters here would work out favourably for you both within the legal constraints laid down previously.' He placed the folder on the desk and reached into the briefcase once more, this time extracting two letters. 'There is one for each of you. He asked that you be given these at the time of his death. As I said, we didn't hear of his passing until a few days ago, hence the delay. Miss Delaney, you may read yours now, but it was his wish, Mrs Delaney, that you read yours in private.'

He handed Harp a letter. The envelope was linen paper, cream and heavy, with her name written on the outside in black ink. She instantly recognised the handwriting. He handed her mother an identical one with her name on it.

'Essentially the purpose of my visit is to appraise you of the situation. Mr Henry Devereaux has written an affidavit claiming paternity of Miss Harp Delaney, and though you and he were not married, he bequeaths this house to her as his heir.'

Rose opened her mouth to speak and closed it again.

'Miss Harp Delaney is Mr Devereaux's daughter, is she not? And therefore a Devereaux and entitled to claim her birthright?' he asked.

Rose cast Harp a glance and swallowed. That look spoke volumes. Harp knew to say nothing.

'Well, yes, yes, of course, but I didn't know he was going to... I mean...I was not... Open your letter, Harp,' Rose said, her voice trembling.

Harp did as she was told. It took several attempts as her hands were shaking, but she extracted the single sheet. At the sight of his handwriting, looped and slanted, she settled and felt calm. Nothing he could write to her would do her harm. 'Shall I read it aloud?' she asked, her eyes locking with her mother's.

Rose nodded.

'Dear Harp. If you are reading this, I am gone, and that is something that here in this sunny office in London in the summer of 1911 makes me exceedingly sad. Not that my life is over per se, but that I will not get to see you every day. For you are surely the brightest star in the firmament of my life.

'I came to London to visit my doctor, but also to make sure that after my death, you and your mother are cared for in the meagre way I can. My heart is weak and getting weaker, and he fears I may not have long left. I haven't told you or your mother because, well, what would be the point? But suffice to say, this trip was necessary.

'I do not have much money. There is some, to which you are both most welcome. I have written to Mr Cotter in Cork and he will see you get it, so go to meet him in his office. But I do have the Cliff House. My mother insisted on it staying in the Devereaux family, and so it will. My brother, Ralph, were it not for this letter and the affidavit I have signed claiming paternity of you, would be my heir.

'So I leave the Cliff House to you, my daughter, appointing Mr Smythe and your mother as guardians of your inheritance until you come of age.

'I wish there was more, but death and taxes, as we know from Benjamin Franklin, are the only certainties. But I can give you this house, our home, and know that with the ingenuity and resourcefulness of both you and your mother, you will survive, and live to do all of the things you dream about.'

Harp swallowed, the tears now flowing freely down her cheeks. She didn't look up, knowing that if she did, she would not be able to continue. She carried on, her voice trembling.

'Live well, Harp. You are very special and unique. Don't strive to be like anyone else, because you're not. You are your own wonderful self, and I am so privileged and proud to call you my daughter. Henry Devereaux.'

Harp gazed at the man sitting opposite her. 'Is this true?' she asked uncertainly. 'That I own this house?'

He smiled. 'Yes, it is very much the case. I sent a copy of the sworn affidavit to Mr Ralph Devereaux's solicitors, and I would, now' – he turned to her mother – 'like to offer you, Mrs Delaney, the opportunity to also swear an affidavit that Harp here is the child of Mr Henry Devereaux, which should copper-fasten the claim on the estate against any legal challenges.'

Rose sat, staring at the letter in her hands. 'Does this letter contain anything that one doesn't?' she asked.

The young man looked bemused. 'I have no idea what it contains, Mrs Delaney. It is addressed to you and was sealed by Mr Devereaux before placing it in our care, and as I said, he wished you to read it in private. But I can tell you that essentially the contents of the letter to your daughter are the reason for my visit today. Mr Devereaux has named Harp as his heir, and as such, she is the owner of this house. As to his other matters, taxes and so on, those will be dealt with by his solicitor here in Ireland and any remaining funds transferred to you.'

'And his brother, Ralph, is in agreement with this?' Rose asked.

Algernon Smythe gave an enigmatic smile. 'I have no knowledge, as of yet, of his position on the matter. All I am able to tell you at this point is that my father, Randolf Smythe, made the will for Mr Devereaux's mother, in which she outlined her wish that the property

70

remain in the hands of someone of the Devereaux family, and that was why Mr Devereaux chose us. If you are willing to sign an affidavit today, corroborating Mr Devereaux's claim to the paternity of Miss Delaney here, then any challenge Mr Ralph Devereaux could potentially make would be unlikely to be successful.'

'And so if I confirm that Harp is Henry's daughter, the house is hers?' Rose tried to keep the incredulity from her voice.

'No,' Mr Smythe said patiently. 'The house has been willed to her, regardless of your affidavit. All your statement would do is strengthen the claim in the event of Mr Devereaux's brother contesting the will. It is a possibility that he could challenge it on the grounds of legitimacy, but we would have to wait and see.'

'And do you think he would, considering that we…we…um…were not lawfully married?'

Harp saw her mother's cheeks blush bright pink at the admission.

'I don't know, Mrs Delaney. He may well do, or he might decide not to – we cannot foretell.' He was gentle yet forthright. 'But Mr Devereaux's will, the affidavit claiming paternity and a similar affidavit from yourself confirming same, while not watertight, would be a considerable legal fight to take on. Especially as the late Mrs Devereaux was most adamant that the house be kept in the family.'

'Would it be easier if I were a boy?' Harp asked, interested.

Algernon considered her for a moment, then gave an enigmatic smile. 'Forgive me, but may I speak frankly?'

She nodded. 'Of course.'

'The issue will be on the legitimacy of your birth, Miss Delaney, rather than your gender. The late Mrs Devereaux only stipulated the house stay within the family. Occasionally an entail will make other demands, such as the estate must remain within the male line, but no such proviso was added here. I suspect she never considered that neither of her sons would produce a son of their own.'

Rose suppressed the urge to give a mirthless laugh. It was likely Ralph Devereaux had several offspring all over the world, given his proclivities.

'Well, given that it is *women* who produce children,' Harp said, 'the

71

idea that either of the Devereaux men could produce a son or a daughter is nonsense, but of course such prejudice is what we have come to expect.'

'Harp!' her mother exclaimed, clearly horrified at her impertinence.

Algernon laughed loudly. 'Please, Mrs Delaney, do not admonish your daughter. She is quite correct, of course. We are by far the more useless species when it comes to populating the earth, and the fairer sex get none of the credit to which they are entitled.'

Harp shared a grin with the solicitor.

'Yes, well, she should not be so impudent nonetheless.' Rose cast a glance at her daughter.

'So to answer her very valid question, the matter of her gender is irrelevant.'

Harp looked around the drawing room. Old Mr and Mrs Devereaux used to throw parties there for the local Protestant gentry long ago, but that all stopped when he died and she took to the bed.

This house was hers. Hers. She tried to take it in. Mr Devereaux must have known she was a Devereaux. It all made sense now, him giving her the pen, saying her name was Harp Devereaux, pointing out that he never made mistakes. But how could he have known that Ralph was her real father? Had his mother told him? She couldn't imagine it. Mrs Devereaux hardly ever spoke to him; Ralph was the only one of her family she spoke about, and she died in disappointment that he never returned, despite several promises that he would.

But he'd called her Harp Devereaux on that last day, and left the Cliff House to her in his will. She repeated the words over and over in her mind. The house, the walls, the stairs…and the floors and the beds and the furniture – everything was hers because she was a Devereaux. Her birth certificate might not show that, but she had a pen with the letters H and D engraved on it – Harp Devereaux.

She allowed the name to swirl around in her imagination. Harp Devereaux. That was her real name.

CHAPTER 9

*A*fter a lunch of tea and sandwiches, followed by a light-as-air lemon drizzle cake, Harp and her mother stood outside the front door as Algernon Smythe drove away. His fancy car and clothes and fashionable haircut all seemed so out of place at the Cliff House, and his news was even more incongruous. And yet it had all happened.

He explained before he left that there would be some more papers to sign on Harp's behalf, though her mother seemed to have signed around ten different documents while he was there. Harp wondered for a moment if it wasn't some kind of a swindle. Was this Mr Smythe really a solicitor and was he telling the truth? But she had the letter and she recognised Mr Devereaux's handwriting, so it definitely was from him, and he would never, ever lie to her. Besides swindling her and her mother would be the most stupid idea ever, as they had nothing worth swindling.

She had become interested in crimes the winter before, having read in the newspaper about a fraudster who had stolen several thousands of pounds from people who should have known better. She spent the months after that reading about various confidence tricksters and fraudsters who had come before the courts, as she wanted details of how they did it. She was intrigued at the ingenuity of some of the perpetrators and the downright stupidity of others. One of her favourites was the true story of John Sadlier, a member of Parliament who created fake balance sheets to swindle thousands from the bank. He ended up drinking poison to end his life but achieved immortality when Charles Dickens based the character of Mr Merdle on him in his novel *Little Dorrit*. Or the Scotsman Gregor MacGregor who came back to London from his world travels claiming to be the leader of the nation of Poyais, in Central America. He wrote a book detailing the delights of the nation, explaining how marvellous a place it was to live, and he was so convincing that people exchanged their money for Poyais dollars with plans to resettle there. Of course the only trouble was that Poyais didn't exist, something that only came to light after several efforts on the part of the new settlers to find it failed miserably.

'I can't believe that just happened.' Rose sat down at the small white table and chairs they sometimes used for tea outside if the day was fine. She was still reeling from the shock of it all. Harp sat beside her on a small wrought-iron stool.

'I wonder' – Harp lowered her voice though there was no possibility of being overheard in the garden – 'should we have been honest? I know it was for us, but Mr Devereaux told a lie. And we went along with it...'

Rose was adamant. 'Old Mrs Devereaux wanted the house to stay in the family, and you are a Devereaux. Mr Devereaux – Henry, I mean – just wanted to make sure you got what you were entitled to.'

'Did he know? About Ralph, I mean?' Harp asked tentatively. Though her mother had been honest that day that *Titanic* was in town, they'd never spoken about it since.

Rose shook her head. 'I don't know how he could have. I certainly never told anyone, and old Mrs Devereaux was in the horrors that anyone ever would find out so she hardly went blabbing. I just can't imagine her telling Henry. She didn't trust him to tie his own shoelaces – she thought he was an imbecile – so she would hardly ever speak to him, let alone confide something like that.'

'If she'd ever taken the time to speak to him, she'd have known he was very far from an imbecile. He was the cleverest person I ever met in my life,' Harp said sincerely.

'Thank you very much,' Rose said good-naturedly, pretending to be offended.

'You know what I mean, Mammy. You're very clever too, of course, but he was different. He just had to read something once and he'd remember it forever. He could list all the prime numbers between one and a thousand.'

'Very handy,' Rose said with a smile.

'There are 168,' Harp replied. 'I could do it, although it would take some time, but Mr Devereaux could just list them off without even thinking. And he could do long division in his head and he knew so many languages and poetry and literature. He read so much and remembered it all.'

Rose squeezed her daughter's hand. 'He was remarkable, no doubt about it. And you're right – Mrs Devereaux was the loser there because if she'd taken time to get to know him, she would have seen for herself what an extraordinary man he was.'

'And Ralph, was he even a little bit like him?' Harp asked.

Rose shook her head. 'No, he wasn't. He was vain and brash and cared nothing for anyone but himself.'

Harp tried not to feel hurt at her mother's description of her father. She wished he was like Mr Devereaux. 'But what if he comes back, Mammy? I know he doesn't know that I'm his child, but still he might guess and then we'd be in terrible trouble.'

'If he comes back, we'll say that Henry Devereaux was your father and that's all there is to it. I know it's a lie, but Harp, it is what he wanted and it was his house. Ralph hasn't been seen for thirteen years. His mother kept saying he was going to come back, that he was planning a visit, but he never did. He let her down, just like he's done all of his life. He took what he could from her and never gave her a second thought.' Harp heard unfamiliar bitterness in her mother's voice.

Though it was horrid that it took the death of Mr Devereaux to change it, their relationship had become one more of equals than mother and daughter. Rose spoke plainly to Harp now, sharing her worries and concerns, but instead of making Harp feel anxious, it had the opposite effect. She liked to know what was going on; not telling her, treating her like a child when clearly they were in a tight spot, only made her worry more. Her mother could fix everything, so if she said it was all going to be all right, then it was.

'At least I look like him,' Harp said, and her mother smiled.

'You really do, and you and he were alike in so many ways, Harp – a pair of peas in a pod.' Rose reached out and stroked Harp's face.

'A very odd pod,' Harp said seriously, and Rose pealed with laughter.

'True enough, but an odd pod I happen to think was absolutely smashing.'

They sat in contented silence for a while, listening to the seagulls caw-cawing overhead, circling in time to meet the fishing boats and steal their feast of guts as the fish were cleaned on the quayside.

'Imagine, Mammy, just like that we have a home of our very own. And not just an ordinary house, but this one, the best house in the whole of Queenstown,' Harp said, gazing up at the façade of the house.

It was originally built in the 1700s but had been extensively renovated in the 1860s in the Victorian style. It had three storeys and an asymmetrical roof that came to four different points along the length. The windows were inset, long and narrow, except for a large bay window that jutted out in front. The façade was constructed in a combination of granite and red sandstone, with marble inlaid in the reveals of the windows. Previous generations of Devereauxes didn't pass on their skills for entrepreneurship and business to either Henry or Ralph, but at the time of construction and renovation, the Devereauxes were very wealthy and the house reflected their status in society.

The front door was five feet wide – with stained glass filling the remainder of the eight-foot aperture – and made of solid teak. It had brass door furniture, an extraordinary extravagance, but it lent the house a sense of importance. Harp and her mother rarely used the main door, coming and going usually through the much-more-modest back door.

The grounds were small for a house so imposing, but that was due to its location, perched on the cliff overlooking the bay. It was a long site, with a carriage gate at one end to the right of the house, stretching some one hundred yards, and a single gate at the other, providing access from the house to the set of pedestrian steps that went all the way down to the town square. There was a lawn to the front, no more than thirty feet deep, and it fell away to sheer cliff face and the lower road below. Behind the house had been dug out from the rockface, the space behind being just wide enough for a large carriage to come through but no more, rendering the back of the house rather dark, and the cliff was steeply stacked, composed of shale and limestone. The view of the entire harbour from the front was spectacular. Harp went to school every day via the steep steps that ran outside the southern gable of the Cliff House. The locals called the steps the Smuggler's Stairs, as they linked the port with the top road out of town.

'It's lovely,' Rose agreed, taking in the house as if for the first time. 'And Henry Devereaux wanted us to have it.'

A small smile formed on Rose's lips, and Harp was struck by how pretty her mammy was. She had been so sad and worried about their future since Mr Devereaux died. The emotions were etched deep on her face, her eyes losing all their sparkle, but today, as the sun shone on the sailboats bobbing about on the harbour and the diamond glints on the sea illuminated the scene before them, the world seemed like somewhere they could go on living.

In those weeks since Mr Devereaux had died, *Titanic* had sunk, with all those lives lost, and the future seemed dark and terrifying. At night Harp would lie awake, wondering how she could live in a world where such awful things happened to people who had done no harm.

But today she felt the beginnings of green shoots. Her heart was still broken and she had regular nightmares, imagining Mr Devereaux on *Titanic*, him locked in a cage beneath the sea, calling to her, begging her to let him out, to help him to swim home, but she couldn't. She woke in tears most nights with her mother's arms around her as she cried for him, for all of the people who were going to America full of excitement, for herself.

'So now we don't have to leave? We have somewhere to live forever? We don't have to separate?' Harp needed to hear her mother say the words, to take back the horrific prospect of them going to work in different houses.

'That's true, Harp, we don't. We have a home of our very own.'

Rose went in and made them some more tea and brought it out to the wrought-iron table and chairs against the western gable, the warmest part of the house in the afternoon as the sun tracked around. Together they sat and leaned their heads back against the wall, allowing the sun to warm their faces.

'Am I dreaming this, Harp?' her mother asked without opening her eyes.

'No, Mammy, I don't think so,' Harp replied, enjoying the sound of a seagull cawing loudly overhead. 'Did you read your letter?' she asked, feeling her letter in the pocket of her dress. She longed to take it out and read it again but somehow felt it wasn't right.

Rose sighed. 'Not yet. I will – I just need to process this first.'

'Why did he do it, do you think?' Harp asked quietly.

Rose thought for a moment. 'Well, he had a connection to you, something nobody else could understand except the two of you really. I was there, I saw it, but even I wasn't part of it. Ever since you were little, he was never anxious around you. Even the way he spoke to you was more relaxed, more at ease than with anyone else in the world. And he never spoke to you like you were a child, but always as an equal. And you and he liked the same things, books, music. He would speak to me too, but not the way he was with you. His mother used to terrify him, the poor man. Whenever she would deign to speak to him at all, she had him tongue-tied and stammering. He wasn't like that with you.'

'We didn't talk all that much. Sometimes we wouldn't say anything for days – we'd just read and listen to music. But I didn't mind. It wasn't awkward.' Harp smiled at a reminiscence. 'I remember once, when I was seven or eight, reading *Pride and Prejudice*. Mr Darcy was enduring Mrs Bennet and her quest to marry off her daughters, and I asked him if he'd ever thought about marrying – he had a fine house and a good family name. But he said he was no Mr Darcy and that the Cliff House was a poor relation of Pemberley, and that the only thing he and Mr Darcy shared was a tendency to social awkwardness.'

Rose nodded. 'He hated meeting new people undoubtedly.'

'He took care of us, though,' Harp said with a smile.

'He did.' Her mother turned to her. 'He wasn't like anyone else, and that's the truth. He wasn't perfect, he had faults, but he loved you, Harp, in his own way, and he took care of us.'

'So does this mean I can go back to school?' Harp asked tentatively. Much as she hated the bullying, she longed for the opportunities to advance that formal education afforded her. She could learn independently, of course – she'd done that all her life – but she'd need to matriculate to get to university, and to do that, she had to go to school.

'Do you want to?' her mother asked.

Harp nodded.

'Even with Emmet Kelly and all of that?' her mother pressed.

Harp thought for a moment. Perhaps her mother knew more about the torment she'd endured thus far than she realised. 'I don't like him teasing me, or the way the others think me strange, and I would like a friend but nobody has ever tried to be my friend. I did try, before, but it never worked. I am different, Mammy, I know that, and not just because of Mr Devereaux and living here. I react differently to other people. It's hard to explain. Sometimes I feel like everyone else knows how to be and I don't. I say the wrong things, or I freeze up when someone talks to me. I try to be like the others, but I never seem to get it right. But I've learned to like school despite all of it. I love learning, I love books and finding things out, and I really want to go to university, so I would like to go back.'

Rose reached over and cupped the side of Harp's face in her hand. 'He was right about you. You are so special and different. And I know that's not much use to you when you go to school, and I know you'd like a friend, but there are people in the world who will love you for who you are, Harp, I promise you that.' She exhaled. 'This is a small place and the people here are good, decent, you know, but they don't trust what they can't understand. And they can't understand you, any more than they could understand Henry. The people of this town, they're not your people, but your people are out there – they really are. People who will understand you and admire you for the amazingly brilliant person you are. So if you want to go back, then of course you can.'

Harp heard a hesitation in her mother's voice. 'But?' she asked.

Rose gave her a small smile. 'Well, getting this house, it's the most wonderful and unexpected thing in the world, but it doesn't solve the problem of us having no money at all. I will need to find a job, and even then, there is so much to be done here.'

'Mr Quinn was looking at the roof when he called to check on us,' Harp said, remembering the kind man's look of pity when he saw the damage the weather had done.

'I know. He told me it would need to be looked at soon, otherwise the timbers will rot completely and we'll need a new roof. But at the time it was going to be Ralph Devereaux's problem and I had enough of my own, so I didn't take much notice.'

'But now it's our problem?' Harp said.

'It is. But we'll figure something out, don't worry.'

Harp watched as a tender approached the quay wall far below. Another ship, nothing as big or as celebrated as *Titanic*, was at anchor in the bay, and people were assembled in order to board it. She wondered what terror was going through their heads. Was fear overriding the excitement? If the mighty unsinkable *Titanic* could go down, then anything could. The sea stretching out before her looked benign, pretty and cheery, but she knew it was not that. The sea could be unforgiving, cold and grasping and did not give up if it wanted you.

'"Full fathom five thy father lies, of his bones are coral made: Those are pearls that were his eyes, nothing of him that doth fade",' Harp recited gently.

'What is that?' her mother asked.

'Ariel's song, from *The Tempest*.'

Rose raised an eyebrow.

Harp smiled. 'Shakespeare. It's about Ferdinand's father, who was believed to have drowned at sea. I was thinking about the people on *Titanic*.'

'It's so sad, but they're in heaven now,' Rose said.

Harp said nothing. The whole town was subdued in the wake of the disaster...or was it? It was hard to tell. She was defeated by loss herself so perhaps it just felt that way. There had certainly been more activity than usual, and even some newspaper reporters had been asking questions and taking photographs, but it had all passed her and her mother by. In the time since the disaster, they had gone out to buy food when it was necessary but nothing else.

The streets of Queenstown were always busy with locals and travellers alike. *Titanic* had garnered so much attention undoubtedly, but every few days a ship was in, either coming or going to the US. They sat, side by side, looking down at the bustling town. Everyone and everything in Queenstown was somehow connected to the transatlantic voyage business.

Suddenly, Rose had an idea. 'What about if we opened a guest house?'

Harp looked at her mother. What did they know about running a place like that? Maybe her mother did, but Harp knew absolutely nothing.

'We can't do that, Mammy. Sure Mrs O'Flaherty has the boarding house below at World's End. She'd have a fit if we set up in opposition to her, and I wouldn't like to be at the wrong end of her. She's a right demon. And the Imperial is lovely but only for the very wealthy who want butlers and footmen and all the rest of it.'

'No, Harp, listen. Not for the third-class passengers – they will always stay at the boarding house – and only the first-class passengers can afford the Imperial Hotel, but what about the middle group, the second-class passengers? Or the better-off third class who don't want to share with all sorts of people, or the less-well-off first class? What about if we opened the rooms upstairs? There are so many empty bedrooms, and what if we did them up and offered more upmarket accommodation than the boarding house but not as fancy as the Imperial with the saltwater baths and the stables and all the rest of it. Something between the two, for people who don't want to sleep six to a room on hard bunks picking up all sorts of things but can't afford the real luxury. We could do it, and they would love staying here, with the views and everything. We could offer a nice comfortable night's sleep in a private room and a good breakfast.'

'But the rooms here are in no fit state for anyone to stay in. They've not been used for decades.' Harp considered her mother's idea and dismissed it. She loved the Cliff House, and even she, not the most observant person when it came to things like that, could see the place needed a lot of work. Besides, the idea of having a whole lot of strangers in their home, touching their things, frightened her.

'But couldn't we make them usable? I mean, what do they need?' Rose was warming to the idea. 'We could make new curtains and bedspreads. The beds and furniture are all there. What do they need except airing and a good cleaning? We have the five big bedrooms on the second floor, and that's not counting the ones on the top floor, although they are in the worst condition, in all fairness, so it's a bigger job bringing them back from the dead. But the ones off the first landing aren't too bad, I think, if we put some elbow grease into it. We could keep the top floor for ourselves, so we'd still have our privacy. That's ten people at two to a room, and if we charge a pound per person for bed and breakfast, that would be ten pounds a night. The breakfasts would be easy – tea, porridge, brown bread and home-made jam. And we could get hens, and we could offer a cooked break-fast of bacon and eggs for an extra charge, and it would be our own business.' Rose's eyes glittered with excitement. 'Imagine, Harp, never having to work for anyone else again? Making our own money? We could control our own lives, Harp, be our own masters.'

Her mother's eyes gleamed with the possibility of it all. Harp swallowed her misgivings. Rose was right – they needed an income and Cliff House was beautiful and in the most ideal location. 'I'm not much good at stuff like that, but I could help before and after school and during the holidays. And maybe if it was busy, we could take someone on for laundry or something, or send it out if we made enough... And I could entertain the guests by playing music for them... And it would mean...'

Harp paused. She had not plucked a string since Mr Devereaux died, but now, for the first time, she felt like she could. Part of her actually wanted to feel the bittersweet heartbreak of the tunes he'd loved and to see in her mind's eye the sheer bliss on his face when she would play.

'If it worked, I could save up and we could afford to send you to university,' Rose finished for her.

Harp coloured. It was her dearest wish to study literature and science and music and art. She had no idea what she wanted to do. Some days she thought she might be an archaeologist, other times a musician or an artist. She had so many ideas, so many plans.

Seeing her daughter's hesitation and embarrassment, Rose placed her hands on Harp's shoulders. 'I really think we could do this,' she said.

Harp nodded. 'Of course we could, if you think we could. And there's a need. Mrs O'Flaherty is always full, even if it is with fellows full of drink looking for a fight or women with loads of children, and there are people coming and going through here all the time. The Imperial is so expensive, almost two pounds a night. For people who are about to embark on a big adventure, even if they're rich, maybe they'd want to save their money but still stay somewhere nice and respectable?'

Rose smiled slowly. 'You know, Harp, Henry was right – you're a marvel. We could go down to the ticket office and maybe put a sign up, and one in the railway station as well. We won't be stepping on anyone's toes – well, except the Imperial Hotel, but I doubt we'd be much competition to the mighty Mr Bridges.'

Harp felt a surge of excitement. 'So we'll do it?'

'I think we should certainly give it a try anyway.' Rose hugged her daughter. 'Henry would want us to stay here and we can't do it if we don't have any money, so this is a way of staying in our home. Imagine, Harp, it's our home now and we can make a living from it if we do it right.'

'All because of Mr Devereaux,' Harp said softly.

* * *

ROSE DELANEY SAT on her bed. Harp was down in Henry's study playing an O'Carolan piece; she could hear her up through the floorboards. Her daughter was entranced by the music, Rose knew, even without seeing her.

The stiff envelope was in her hands, still unopened. What was stopping her? She didn't really know, but there was no way she could put it off any longer. She slid her finger under the flap, opened it and extracted a single sheet.

Dear Rose. She smiled at that. He hardly ever used her name, and when he did he always blushed and mumbled.

I had to leave, it seems. Something that will break my foolish and, as it turns out, distinctly defective heart. A family failing, apparently – the same complaint got my father. Though I suspect he was happier to check out than I, a final welcome finale to my mother's endless carping.

My death means I can finally say the words I could never utter in life.

I want you to have written in black and white the truth of my feelings for you so you might never doubt them as the years slide by. Rose, you and Harp are all I care about, the only people on earth I ever loved.

I know the truth of her parentage. I found a sworn statement among my mother's papers after her death last year, a horrible document she made you sign, forcing you to silence on the subject of Harp's father in return for allowing you and Harp to stay here. Though the document didn't name

84

Ralph, it wasn't me, my father was dead, and so it could only have been my brother.

Despite that difficult start, and your appalling treatment at the hands of my family, we created a world inside these walls where we were just three people living happily together. I loved those years and hated anyone to enter our bubble, fearing that to bring our perfect little family out into the cold, harsh critical light of the world would somehow break the magic spell. Perhaps you saw me as just the last Devereaux, the peculiar son who rejected the world in favour of books – you have no reason not to. But know that for me, you and Harp were my whole world.

I know you both thought me odd, and I was. How strange to refer to yourself in the past tense! But the world confounded me in ways I couldn't explain to you in life. I feel compelled to try now.

When I was a child, my father was aloof and distant, my mother nagging and haughty. Ralph and I were nothing more than a necessary inconvenience. People like them were bred to breed, and we were the result. There was no love between my parents. Not even affection, I'd wager. A succession of British nannies and governesses were shipped out to Japan for our youth, all authoritarian, some violent and others negligent, and they were followed by excruciating years at boarding school in England, where every aspect of my being was assaulted – physically, emotionally, intellectually.

Returning to the Cliff House after school was a mercy, and by then I believe my parents had given up any faint hope that I would make anything of myself, and so I was left alone with my books. It was bliss.

Ralph and I were not close; we might as well have been different species altogether for all we had in common. He and I lived here for a time as young men, but he was sent to India soon after you came to work here. Now I know why, though there were other reasons too, I think. Other women, debts and so on. Nothing was ever said outright, but when you say as little as I do, you hear and notice a lot.

Within a year of Ralph's departure, as you know, my father was dead, of the same condition that now besets me, having not uttered more than a few syllables to me since I returned from school.

Then we endured all those years with my mother, and when she took ill and died, I'm not ashamed to say I felt nothing but relief. It would be just me and you and Harp. Though my mother was confined to her bed for the last years of her life, her cold, malevolent presence was as pervasive as smoke. It might sound harsh, but she never loved me, or even liked me much, and the feeling was mutual. Her treatment of you, my dear Rose, is testament to the fact that my perceptions of her were completely accurate. You are the polar opposite of her as a mother. You are what a mother should be – warm, loving, gentle...yet strong.

What a wonderful girl Harp is, Rose. You should be so proud. I never in my life met anyone like me, but Harp is. She's lovely and friendly, where I am neither, but she understands me, and I her.

I love her, Rose, and I love you. I know I could never have been a man worthy of your affection in that sense, and I would never have had the audacity to suggest it, but know that you were treated badly by one Devereaux brother, for which I am incredibly sorry, but you were adored by the other. Completely and totally.

Rose didn't realise she was crying until a tear smudged the ink. Henry was an unusual man, and he was right – she'd never thought of him in that way – but he was ten times the man his brother was. She should have seen it. Maybe things could have been so different. But she didn't, and because he was such an insecure and sensitive adult who never wanted to hurt anyone, he never said.

And so, my love, I have had to leave you and Harp. The Cliff House is your home and I hope it always will be. I love the thought of you living happily here. Please, Rose, continue to care for Harp as you have. Love her. Do not allow anyone to dim her light. She is special, Rose, and though I don't have a right to be, I am so proud of her.

Marry if you meet someone worthy of you and Harp. Be happy, my love, please. You deserve so much.

I am leaving you both the house. It is bequeathed to Harp because of the proviso in my mother's will that it must go to a Devereaux, but I know you two will stick together. I wish I could leave you more. Perhaps if I'd been braver, I could have.

Live a long and happy life, my darling.

All my love,

Henry

86

Rose folded the letter and placed it carefully in its envelope. It explained so much. She'd never had an inkling of his feelings for her, but she now took comfort in the afterglow of his love. Though nobody would see it as such, he was a father to Harp all of her life, not just since he discovered she was his niece. He was kind and constant and noble, cherishing and nurturing her, and Rose knew she was doing the right thing by accepting his last gift to them.

CHAPTER 10

The next three weeks passed them by in a blur of sewing and cleaning and dusting and polishing. The rooms had to be aired and repainted, the floorboards sanded and polished, but they did it, the two of them, working day and night.

They used what little money Rose had saved to buy paint, and when Mr Quinn heard of their venture, he cleared out his shed and found all sorts of tools and paintbrushes and even some paint left over from his house. He and Brian arrived one day in overalls ready to help out, and Rose and Harp were delighted to have strong men around for lifting.

Mr Quinn was a tall and quiet man and restful to be around and Brian was very nice, and as they sanded the floor together, Brian told Harp how he was going away to university next year to train as a doctor. She envied him all the opportunities he had and told him so.

'Sure won't you want to stay and run this place with your mother now?' he'd asked when she said that.

'No, that's not my dream. I want to study, get a degree, travel,' she said, wrapping the sandpaper around a wooden block as Mr Quinn had taught her and rubbing the floorboards vigorously.

Brian gently took the block from her hands and turned it around.

'Sand with the grain, not against it.' He smiled. 'Well, Harp Delaney, if anyone can do that, it would be you, sure you're a pure genius,' he said with a lopsided grin.

'I'm not,' she protested, colouring at the thought and getting flustered. 'I just read a lot, and Mr Devereaux taught me lots of things so I –'

'Harp, it was a compliment.' Brian smiled again, throwing some sawdust at her. It lodged in her wavy hair and she started to giggle as she extracted it. 'You're the cleverest person in that school, by a million miles, and some people resent it, but I don't. I think you're amazing.'

'I'm not,' she began again. 'And you're not even in my class, so how could you know –'

'Harp Delaney is a legend in the school, surely you know that?' He went on sanding. 'You know Mrs Barry, who taught you in third class, is my aunt, don't you? She said you were a child genius.'

Harp blushed to the roots of her hair. She'd loved being in Mrs Barry's class; she was such an inspiration. All the other teachers were either men or nuns and they asked the boys the more difficult questions and often ignored the girls altogether. Mrs Barry was married to the master, who taught Brian.

'So Master Barry is your uncle?' she asked.

'Well, uncle-in-law. Mrs Barry is my aunt Kate – she's my mother's sister – and she married Ted Barry.'

'Is he nice at home?' Harp asked. The headmaster always seemed forbidding and unapproachable. He taught the senior class, so she'd had no direct dealing with him.

Brian nodded. 'He is, and in fact he had great time for your Mr Devereaux. He and Henry Devereaux were pals as lads, I think, after the family came back from Japan, but neither Mrs Devereaux nor Mrs Barry thought it was a good idea. And so then Henry was sent off to some fancy boarding school in England. He always said he would have liked to renew the acquaintance, but since Mr Devereaux never came out, he didn't like to intrude by calling, so he never got the chance.'

Harp felt profound sadness at that. She would have liked Mr

Devereaux to have a friend. 'He was sent to Stonefallow, a boarding school in the New Forest. He hated it.' Harp remembered him telling her the horror stories of boarding school, where the PE master made them do midnight runs in the dark and the rain, of the poor food and regular beatings that were the norm.

'Poor fella. I'd say it was bad, all right. Uncle Ted and Master Barry always said to those of us in school that he was great, funny and interesting.'

'He was,' Harp confirmed, glad to have some tenuous point of contact between Brian and Mr Devereaux. 'He was very clever, and he always had time for you, to explain things. He never spoke to me like I was a silly child like most grown-ups do. And he knew everything.' Brian smiled and she insisted. 'Honestly, he knew every single thing. I never asked him something he didn't know the answer to.'

'I'm sorry I never met him,' Brian said, and Harp nodded.

'You would have liked him very much.'

That evening, after Brian and Mr Quinn left, Harp tuned the harp in the guest room that had once been Mr Devereaux's study for the first time in weeks and played some slow airs, finishing with O'Carolan's concerto. She rested the soundbox on her thin shoulder, her fingers reaching through all the strings from soundboard to pillar effortlessly, instinctively finding the strings without looking or reading notes. She'd tried to read sheet music, and she could if pressed, but the music was so intuitive for her, so much a part of who she was, that the pages of black dots seemed superfluous, an unnecessary hurdle between her and melody.

She'd been avoiding playing, fearing it would be too painful, but she found to her surprise that it had the opposite effect. She was comforted by the familiar tunes and could almost feel Mr Devereaux's presence in the room. He would have dismissed it as a fanciful notion, a fiction made up by those who could not face the fact that the mortal realm was all there was, but she smiled and played and felt him there with her.

* * *

THE WEEKS FLEW by in a blur of renovation and cleaning, and soon the town was at its peak of hustle and bustle. The summertime was the busiest around Queenstown, people preferring to make the transatlantic voyage when the seas were calmer and less prone to storms, especially in the wake of *Titanic*. But there were also lots of people just taking the sea air on their holidays in Queenstown, and her mother planned to take advantage of that market too.

They'd received some cash from Mr Cotter, the solicitor, the funds left in Mr Devereaux's estate, and had used it to patch up the worst of the wear and tear on the house and to take out an advertisement in the *Cork Examiner* and the *Irish Independent* announcing the opening. The trust fund set up by Mrs Devereaux that had paid Rose's wages and the upkeep of the house had reverted to Ralph, such as it was. They lived as frugally as they could, using the furniture and china of the house and darning moth holes in ancient sheets and blankets. Buying something new was a last resort.

They had received so many enquiries by post that they were booked solid from the 21st of June. They had one week left to turn the house into the beautiful guest house they'd promised.

They bought fabric – yellow gingham and white cotton were the cheapest they could find – for Rose to make curtains and bedspreads. Harp polished the old furniture with beeswax until her arms ached. The house was very slowly coming back to a slightly shabbier version of its former glory. The leaks were disguised and thankfully were not that noticeable in the new guest bedrooms; at least in summer they weren't. Hopefully by winter they would have made enough money to do a job on the roof. The worst of the rot on the windows was patched up with paste and painted over. The plan was that they would be able to invest in a man to come and do repairs next winter if they made it through the summer season.

They'd contacted Mr Quinn to see if he would consider running a taxi service with his carriage from the station for their guests, and he was happy to do it. The steep pull of the hill would be a bad start to a guest's experience at the Cliff House, especially with luggage. His hearse was lying idle most of the week, so he was glad of the business.

Harp and her mother worked night and day, falling into bed each night after midnight, their limbs aching, only to wake again at six to tackle the house once more. Word got around about their good fortune, and though undoubtedly it had set the tongues wagging behind their backs, to their surprise there was no sneering or smart remarks.

Harp noticed that Mammy had started to dress slightly differently – still very proper and ladylike, of course, but with a little more flair. She didn't dress all in black any more, as was befitting a housekeeper, and now wore pastel blouses and neutral-coloured skirts. Harp hid a smile when she and her mother walked into the cobbler's a few days earlier to have their boots heeled and Mrs Deasy, the cobbler's wife, was passing a remark to her husband about how Rose was looking very pleased with herself these days. Her back was turned to the shop door as she spoke, and she nearly died when she turned to see them standing there. Harp almost felt sorry for Mrs Deasy, who blushed bright pink when she realised Mammy had heard every word she said. Mr Deasy, a nice, polite man not given to gossip, hid a grin at his wife's discomfiture and took their boots.

Harp had noticed that a lot, how some women seemed to be a bit resentful of her mother while men admired her. It wasn't as if Rose was flirtatious or anything like that; she could never be accused of that. She was polite and courteous but a bit distant, Harp supposed. It was just that people always noticed her mother as she was so striking. Now that she was dressing like a business owner, she seemed to really irk the women, whereas the men just gazed appreciatively. Having notions above your station was a very grievous sin in Queenstown, and even before the inheritance, Harp imagined she and her mother were suspected of having outlandish notions. Harp considered it sometimes, wondering if there was merit to the way the people there thought, that one should know their place, but she decided there wasn't. If nobody had ever tried to advance, to better themselves, to educate themselves, then mankind would still be living in caves. She wanted better for herself than she was entitled by virtue of her birth, and she would never apologise for it. Her mother too should, by the ideology of a small Irish town, be hanging her head in shame to have borne an illegitimate child of a Protestant gentleman and then, to add insult to injury, inherited his house. But Rose held her head up; she always did and always would.

Rose's admission in school that Harp in fact was a Devereaux would be general knowledge by now, and so the fiction of Rose's dead husband would have been exposed. But Mammy said the people of Queenstown were nothing if not business-minded. A guest house such as theirs could only elevate the status of the town as a destination, and so all businesses would benefit. Besides, they were not bad people. Gossip was the fuel that drove social interaction. She and Harp were headline news now, but next week their story would be forgotten in favour of someone else. It was just a case of riding it out. As usual she was right.

Mrs O'Flaherty from the boarding hostel even wished them well when she saw the advertisement in the newspaper for the Cliff House and said she would send anyone she thought could afford it up when she was full. To their utter astonishment, even the haughty Mr Bridges, the town magistrate and owner of the Imperial Hotel, called one day to see the progress and with a gift of a lovely leather-bound guest book for their hall table.

Mr Bridges was one of those Irish men who was more English than Irish, though to Harp's knowledge he had lived all his life in Cork. His wife and the wife of Lieutenant Colonel DeVeers, the Royal Irish Constabulary senior officer stationed in Queenstown but who oversaw the entire lower harbour area, were sisters, the daughters of some high-ranking British official in Dublin Castle apparently.

The rank and file of the RIC were made up of locals mainly, though their quasi-military way of policing was different to other parts of the United Kingdom. Ireland had rebelled so many times under British rule, it was deemed necessary, but in general the constables were all right. The senior officers, though, were almost all Anglo-Irish Protestants. And the DeVeers and the Bridges families were certainly that.

'You're filling a niche in the market, Mrs Delaney. Well done,' Mr

Bridges had said warmly. 'The people you are aiming at currently don't stay in Queenstown – they stay in Cork and come down on the train – but if we can put them up here, well, they will use the local shops and services and they might pop into the hotel bar for a drink. So as I frequently say to Mrs O'Flaherty, a rising tide lifts all boats, Mrs Delaney. We are allies and friends, not enemies. There is business enough in this town for us all, and much better we pull together than separately, so if there is anything I can help with, please don't hesitate.'

The idea of the impeccably groomed Mr Bridges having anything in common with the wild and frequently terrifying Mrs O'Flaherty was one that tickled Harp. The boarding house owner was well known in the town as being more than a match for any drunkard or man spoiling for a fight. Despite the rough-and-ready appearance of O'Flaherty's, it was a well-run establishment and any nonsense was dealt with by the proprietress swiftly and severely. Mrs O'Flaherty had been married four times, each husband dying prematurely, though it would be a very brave or foolhardy man or woman who would remark upon it. But no matter what the state of her romantic life, Mrs O'Flaherty always managed well enough. She had a number of sons and daughters from those marriages, but the boarding house was her own, and she ran it alone.

They'd accepted Mr Bridges' gift graciously and laughed when he was gone at what kind of a friendship could exist between the ruddy-cheeked, straight-talking Mrs O'Flaherty and the oh-so-perfect Mr Bridges. While her mother reminded her of the wonderful Hester Prynne in Nathaniel Hawthorne's *The Scarlet Letter* in the way that she refused to be cowed or made to feel inferior in a society that demanded that she should, Mrs O'Flaherty was more like Moll Flanders in the story by Daniel Defoe.

Mammy remarked how relieved she was that Mrs O'Flaherty was now too an ally of theirs rather than an enemy, for she would be a formidable one.

* * *

THE NIGHT before the first guests were to arrive, Harp and her mother did one last tour of the house.

The front door no longer scraped across the tiles since Matt had taken it off the hinges and planed it to make it fit better, the wood having expanded over the years. The tiles shone after Harp scrubbed them using baking soda and bleach to rid them of decades of staining, and the rosewood hallstand gleamed with polish. The mirror was age spotted, but there was nothing to be done about that. The hatstand and umbrella holders were brass and looked like new after Harp's rubbing with Brasso, which she then polished off with a soft cloth.

They'd revarnished the bannisters, and the royal-blue and gold stair-runner carpet that was threadbare on the corners had been released from its grips on the top and pulled down, then retacked, so the risers were now the treads. It wasn't perfect, but it was the best they could do.

Old paintings that had been in the family for years – that Henry had hated, claiming his ancestors were glowering at him from the walls – were retrieved from the attic, their gilt frames cleaned first with a soft brush to remove the dust and then washed with lukewarm soapy water. Harp agreed with Mr Devereaux as she washed them under her mother's watchful eye – they looked very grumpy and sour – but her mother insisted they lent the place an air of sophistication; besides, they covered up the damp patches.

The kitchen was largely ignored in the work as the guests would not see it. They had four fully ready bedrooms, two bathrooms, the kitchen, a dining room and a drawing room. The other rooms were too badly in need of refurbishment, so they remained closed for now.

The dining room had to be supplemented with other tables and chairs gathered from the rest of the house to ensure seating for all the guests, and while they were not matching in design or height, Harp and her mother agreed that when the tables were all covered in their signature yellow gingham tablecloths and the seat pads all covered in yellow serge, one almost forgot that all the furniture was mismatched. They had, with Mr Quinn and Brian's help, dragged a large sideboard from the drawing room to the dining room to be used as a serving table for breakfast and to store the condiments and cutlery. The windows of the dining room overlooked the bay, and so it would surely delight guests to watch the comings and goings of the harbour as they enjoyed their breakfast.

The hens were installed in a pen behind the house; Harp hated them with their beady eyes and the way they rushed at her when she went to collect the eggs.

The drawing room looked lovely now too, Harp thought, and had almost completely lost the musty smell that she'd associated with it for her entire life. Under the white dust sheets, the furniture had fared reasonably well over the years, though it had broken their hearts to burn a beautiful writing bureau. But Mr Quinn pointed out that it was riddled with woodworm that would spread to everything if they didn't destroy it. They discovered the attic full of furniture and rugs and even two full Royal Doulton dinner services, and everything they found was pressed into commission.

The huge fireplace with its red Cork marble mantelpiece and carved lions either side of the hearth was a focal point around which they'd placed four Queen Anne chairs, each upholstered in royal-blue velvet, and several mahogany and walnut side tables, and it made a welcoming place for guests to read or relax. The sofas were horribly uncomfortable, upholstered in gold brocade and stuffed with horsehair, but they looked nice.

Mr Devereaux's study was now a suite, with a bedroom and a sitting room attached, for which they had already had several bookings, so they'd removed the gramophone and the harp and placed them in the drawing room on the ground floor for guests to enjoy in the evenings. Harp had spent a lovely afternoon curating a library and placing an eclectic selection of books on a bookshelf for guests to peruse. She was careful not to include any of her favourites, though, for fear someone would try to take them. She enjoyed those kinds of jobs so much more than polishing or sanding, but she tried her best to be helpful to her mother nonetheless. They had a more extensive library upstairs, but they had decided to keep that closed for now.

'After you.' Rose smiled as Harp climbed the stairs to go to bed.

The whole house smelled lovely, clean and welcoming, and the grounds were neat and clipped, with a few pots of colourful flowers dotted here and there. It felt so strange to know that the next night there would be five strangers sleeping under their roof.

In addition to Mr Devereaux's suite, there were three bedrooms on the second floor, one with twin beds and two with doubles. One room had a settee that could be pulled out to make another bed should a family wish to stay together. The beds were old but perfectly functional, and Rose and Harp had dragged the mattresses outside one by one to beat them of any dust and to air them after decades of neglect. They had found lots of woollen blankets in a chest in the attic, incredibly only partially nibbled by moths or mice.

'Remember the inhabitants of this room?' Rose asked, opening the large double in the front.

Harp shuddered. Though the entire house played host to mice, the largest of the rooms had been particularly infested. Mr Quinn had very kindly put down poison, and they had only to clean up the evidence. It was the worst of all the jobs. She'd tried so hard to visualise the protagonist in Dorothy Kilner's *The Life and Perambulations of a Mouse*, embarking on exciting adventures while all the time outwitting enemies to prove itself valiant and honourable. But when she spotted a fast scurry out of the corner of her eye, or swept the droppings into a pile for brushing onto a shovel, their home invaders felt much less like small, brave, noble creatures than terrifyingly disgusting rodents.

'They're gone now anyway, and it was just mice, not rats,' Rose reassured her, checking under the bed to be sure.

Harp shuddered. 'St Francis of Assisi loved all animals but he saw mice and rats as the devil's agents,' she said darkly, and her mother chuckled.

'He could be right,' Rose whispered as she shut the door. 'Maybe we should get a cat.'

'Or a terrier?' Harp said hopefully. She would have loved a pet but Rose had never allowed it.

'A cat is as far as I'm willing to go,' her mother replied sternly. 'And even that's a stretch for me.'

There was a large shed at the back that had been a dumping ground for all manner of things going back years, and they had been tempted to investigate until they saw a rat run out of it one day. Both of them baulked. A mouse they could just about stand, but they drew the line at a rat.

They opened each bedroom and inspected. On each nightstand there was a candle in an ornate holder, a small bud vase with a sprig of fuchsia and a bit of fern, and a pitcher of water and some glasses. There was a warm rug on the floor beside each bed on which to place feet in the morning and a wardrobe containing extra blankets. Rose was sure everything was perfect, clean and comfortable.

There were two more rooms on the third floor, as well as their own, that they could use should the need arise, but for now, if they could fill four rooms, then that would be enough.

Mr Quinn would collect their first guests the next day from the one o'clock train. There were two women travelling alone, a man with his fourteen-year-old boy and a single man. They had hoped for double occupancy, but the nature of the type of business they were going for meant a lot of lone travellers. Rose had researched the idea of a single occupancy supplement, and so far people didn't seem to mind.

'We'd better get to bed, Harp. It's going to be a big day tomorrow,' Rose said, closing the last bedroom door and smoothing a wrinkle in the curtain on the landing.

'It's going to be great, Mammy, don't worry.' Harp squeezed her mother's hand.

'When did you get so grown up, Miss Harp Delaney?' Rose asked as they mounted the stairs to their own quarters, nothing as fancy as the new guest rooms but cosy and comfortable.

'I was always grown up. I think I was born old but you wanted me to be little,' Harp said seriously. 'I certainly never felt like a child, though I'm not sure what it is to feel like a child, so perhaps I did.'

Rose kissed her forehead and placed her hands on Harp's shoulders, looking into her eyes. 'Well, I don't know about that. Maybe none of us feel like we truly fit in – I know I don't. But I do know this – you're turning into a very intelligent and poised young lady. I...I'm so proud of you, Harp. I would never have done this without your help.'

'He would want us to stay here and be happy, Mammy. I don't know if he's watching over us – he didn't believe in any of that, as you know – but sometimes I can sense him or something. But I know he's proud of us both.'

Rose drew her in for a hug. 'I think he would be. Sleep well, my love. We have a lot to learn, but we can do it.'

CHAPTER 11

*R*ose shut her bedroom door and wearily undressed for bed. Harp slept in her own room again these nights. She brushed her long dark hair out. It fell four inches past her shoulders but nobody but Harp had seen her hair loose for years.

She pulled her dressing gown on and stood at the window, opening it and allowing the warm night breeze to cool her, too anxious to sleep, the ache of apprehension eating away inside as it had since she embarked on this plan. What if it was a disaster? There were plenty in this town who would like to see her fail; some people didn't like it when someone dragged themselves out of the boxes society had made for them. But she had to do this, if not for herself, then for Harp. Her daughter deserved a future. She could do something remarkable with her life if she got the chance, and nobody else would give her that chance. Henry had opened the door; now Rose had to step through.

The stars were out that night over the water, twinkling brightly. The metal off masts making a 'tink, tink, tink' sound that wafted up the hill, the gentle lapping of waves against the quay wall, the odd glimpse of a man going home from the pub on the road below, the salty smell of the sea... Her senses had become so accustomed to this place, it was hard to believe she'd grown up somewhere else, somewhere poorer, somewhere harder. Nobody from there would recognise her now, and she wondered if her parents or siblings ever thought about her, wondered how she and her child were faring. She was the eldest of the family. Her three brothers and two sisters were lost to her as well as her mother and father. She killed the thought immediately – of course they didn't. They were shamed by her coming home in that condition and threw her out. There was a part of her that would like for them to see her now, in this fine house, damp patches and all, but that was silly. Besides, they would just see it as further proof of her fall into sin. No, this was home, Harp was her family, and she needed nothing else.

'Henry, watch over us if you can, if you are somewhere. Please don't have us make fools of ourselves with this venture.'

She closed the window, drew the curtains and lit the candle, extracting the letters once again, reading them slowly as she did every night.

The one from Algernon Smythe had arrived two weeks ago, saying that there had been no correspondence to his office from Mr Ralph Devereaux and that he had registered Harp's name, albeit in trust, as the beneficiary of the Cliff House with the Land Registry in Dublin. He would forward a copy of that document once it was provided to him. He wished her well in the guest house venture; she'd written to him thanking him for his visit and informing him of their plans.

The second letter had arrived three days ago. Her relief was short-lived. She opened the envelope, a thin wisp of paper, not the stationery of someone well-to-do, but she was probably reading too much into that. Maybe all paper in India was like that.

Dear Rose,

Well, it has been a long time, and I was astonished to discover your good fortune in regards to the inheritance of the Cliff House.

I had no idea that you'd managed to beguile both Devereaux brothers – you truly are a woman of many talents. My late brother, Henry, and I share you in common if nothing else.

Of course, this new-found prosperity of yours and your child has rather scuppered my plans, but we can discuss that in due course.

I look forward to coming home to the fresh Irish air after the stifling oppression of the Indian sun.

Regards,

Ralph Devereaux

She felt the familiar thumping in her chest. What did he mean, 'We can discuss that in due course'? The phrase chilled her blood. He was coming to claim his house surely? The tone was unmistakable. He was accusing her of being a gold-digging jezebel who seduced not one but two Devereaux men, which was nothing approximating the truth. She'd been an innocent, a seventeen-year-old girl star-struck by the son of the house, a man who'd shamelessly used her and cast her aside. She'd been foolish and naïve but she was no harlot. Ralph Devereaux was the first and last man to touch her. As for Henry, well, she was still reeling from his letter declaring his love; she'd had no idea. She wondered if she had, would it have changed things? Perhaps. It was too late now anyway.

The solicitor said that Henry's affidavit claiming paternity, combined with her corroboration of that fact, should provide a robust resistance to any claim against the estate made by his brother, but she wasn't sure. The letter certainly suggested he wasn't going to take it lying down.

How could a single woman and a child withstand someone like him? He was of that ruling class and this was his parents' house, going back generations; a judge was surely never going to find in favour of a working-class Irish woman and her child over a member of the gentry, was he? She'd invented a dead husband, a father for Harp, but that story was proved untrue by Harp's admission at school that she was a Devereaux. If Ralph chose to press that advantage, paint Rose as a devious, duplicitous woman capable of telling such lies, then surely it would not be such a leap to imagine her manipulating a vulnerable man such as Henry was perceived? He could say that Rose swindled Henry or seduced him and then pressured him into leaving her the house. That's if he even believed Harp to be Henry's child.

At least the mathematics of it wouldn't add up. Mrs Devereaux had insisted Harp's date of birth be registered six months later than her actual birthday. How she'd managed that, Rose had no idea; she'd arranged it with some official, no doubt. Rose had been summoned one day when Harp was a baby and was informed that the child's birthday was registered as the 14th of August, not the 3rd of March, and that was all there was to be said about it.

She wished she had someone to talk to, anyone she could confide her worries in. Harp was such a good girl, and Rose was honest when she said she wouldn't have done any of this without her, but she was ignorant of the ways of the world. Harp was just a girl. And men had all the power. And money and social class spoke louder than anything else.

She lay on her back, staring at the ceiling, knowing sleep was impossible. She willed herself to try – she would need to be alert and organised the next day – but round and round it all went as she imagined scenarios of humiliation. At no point in her imaginings did she ever consider the possibility that Ralph would have changed, that he would be kind or even just grudgingly accept the will. He might have been gone thirteen years, but she knew what he was and who he was, and there was not one shred of common decency in that man. Of that she was definite.

Would he come and throw them out? If he did, what could she do about it? She had no money to engage a lawyer, and even if she had, she doubted she would find one to take her case on. She couldn't afford the fees of Algernon Smythe, she was sure, and old Mr Cotter in Cork, even if they could afford him, didn't strike her as the type to be a courtroom viper. Besides, he was a Devereaux lawyer, not hers.

She had to hold firm to the idea that Henry was Harp's father. She would have to confirm that she'd almost immediately begun a relationship with him when Ralph left and became pregnant as a result. The thought of such an admission churned her stomach with anxiety and shame. People knew about the alleged relationship with Henry, and that was bad enough – what if Ralph told people that he'd had her first? Her cheeks burned in the dark night.

She mentally pulled back from that familiar and pointless line of thought. She would have to deal with it as it happened. Henry left the house to Harp, it was hers legally, and Ralph Devereaux could do his best but she would hold on for dear life. She would hold on for Harp.

She folded Ralph Devereaux's letter and placed it beside the one from the solicitor, keeping, as she did every night, the letter from Henry until last. Like Harp cherished her letter, Rose treasured hers, and she was careful not to overly crease it. She would read it every night for the rest of her life, even if it was battered and torn.

She knew it by heart now, but still it gave small comfort to see his handwriting. Her feelings for him were changing. She'd always liked him and thought him a fine man, a decent person the world didn't understand. But she did, and Harp did too. They'd talked at night sometimes, when Harp was in bed, about this and that, and while he wasn't a conversationalist, he was interesting and he listened, really listened. He had that ability to make one feel like they were the most fascinating person in the world, that he wanted to hear their thoughts, that he had all the time in the world for them. She wished he'd have said something sooner, because the more she thought about it, the more she realised that loving Henry Devereaux would have been a very easy thing to do. He was not the dashing rake that Ralph was, but there had been something very attractive about him, with his intense grey eyes, his sensitive hands, his full mouth. They might have been happy together, if only he'd been braver or she'd been less blind.

Her eyes lingered over the words.

You were treated badly by one Devereaux brother, for which I am incredibly sorry, but you were adored by the other.

She sighed and kissed the page, folding it carefully, and placed the envelope in the drawer of her bedside locker. She blew out the candle and tried again to sleep.

CHAPTER 12

*M*olly O'Brien tried to ignore the crick in her neck; she dared not look up from the prayer book she had open on her lap. If she caught anyone's eye, they would surely read the furtive, hunted look on her face. She had tucked her unruly red hair up inside her hat and pulled the brim down as much as she dared. Bits were springing out, she could feel it, but she dared not fidget too much as that was a sign of someone up to no good. She frequently wished that she was physically smaller, but never so much as now. Tall and heavy, she took up a lot of space, and her colouring didn't help. The last thing she could be described as was inconspicuous. A tall, broad, good-looking lad about her own age, maybe a year or two older, sat beside her, and she wished no part of her needed to touch him, but alas that was not the case. She was wedged in beside him, every part of her squeezed up to him. It was mortifying. She knew she was taking up more than her portion of the seat. Thankfully he seemed distracted and made no effort to converse.

'Beef to the heel like a Mullingar heifer,' her brothers used to tease her. Mammy had tried everything over the years – corsets, half starving her to death – but it was no good. Molly was fat.

'She got it from the O'Brien side,' her mother would mutter in frustration. 'Sure wasn't your father's sister Julia the size of half a house? And his Auntie Patricia has a behind like a barn door.'

Mammy had been terrified her daughter would never get a man, something that cost Molly not a moment's thought. She needed a man like she needed a hole in the head, but her protests fell on her mother's deaf ears. Mrs O'Brien would moan to her husband that a big-boned girl with flame-red hair and a round freckled face was not going to stand a chance beside the likes of Madge Donnelly with her slim ankles or Meg O'Hara with her sleek black curls, both admired by every bachelor in the parish as they went up to receive Holy Communion at Mass each Sunday.

She played the scene she imagined unfolding in her home as she travelled south on the train. Her mother would call up the stairs for her to come down and help to get the breakfast on the table for her father and three brothers, who would have been up milking since five. There would be no sound, so she would call again, sharper the second time, muttering how good Molly had it lazing about in bed while everyone else in the family was hard at work.

By seven o'clock her mother would march bad-temperedly up the stairs and burst into the bedroom. Molly was the only girl she knew with a bedroom of her own. It wasn't because they were wealthy – well, they were strong farmers, milking a hundred cows on eighty acres, but not gentry or anything – but she had no sister so she got the small room under the eaves to herself while her brothers shared the big bedroom.

Mammy would let out a roar that Molly was to get out of bed that minute and then she would see it. Or would she? Molly had put pillows in the bed, so maybe her mother would be in such a rush back down to the porridge and the boiled eggs that she wouldn't go as far as the bed. She'd know soon enough either way. They definitely knew by now. But hopefully it was too late.

She'd prayed most of the way on the predawn four-mile walk to Limerick Junction. Not one person passed her by, but it was so early, it wasn't that surprising. She prayed to the Virgin Mary to protect her, and to Saint Christopher, the patron saint of travellers, though she'd hardly be classed as a seasoned traveller, considering she had never once been outside of the parish in all of her eighteen years. She put her finger to the medal she'd bought the day she paid for her ticket. It was a beautiful gold St Christopher medal inscribed with the words 'may you go in safety'. She needed all the divine assistance she could get, but perhaps it was wrong to seek help to break a commandment. The Fourth Commandment said to honour thy father and mother, and this vanishing act was the very opposite.

Waiting on the platform at the station would have been too risky, as someone might recognise her, so she waited behind the goods shed until the train to Cork was due, then scurried out like a rat up a drain-pipe – or at least she scurried as fast as her lumbering frame would allow – onto the train. She knew she could buy her ticket from the conductor.

She would return the money she took from the housekeeping jar when she wrote to them, once she was far enough away, once she reached America. Though how, she had no idea. It wasn't as if she was planning gainful employment. She felt the familiar frisson of terror mixed with excitement. She was doing it. Not just talking about it, but actually doing it. She was leaving. She was doing the right thing, she knew it, but undoubtedly her family would not see it that way.

Imagine if Father O'Rourke had never brought Sister Brid in to speak to them? Or if she'd been kept at home that day to thin turnips or save hay? It didn't bear thinking about.

She fought the feelings of guilt. Her mother and father had allowed her to remain at school for much longer than any of the other girls except for Agatha Gray, the doctor's daughter, and Miriam Woolton, who was raised Catholic by her mother despite her Protestant father. Molly had begged to be allowed to stay on at school, and while Mammy wasn't keen, she knew her daddy could refuse her nothing. Besides, there wasn't exactly a queue of lads at the farmyard waiting to take her out with a view to marriage. She was allowed to stay and study for her exams, and she ignored the snorts of derision from her brothers, who'd all left at fourteen to farm at home. But she wanted to be a teacher, and leaving school wasn't the way to achieve that.

Daddy always stood up for her and gave out to the boys for teasing her, and she knew he was happy at how well she did in her tests. The Reverend Mother had even stopped her parents after Mass a few weeks ago to tell them they should be so proud of her, that she was so diligent and studious. Daddy had blushed beetroot red at that, muttering something non-committal; compliments were not easily received or distributed in Seamus O'Brien's world. But she knew he was pleased as punch. Neither he nor her mother had had much schooling, so knowing his daughter was as smart as paint was a source of tremendous pride to him.

Her father's kind, careworn face swam before her eyes, and she blinked back a tear. He would be heartbroken. But he didn't understand any more than Mammy or Finbarr Clancy or Father O'Rourke did. It wasn't that she was being difficult; she just couldn't do as they commanded. She had no choice but to get away.

Would she ever again see her home, that little village of Ballymichael, with one shop, one pub, a church, a convent and a primary school? It might mean nothing to someone passing through, but to her it had been her whole world. She walked from the farm to Mass every Sunday, and every day in Lent, and she had memories of the town from even before she went to school. The church was her favourite place, so peaceful, and as a girl she would often duck in after school or if she'd been sent on a message just to say a prayer or to be still and feel God's presence. When her friends got older and became less interested in the liturgy and more interested in the boys that were loitering down the back of nine o'clock Mass, she'd felt profoundly sad. She loved everything about the Sacred Heart Church of Ballymichael, the beautiful altar, the smell of incense and polish, the sound of Miss Devine playing the organ in anticipation of the three Masses on Sunday morning. Sometimes if one were lucky they would hear the choir practising. The nuns had their own choir and the parish had another, both wonderful.

Her whole life had been punctuated by the events of her faith. The four weeks of Advent, each one marked by the lighting of the candle on the Advent wreath as the entire parish prepared for the birth of

Jesus, then Christmas itself and all that entailed – midnight Mass, the carols, the life-size crib in the corner of the church. Then Lent, in preparation for Easter, and Ash Wednesday, when the priest marked every forehead with ashes with the words, 'Remember that thou art but dust and unto dust thou shalt return'. It had frightened her as a child, but her mother had explained that nobody she loved would be returning to dust for years and years and she need not worry about it. Palm Sunday brought the palms to be blessed, then Holy Thursday, and then the Stations of the Cross on Good Friday. The other girls in school would complain that during those days around Easter it felt like they were never out of the church, but Molly loved it all.

One of her favourite feast days was Corpus Christi, right after Easter. The weather was usually nice and there was a procession through the town, the children spreading petals and the altar boys carrying the Blessed Sacrament under a canopy. The local confraternity band would play, and there was such an air of joy and reverence combined.

She never knew why she had been slow to reveal her vocation. She'd foolishly assumed they all knew and took it for granted. Perhaps, if she'd been more forthcoming earlier, she wouldn't be in this mess now.

When the nuns at school talked about other religious people having a vocation, it was always something dramatic like a dream or a vision, or they were after doing a terrible thing and realised that they needed to repent and then dedicated their lives to God. But Molly didn't have any of that. She just knew from as far back as she could remember. She knew it as sure as she knew the sun rose in the morning and set in the evening. She was going to be a nun.

In first class, aged only seven, as the girls and boys were prepared for their first Holy Communion, she knew that one day, such days would be her life. Praying, meditating, working for the Lord – it was all she ever imagined she would do; nothing else ever entered her head.

Her family knew she was devout. Her brothers had to be hunted up the road, complaining and giving out, to Mass every Sunday, and

Daddy nearly murdered Kevin when he heard that he and the Casey twins were smoking in the churchyard instead of inside praying. Mammy was mortified as well, thinking the whole place was talking about them. But Kevin couldn't give a hoot. Billy and Pius couldn't either. They were just obsessed with farming and land and thought anything that distracted from that was a waste of time. Not that they'd dare say that out loud – there would be a queue of people lining up to give them a hiding for such sinful thoughts – but she knew how they felt.

The Caseys owned the farm beside theirs, and the twin boys, Finbarr and Con, were great pals with her brothers. They were nice lads, and good-looking, she supposed, average height and broad, with sandy hair and green eyes, but she never considered for one second that they would be anything but her brothers' friends and neighbours.

When the girls at school talked about going to dances, or liking this lad or that one, she never joined in. She knew they thought her a goody two shoes, but she couldn't help it. She felt her faith in every cell of her body, and for her only one life was possible.

She'd assumed everyone knew of her plan. She'd never said it outright, in their defence, but how could they not have known?

She'd never forget the look on Mother Raphael's face when she went to her two weeks ago to tell her about her desire to enter the convent and begin her postulancy. The school principal had looked shocked, then troubled. Molly had never had cause to be in her office throughout her time in the school for any reason, but now, instead of the warm welcome to the religious life she'd fantasised about, she was met instead with confusion and a furrowed brow.

'I thought I might like to join the Ursulines because I would like to become a teacher. And while I'd be happy to remain in Ireland should the Order so wish it, I would also welcome the opportunity to work on the missions.' Molly had progressed with her prepared speech, trying not to focus on the Reverend Mother's face. She stopped talking then, and the silence was heavy and awkward.

'And your parents, have they said anything about this?' the Reverend Mother asked.

Molly had always seen Mother Raphael as a benign force in the school. She wasn't one for giving out slaps or admonishing anyone too harshly, though Deirdre Kelleher was sent to her for being cheeky to Sister Rosario and did come out in tears, so perhaps there was another side to her.

'Er...no, Mother Raphael, I haven't told them yet, but I'm sure they'll be delighted...' Molly had replied.

'And have you been thinking about this for long, Molly?' the nun asked kindly.

'Well, I always knew, I think, but the day Sister Brid came in, when she was home from Boston, and she was talking about all the good work she and the other sisters are doing in America, that really made up my mind.'

'I see,' the Reverend Mother said, but the words seemed to mean more.

That evening, on the Reverend Mother's instructions, Molly waited until Kevin, Billy and Pius were outside baling hay, taking advantage of the fine dry spell, and she caught her parents together and alone. Daddy was reading the paper beside the fire, enjoying a cup of tea and a slice of apple tart, his boots off and his stockinged feet crossed on the rug before the hearth, and Mammy, sitting opposite him on Nana's old rocking chair, was pulling out her knitting.

Her father grunted in displeasure as he read about the Home Rule Bill, and she knew she would need to pre-empt any tirade on the folly of the current political plan. Her father's favourite topic of conversation was how it would be much better if fellas above in Dublin minded their own business and didn't give their lives trying to change everything when it was working perfectly well. It wasn't awful being ruled from England, and sure maybe the crowd in England were doing a better job of it than the hotheads in Dublin, demanding Irish sovereignty, could ever do.

Pius and Billy were forever arguing with him over it. They loved the idea of Irish independence, but their father was having none of it. Mammy had banned the subject at the dinner table.

'Mammy, Daddy, could I talk to you both about something?' she began, feeling nervous.

Looking back now, she must have known on some level that there was going to be a problem, but for the life of her then, she couldn't imagine what it could be. Surely they would love the idea of a nun in the family? They were good people, they said the rosary every night, making the boys kneel down and say the responses properly, they never ate meat on Fridays, and they went to Mass every morning during Lent. Inside the front door was the St. Brigid's cross Molly had made from the rushes growing in the bottom field; beside that was the dried palm from Palm Sunday. Her parents lived their faith properly and devoutly. Having a priest or a nun in the family was every Irish mother's dream. The boys certainly showed no sign of interest in the priesthood, so all the more reason to be happy that she wanted to devote her life in that way. God knew, Mammy moaned often enough, how difficult it would be for them to find her a husband, looking as she did, so maybe her becoming a Bride of Christ would be weight off their minds. Maybe if they accepted she was going to be a nun, her mother would stop looking disapprovingly when she went for another potato and mashed a big blob of yellow butter into it, or poured cream and honey all over her morning porridge.

Her mother put down her knitting, her face pale. Her father was engrossed in the paper, and his wife had to pull it down to get his attention.

'What is it?' her mother asked, looking worried.

'I...' She swallowed and tried to force a cheeriness she didn't feel into her voice. Maybe God was making it difficult for her to test her vocation? If so, she would not let Him down. 'I spoke to Mother Raphael today about wanting to enter the convent as a postulant, and she said I should talk to you both first.'

Her parents exchanged a glance, and she knew instantly there was something they weren't telling her. Her father threw another block of timber on the fire, the sparks flying up the chimney. It was summer-time so not really cold, but there was always a fire in the hearth, all year round.

Seamus O'Brien was a man of many words on the subject of politics, but when it came to his daughter, his only girl, he was dumbstruck. Molly watched her mother plead with him with her eyes, but he looked away, poking the fire instead.

'What's the matter?' Molly asked. 'Surely you'd be happy?'

Her mother inhaled, as if to speak, then opened her mouth and closed it again. 'We would be, of course, and you're a very good girl, never gave us a moment's trouble, not like those three *bosthúns* out there.' Her mother rolled her eyes and nodded in the direction of the yard, where her brothers were now kicking a football instead of working. Molly knew her mother adored her sons, but she was never done giving out about them all the same. She paused and Molly fought the need to urge her on.

'And God knows you have great faith, so you do, never had to get you out of bed for Mass or a bit, always first up, and praying and the choir and all the rest of it. You're a great girl, Molly, and we couldn't have wished for better, sure we couldn't. Seamus?' Nora O'Brien made a face at her husband, one that said, 'Help me out here.'

'Oh, you're a grand girl, right enough, never a minute's trouble,' Seamus concurred, and Molly wondered what on earth this had to do with anything. They were hiding something, but what?

Her mother swallowed conspicuously and darted another glance at her husband. Realising he wasn't going to help her, she spoke again. 'It's just that, well, we have some great news for you. We were not going to say anything until it was all finalised, but it's as good as done now, so you might as well know. Your father and I were thinking, and... Well, it was Dinny Casey actually suggested it, and it would be really good, you know, because our bottom ten acres are boggy, as you know, so the top would be much better. We wouldn't rely so much on it. And with five boys between us to try to fend for... And we thought you might have trouble finding a man, but this is a perfect solution really...'

Molly had no idea what her mother was going on about. She was wringing her hands on her apron and her face looked pinched. Her father continued to poke the fire.

'And sure he's a grand lad – there's plenty would be delighted to have him. And sure you'd be right beside us here and it would be fine, and it would mean the boys could farm the land between them. There'd be enough for the two families. And then if Dinny Casey buys the Quinlan place, and the widow has it promised to him, 'twould make a fine job of it altogether…'

'What are you talking about, Mammy? Who is a grand lad? And what has Dinny Casey's or Mrs Quinlan's farm got to do with me entering the convent?' Molly had a sick feeling in the pit of her stomach.

'Ah, Nora, we should have just said it outright,' Seamus interjected. 'Look, Molly, you're to be married to Finbarr Casey when you finish school next month. The match will join our farm to his, and then he'll buy the Quinlan's, and between us we'll have enough land to keep the Caseys and ourselves in work.'

Molly could hardly formulate words. Her brain was refusing to cooperate and come up with an appropriate response. Before she could object, her mother spoke again, soothing this time.

'I know it's a bit of a shock when you had thought you might do something else. But sure you were only thinking of the convent because… And you're a fine girl and we're very fond of you, of course, but 'tisn't every lad would like a girl so big and strong, but Finbarr Casey doesn't mind a bit. He's a grand boy and he always liked you growing up, and his father agreed to the match, so it's great news really.' She smiled, too brightly. 'And we'll go to Limerick and get you a lovely frock to wear and we'll have a fine big spread on the day, invite everyone, and there'll be cake and everything. And you'll be the belle of the ball.'

Molly shook her head and said quietly, 'But, Mammy, I don't want it. I don't want to marry Finbarr Casey, or anyone.'

'Ah, hush now, Molly. That's only the surprise talking. You were wise to have a plan for fear the marriage thing didn't work out, but now it has, and sure you'll be all excited like any bride next month when it's all arranged –'

'No!' It came out louder than anyone expected. Molly had never raised her voice to anyone in her life before, and especially not her parents, but she wouldn't do this. She couldn't.

Her father stood, and for the first time, she saw the greed for land in his eyes. It was a feature of life round there, men who dedicated their lives to the acquisition of land by fair means or foul, but her daddy wasn't one of those men – or at least she used not to think so. Her father loved her. He brought her sweets from the mart and always hit the boys a clatter if they were teasing her. He would never want her to be unhappy, of course he wouldn't. He just didn't understand how deeply she felt her vocation.

She tried to keep her voice calm but failed. 'I won't, Daddy. I won't marry him. I have a vocation. I belong to the Lord and I want to dedicate my life to Him. I can't marry. I don't want to.' The last words escaped as a sob.

'Molly' – he moved to stand before her and he held her arms, but not hard – 'the deal is struck, I've agreed, the papers are drawn up and everything. It's all arranged. You'll marry the Casey lad next month, and that's all I want to hear about it.'

Molly wrenched herself free of his hold as she fought back the tears. 'I'm not a cow you can sell at the mart, Daddy. I don't want to marry anyone. I don't care what you or Mammy say, you can't make me. I'll tell Father O'Rourke that I'm being forced into it, and he'll stop it and –'

The sting across her cheek was more shocking than painful. Daddy had taken the belt to the boys so many times she'd lost count, but he had never once slapped her. Mammy neither. She never gave them cause.

'Seamus!' Her mother rushed to her side and put her arm around her.

'She'll do as she's told,' he barked, and went out of the kitchen door into the yard, where he roared at the boys for slacking off work, slamming the door behind him.

The remainder of the night was spent with her mother cajoling and wheedling, going on about cakes and dresses and shoes, but Molly didn't respond. Surely she couldn't be forced to marry someone?

Surely it wasn't allowed? And even if it was, her parents, the people who were supposed to love and protect her, they wouldn't do it to her, would they?

It became evident that everyone was convinced the wedding was going ahead. Father O'Rourke had mentioned it to Mother Raphael before Molly even knew herself, she'd discovered, which is why the principal seemed reticent. Molly had tried several times to speak to her father, but he ignored her and left the room. The atmosphere in the house was horrible, and even the boys had stopped teasing her. In record time, a dress had been bought and shoes and food ordered for the wedding breakfast, and Molly felt like she was living a nightmare. No matter how much she cried or begged or pleaded, it fell on deaf ears. The plans for the wedding went ahead. Nobody, not even Father O'Rourke, who she waylaid one morning after early Mass, was willing to listen to her side.

The previous week, Finbarr came around for tea, in a clean shirt and with a cut on his face where he'd nicked himself with the razor. The boys were warned to within an inch of their lives that there was to be no messing or smart talk, and her mother made Molly wear a corset under a flowery dress. She could hardly breathe, it was so tight, and she felt so self-conscious because squeezing her middle made her breasts look even bigger. She voiced those concerns to her mother, who dismissed them, but she knew the moment she walked into the kitchen she was right. Her brothers looked mortified, and Finbarr seemed to fix his gaze into the corner over her head.

After tea everyone was moved into the good room, only used at Christmas and for the Stations, the annual Mass in the house. Pius and Billy were excused to hose down the milking parlour, and Kevin, who was the same age as Finbarr, looked uncomfortable on the over-stuffed armchair with the antimacassars. The room smelled musty and vaguely of damp. Mammy wittered on about some nonsense, while her father, Finbarr and Kevin remained silent, each balancing a cup of tea in the good china dusted off for the occasion. Molly felt like she was in a play.

Afterwards, her mother suggested that she and Finbarr go to check

LAST PORT OF CALL

on the calves, an activity Molly had never once engaged in before, so it was obviously a way of getting her and Finbarr alone together.

She hated every second of the evening – the horrible dress that was too tight, the way her mother had clipped her hair back from her face, the way Finbarr looked at her. He was all right, a nice lad, and she was sure he'd not been given much choice either.

She and her father had not spoken since that night he slapped her. The boys knew what was going on but they would never take her side; they wanted the land as much as her father did, even more maybe.

She remembered the cool breeze that night as they rounded the yard. It had rained all day and the ground was wet and muddy under-foot, the familiar smells of milk and dung combining. The calves were lowing in the barn, having been taken from their mothers. Her father cared no more for her feelings than he did for the poor little calves.

Daddy was in foul form, as he was trying to save all the hay and it was vital the rain stayed off, but Mother Nature had other plans and it had poured for days. The temperatures were much lower than normal too, and Molly felt like the world was in sympathy with her plight. She pulled her cardigan around her and Finbarr asked her if she was cold.

'I am,' she said sullenly. 'Will we go back in?'

'Or we could go to the barn,' he suggested. 'It's nice and warm in there. I got you some barley sugars in the shop – Mrs Farrell said you liked them.'

Molly cursed Biddy Farrell for her nosey ways. So what if she liked barley sugars; there was no need to go blabbing her business to all and sundry.

She didn't want to go to the barn with Finbarr, but if she went back in now, so soon, there would be questions. 'All right.' She sighed.

She walked quickly and he followed, he barely two inches taller than her and broad-shouldered, with a pleasant, open face. His nose was crooked where he'd had it broken playing hurling. There was a rumour he was good enough to make the county team. She knew some of the girls in school thought the Casey twins handsome, but she couldn't see it. Mammy was right about one thing: If she had been looking for a husband, Finbarr would have been out of her league. He could have had any one of the pretty girls in Ballymichael, and if there wasn't land involved, she was under no illusion that Finbarr would have looked sideways at her. Part of her felt sorry for him too; he could do so much better than her. She tried to reserve her resentment for her father and Dinny Casey, because Finbarr was just a pawn in the game of getting more land the same as she was. He should be allowed to pick one of the pretty girls for himself, because she knew he wasn't interested in her. She'd heard Pius sniggering about it with Kevin, wondering if she would crush him on the wedding night.

She stepped into the barn, where at least it was warmer. It was turning dusk, so she lit a lamp and sat on a bale. Finbarr took out the paper bag of wrapped barley sugars and handed it to her.

'Thank you,' she said. An idea occurred to her. 'Do you want to marry me, Finbarr?' she asked bluntly.

'I do, of course. Sure you're a fine hold of a girl, and you'd produce good strong boys.' He now seemed mesmerised by her bust, and she pulled her cardigan tighter.

'Really?' Molly fixed him with a stare and he reddened.

'Yeah, sure, why not. And 'twill make a grand job of the farms, joining them like we will. And sure as I said, you'd be well able to help with working the farm, not like the town girls running at the sight of a mouse. You're a great cook, and sure what more would a man want from a wife?'

'But you could have anyone, Finbarr...' she began, hoping to lure him away from the marriage, which might be her only hope.

'But I want you,' he said, slowly moving towards her. He tried to kiss her but she recoiled. To her amazement he just smiled.

'I'm sorry, Molly. I should have known better. You're a good girl and you don't want any of that till we're married. Fair enough.' He ran his hand through his hair. 'We'll be happy out, Molly, I promise. I'm a simple man. I want to work the farm, have children with you, a good feed in my belly every evening and a woman in my bed at night and that's all I want from life. I'll be good to you, I swear.'

She couldn't bring herself to answer. Finbarr may have been used too, but he would benefit from it. He would never call it off, that much was sure.

'I'll go back in now,' she said, her voice sounding strange to her own ears.

She ran out of the barn. It was raining again but she didn't care. She walked across the yard, allowing the cold summer rain to trickle down her neck, to soak the awful dress. Her feet squelched in the muddy puddles, but she just walked on slowly. The yard was neat, as her father insisted that everything be stored away at the end of each day. She passed the hens sheltering from the rain in the henhouse. The lush green fields of her home were being drenched, which would just promote more grass, more feed for more cows, more cattle, more money...more, more, more. That was all they cared about. She walked down the lane and leaned on the gate. Their bottom fields were waterlogged right enough, and the hilly part of this area was owned by the Caseys, so their land was better. She'd seen her father eyeing it jealously for years. There was a valley between them and the village, and Mrs Quinlan owned 105 acres of it. It was fine land, hilly but not too steep, with a spring too so they wouldn't have to draw water. With their own eighty acres, and surely the Caseys had another eighty, and a hundred from Mrs Quinlan, they'd have the biggest farm for miles. She was the only fly in the ointment, the only thing standing between her parents and the emigrant ship for her brothers.

Could she become a farmer's wife like her mother before her? Cook dinners every day, bear his children? She thought of the only marriage she knew, that of her parents, and it was good. They might not have been Romeo and Juliet, but Nora and Seamus were a team, and in their own way, they loved each other. Nora even enjoyed some aspects of farming, and she did the books for Daddy, who was terrible at maths. Sometimes when they thought there was nobody looking, Daddy would kiss her cheek or squeeze her hand, and they had four healthy children, so that end of things was probably fine. They were a match – Nora's father and Seamus's widowed mother did a deal – but it had all worked out. And Molly remembered Nana O'Brien living with them until she died, and she and Nora got on well. She was lovely, and Molly missed her.

She heaved herself off the gate, thoroughly soaked, walked back to the house, let herself in the back door and went straight to her room. She pulled off the horrible dress and corset and changed into her nightdress and woollen dressing gown.

Her mother came up a little while later, but Molly pretended to be asleep. She couldn't listen to any more platitudes about how it was all going to be fine, how it was for the best. Best for them. Not best for her.

As she lay on her narrow bed in the dark that night, she knew. She had no choice. She had to get away.

The guest house in Queenstown that the lady in the ticket office had mentioned sounded nice, and also it was a bit out of the town and newly opened, so they might not look for her there. Molly wrote to book a room and watched for the postman every day for fear someone would intercept the reply. She met him on his bike up the lane and took the post with a sigh of relief.

The lady that owned it said a man would collect her with her baggage off the train and would take her there. Her plan was to remain in the guest house, in her private room, until tomorrow at midday, when she would present herself at the Cunard Line ticket office. Her ticket said the tender would leave at two o'clock and the ship would sail at 6 p.m. on the evening tide.

She would never have thought herself capable of the duplicity she'd shown in recent weeks. She'd gone to Limerick to Ryan's, the agent on Sarsfield Street for Cunard and White Star as well as all the other companies that sailed all over the world, trying to look confident, and bought a second-class ticket, one-way, from Queenstown to Boston, sailing on the 22nd of June, 1912, on the Cunard ship the *RMS Laconia*. The man selling the ticket had made some soothing noises about her having nothing to fear after *Titanic*, but she didn't really pay attention. Her father had said the safest place in the world to be after *Titanic* sinking was a ship now; they'd not make that mistake again.

She paid the money and took her ticket, hiding it in her skirts and later under her mattress.

She'd packed her bag slowly, as she didn't want her mother to notice anything missing, and stored it in the outhouse, under the old trap they used to use to go to the mart before Daddy bought the new one. He was loathe to get rid of it, but everyone knew it would just sit in the shed and rot. Nobody would ever look there.

Outside the window of the train, the green fields sped by. Would she ever see Ireland again? Her prayer book was open to the *Memorare*. She didn't need to read it – she'd known that prayer since she was a child – but just looking at it gave her peace. The opening lines soothed her soul, making her feel less alone.

Remember, O most gracious Virgin Mary, that never was it known that anyone who fled to thy protection, implored thy help or sought thy intercession was left unaided. Inspired by this confidence I fly unto thee, O Virgin of Virgins, my mother...

Surely Our Lady would stay by her side?

CHAPTER 13

ourteen-year-old JohnJoe O'Dwyer gazed out the window at the fields and small farms. His reflection stared back at him, with his small face, dotted with freckles, and his red-blond hair that would never lie flat no matter what he did with it. He knew he looked like his mammy, small and with a round face. His mammy used to smile and laugh all the time, and she was so tiny compared to his father. Some of the lads said they forgot what their parents looked like, but JohnJoe could picture her like he'd seen her yesterday. He could visualise every contour of her face and remembered the feel of his face against her jumper when she hugged him. But he couldn't hear her voice in his head any more. Try as he might to recall her voice, it was gone. The only way he could remember what she sounded like was when he heard a certain song. He wished he had a recording of it, and he'd heard it only once in the years since she died.

The boys from the borstal were sometimes sent out to local farmers to pick potatoes or stones from the fields, and one time he was called in by the farmer's wife for some dinner. It was a lovely warm kitchen and she put out a big plate of stew with meat and carrots in it, the nicest dinner he'd had in years. She'd had a gramophone playing that song. He tried not to cry but it was impossible. He told her how his mammy had died giving birth to his sister and how an aunt in England had taken his older sister, Kitty, and the new baby, Jane, but didn't want a boy so he'd been sent to the borstal. His da wasn't much of a worker, and he fell to pieces when Mammy died. It had been Mammy's parents' farm they lived on, and she was the worker in the family. She kept sheep, goats and hens and a huge vegetable garden. Daddy was only good for drinking and fighting.

She'd been so kind, the farmer's wife, giving him a big chunk of cake when he was leaving, and he longed to be called back to work there, but it never happened. The priest saw him with the wedge of cake in his pocket and had cross-examined him, so JohnJoe knew they'd put a stop to that.

What would a city be like? Danny had shown him a picture of Boston in a book he'd brought, and it looked so different to even Cork City, where he'd been twice.

His cousin – apparently Danny was a cousin of his now – was talkative after he'd collected JohnJoe from his father's house, but now Danny was sleeping. JohnJoe didn't give a hoot where he was going; it could have been the moon if it meant getting out of there.

His father had come to the borstal, and JohnJoe was called to the dean's office. JohnJoe hadn't seen his da since he was nine, when Mammy died and his sisters were taken away. There was a smell of whiskey off Johnny O'Dwyer, and he looked so much older than JohnJoe remembered.

'You'll go now with your father,' was all the dean said to him.

He didn't think to question it; he was sure he was being called in for fighting again, so anything other than the strap was a good result as far as he was concerned. He had to fight; they all did. It was that or be a victim. There was no choice.

His heart leapt – he was going home, to Kitty and Jane too, maybe, and his lovely warm farmhouse by the sea. He knew his mother wouldn't be there, but at least he was away from the beatings and the cold and the hunger of the borstal. But in the trap on the way back home, his father had told him he was going to America.

'What? Why?' he asked, astounded.

'Your mother's brother Patrick lives there, and he has no child, his wife is barren, and he wants a lad to train up in the business like. So he wrote to me and asked if I'd send you.'

JohnJoe had rarely heard his father speak such a long sentence. 'What kind of business?' he asked.

His father shrugged and pulled the stopper out of a bottle in his pocket, swallowing the amber liquid and belching loudly. 'I don't know, and if you have sense, you won't go around askin' too many questions. And no fightin' or blackguardin' either, d'ya hear me?'

'And how long am I to stay there?' JohnJoe asked.

'I don't know, for good if you're lucky.' His father gave the old mare a flick of the stick and she trotted on.

'And are Kitty and Jane going too?' he asked, daring to hope.

'Who?' his father asked.

'Kitty and Jane, my sisters?' JohnJoe wondered if his father was a bit slow in the head. He never used to be. He had some good memories of him and Mammy, and despite all his faults, Mammy loved him. JohnJoe's granda couldn't stand his son-in-law, thought him an idle waste of time, but Mammy saw something in him. He looked very different now, though; his face was bloated and he'd put on a lot of weight. His hair was unkempt and he smelled terrible.

'No, they're not, of course.' His father sounded irritated now, and JohnJoe instinctively knew it was best to stay quiet.

He longed to know where they were. Kitty would be sixteen now, and Jane five. Maybe they were at home? He felt a pang of pain. 'So where are they?' he asked tentatively.

His father exhaled impatiently. 'Where are who?'

'My sisters.' JohnJoe tried to keep his voice respectful.

His father took another drink. 'In England, I suppose.'

'Do you know where?' he asked hopefully, thinking maybe he could write to Kitty.

His father sighed exasperatedly as if JohnJoe's requests were the height of inconvenience.

'No, with your mother's sister probably, but I lost the address.'

They made the rest of the journey in silence, not stopping for any food, though JohnJoe was ravenous. Eventually, late that night, they arrived at the old stone house on the edge of Kilrush. He barely recognised it. He'd been happy there one time, with a few cows in the byre, hens running about the well-kept yard and the side garden tended carefully into rows of different vegetables. Nothing had been done for years by the looks of it, and the entire place was run down and overgrown and choked with weeds. His mammy and his granda would be turning in their graves to see the state of the place now.

He climbed down and went for the door, but his father threw the reins at him. 'Untack and feed and water her,' he barked, and went inside.

JohnJoe did as he was told, leading the horse to the stable and piking in some hay. There was an old barrel of water there and she began to drink thirstily. When she was settled and the trap pushed inside, he went to the house. It was cold and smelled dirty.

Of his father there was no sign; the only indication he was there was a loud snoring coming from upstairs. JohnJoe looked for a candle but found none, so he rummaged in the dark for a piece of bread or anything to eat. There was nothing, so he sat in the chair by the empty hearth and fell asleep.

The morning dawned bright and clear and he had a chance to look around. The kitchen was filthy and smelled of something horrible. The last time he was there was the day of Mammy's funeral; he and the girls were sent away the day after. He tried to shut his eyes tight and remember it as it was – the fire burning in the hearth, a loaf of soda bread on the bastable over the fire, Mammy sitting by the fire in the evenings, darning or knitting. Everything smelling warm and clean and safe.

The last thing he'd eaten was porridge the previous morning at the borstal, and he was so hungry he felt he might faint. But there was nothing in the house. He went outside, hoping he might find something. He spotted some strawberries – his mother used to trail the plants up the garden wall to avail of the summer sun – and so he dived on them, eating all he could find. His father was gone and so he waited. He decided to sit outside rather than in that house where only ghosts and memories lay. In there he was reminded of all he'd lost – his mother, his sisters, his family, his home.

At least he was free.

He had no way of knowing how long he waited there – hours probably. The sun was high in the sky by the time a motor car appeared in the yard. JohnJoe had only seen a few motor cars in his life and they fascinated him. He'd never even looked inside one before, and there one was, in his father's yard.

Intrigued, he watched as his father got out one side of the back and a man he didn't recognise stepped out of the other door. There was a driver who remained in the car.

'So this is the famous JohnJoe O'Dwyer, huh?' The young man spoke with an American accent, and JohnJoe thought he was like the carmaker Henry Ford – he'd seen a picture of him once. The man wore a suit with a matching waistcoat and a shirt with gold collar studs. He took off his hat and raised it in a gesture of greeting. His dark hair was cut in a fashionable style, longer on top, and JohnJoe got a whiff of a spicy cologne. He was the most exotic person JohnJoe had ever seen.

'Yessir, I'm JohnJoe,' he answered, though he was most certainly not famous. The man said his name like it was two names, John and Joe, when everyone he knew ran the two together.

'Nice to meet ya, kid.' He smiled, extending his hand. 'My name is Danny Coveney. I'm your cousin.'

JohnJoe was perplexed but shook the man's hand. A cousin? In America?

'My Aunt Kathleen is married to your Uncle Pat, your mom's brother, so we're more like cousins through marriage, but let's not get too hung up on technicalities. He sent me here to get ya, take you back to Boston. Whataya think of that, kid?'

'I...I'd love it,' he managed to blurt.

The man chuckled and punched him playfully on the shoulder. 'Sure you would. OK then, let's get outta here.' He looked at JohnJoe questioningly. 'Go get your stuff.'

'I don't have any...stuff, sir...' JohnJoe said, hoping this wasn't a mark against him.

The man shrugged. 'OK. Whatever. Get in the car – we got a train to catch. I just need to talk to your father. I'll be right there.' He said father like 'faahthaa', and JohnJoe wondered if all Americans sounded like that.

JohnJoe approached the vehicle with a combination of awe and trepidation. Was this really happening, an exotic stranger with lovely clothes turning up and telling him he was going to America? But first he'd get to ride in a real motor car and then a train? He'd never been on anything but a pony and trap before. He did as he was instructed and walked to the shiny black automobile. The driver stared ahead. His dark-green uniform was magnificent. On his head he wore a hat like the senior officers of the police wore, with a peak and a black band and everything. JohnJoe was transfixed.

The vehicle had no roof. He opened the door and climbed up. The interior was black leather that squeaked as his bare legs in his short trousers inched across the seat.

Sure someone was about to give him a clip around the ear for having the impertinence to be near such a vehicle, he watched as the man, Danny, gave his father some money. JohnJoe wondered what on earth was going on. Yesterday he was facing years of the borstal, followed no doubt, according to the priests who ran the place, by prison because of his bad character and criminal disposition. And now here he was sitting in a motor car on his way to America. He should feel sad, he supposed, leaving his father and all hope of being reunited with Kitty and Jane, but his father clearly didn't care where he went and Kitty and Jane were in England somewhere so he would never have been able to find them. The farm was a sorry version of how it once was, and it broke JohnJoe's heart to see all the work and pride his mother and grandfather put into it wasted.

Danny exchanged a few words with JohnJoe's father, who pocketed the money, and JohnJoe wondered if he would ever see his father again. He found the thought wasn't really painful. Would he come to the car to say goodbye? Surely he would. JohnJoe sat up straight and put his shoulders back. He wanted his father to see a good boy, someone he could be proud of. But after the short exchange between him and Danny, his father just went into the house; he never even looked in his son's direction.

Moments later Danny sat down beside him and grinned. 'Let's get outta this dump, eh?' He winked.

* * *

THEY HAD ARRIVED TO ENNIS, the biggest town in County Clare, early enough to go into a gentleman's outfitters before crossing to the station. JohnJoe was now dressed in the finest clothes he'd ever seen. He had polished shoes, stockings, long trousers and a jacket. His shirt and tie were fitted most carefully once the man in the shop saw the wad of cash in Danny's wallet. Danny even bought him a lovely hat. JohnJoe felt wonderful.

'We can't bring a ragamuffin to Uncle Pat now, can we?' Danny had said as he paid for the outfit and several other garments as well – sweaters, pyjamas, underwear, some spare shirts and even a coat, something JohnJoe had never owned before. And then he bought him a leather travelling case to put it all into.

The train was another excitement. Danny bought them first-class tickets, so they had a compartment to themselves.

'Mr Coveney.' JohnJoe nudged him, fearing his reaction at being woken but badly needing the toilet.

'Hrrmh…' he groaned, and then opened one eye. 'Oh hey, JohnJoe, you OK, li'l man?'

'I… Mr Coveney, sir, I need the toilet.' He blushed.

'Well, don't let me stop ya, kid.' He stood up and gestured that JohnJoe should pass.

'I… Is there one on the train?' he asked, feeling very foolish, but he didn't like to admit to Danny that it was his first trip on a train as well.

'Ain't you never been on a train before?' Danny asked with a grin.

'No, Mr Coveney…' JohnJoe began.

'OK, first off, call me Danny, everyone does. No more with this Mr Coveney. Only my old man is called that. Secondly, if you go to the end of the carriage, there'll be a door, and in there is the can.'

Seeing JohnJoe's look of confusion, he added, 'The bathroom, the john, where you go pee-pee.' He cuffed JohnJoe across the head playfully. 'Where did they keep you, kid? Under a rock? Now git.'

JohnJoe left the compartment and walked in the direction of the back of the train. He caught a glimpse of his reflection in the glass and could hardly recognise himself. Just as Danny predicted, there was a toilet in a cubicle, and he went in. On the way back he saw a woman pushing a cart laden with buns and sandwiches.

He was so hungry but didn't like to say it, after Mr Cov – Danny had been so generous. But when he got back to the compartment, he was delighted to see Danny had bought some sandwiches and three different kinds of buns, as well as two cups of tea that were on a tray with some biscuits.

Danny handed JohnJoe a cup of hot tea and thumbed at the pile of food on the seat. 'Help yourself, kid. I didn't know what anything was. The old lady selling it was talking Gaelic or somethin'.' He picked up a sandwich and examined it. 'They sure got some strange food here, so I got a bunch of things.'

JohnJoe descended on the sandwiches wrapped in waxed paper. He sank his teeth into the bread, delighting in the creamy butter and salty ham inside. He slurped the tea and swallowed the sandwich in two minutes flat.

'Keep working on it – you look like you need it.' Danny chuckled, then lit a cigarette and sipped his tea. 'Urgh.' He winced. 'What is this stuff?' He looked at the tea. 'Oh man, it tastes like boiled weeds. Get me back stateside. This place...' He shook his head and shuddered.

JohnJoe smiled. 'Try putting milk and sugar in it, it's nice.' He took the small jug of milk from the tray and poured it into Danny's tea and then added two spoons of sugar from the bowl, stirring it.

Danny tried it, wincing again. 'It's not coffee, but it's OK.' He smiled as JohnJoe began on an egg sandwich. 'So story goes you're a bit of a hellraiser, huh?' he asked, sucking on his cigarette.

'I don't know what that is,' JohnJoe answered truthfully.

'Sure you do.' Danny winked. 'How comes you wound up in juvie?'

JohnJoe hadn't the faintest idea what he was talking about.

'The place where you were, where your old man went to get you?' Danny looked at him as if he were slow.

'Oh, borstal? I was sent there when my mammy died. My aunt in England took my sisters and they sent me there 'cause my da was a drinker, still is.'

A softness crossed Danny's face and JohnJoe felt safe. Danny was the nicest person he'd ever met, apart from his mammy, of course.

'Jeez, kid, you didn't do nothing wrong to get sent there? No stealing or nothing? What was it like?' he asked gently.

JohnJoe shrugged. He didn't want to remember. 'Terrible.'

It was the truth, of course. It had been horrible. But there was no point in bringing all that up here. He was going to America with Danny, and he had fancy new clothes and lots of food. Things were good, so best leave the past where it belonged.

'I bet it was. If it's anything like the place they sent me when I was your age, juvie, y'know… And that was only for six months, but it sure felt longer. The Lyman School for Boys, out near Westborough, but you don't know where that is. Man, that was bad, real bad. The old guy and his wife that ran our cottage, he was vicious and she wasn't much better. One stint there was enough for me.'

'Why did they send you there? Did your mother die?' JohnJoe asked. He'd never been so forward with an adult before, but Danny seemed not to mind.

'Nah, she's still kickin'.' He grinned. 'Kickin' my old man mostly.' He chuckled. 'I didn't like school much, so I didn't go, and eventually they got the truant guy after me and they locked me up, taught me some manners.' He lit another cigarette, and as he did, JohnJoe saw the tattoo on his wrist. It was of a shamrock, the three-leaved emblem of Ireland.

'And did you just get out after six months? They let you go home?' JohnJoe asked, then took a bite of a currant bun.

'Yeah, but my old man knew there wasn't no point in sendin' me back to school, so I went to work for Uncle Pat.'

'What sort of work was that?' JohnJoe was intrigued.

'All sorts of things. Uncle Pat's a powerful guy, JohnJoe. He got fingers in lots of pies, y'know?'

JohnJoe nodded, though he had not the faintest clue what Danny was referring to. Was he a pie maker? Maybe if he made pies, there would at least be lots to eat.

Danny looked out the window. 'It's so green everywhere,' he remarked. 'Back home they say it is, singing songs about the green fields and the rivers and mountains and stuff, but it's real, huh?'

Again JohnJoe didn't know how to reply. Yes, the fields were green – what other colour would they be? Weren't American fields green too?

'Oh wow, look there, what the... What is that?' Danny pointed excitedly out the window at the large McNamara castle standing in a field beside the track.

'It's a castle. Don't you have them in America?' JohnJoe asked, glad that the Irish countryside was delighting his cousin so much, even if he couldn't really understand why.

When he was small, his mammy used to take him and his sisters for picnics to the fairy fort on their land. She used to tell them how neither his daddy nor his granda, nor his before that, would ever allow cattle or sheep in there, nor would they use it for growing crops, because it was owned by the fairies and you wouldn't want to get on the bad side of them – terrible things could happen to you if you did. There was a hawthorn tree – everyone knew they were magical – right in the middle of the ring fort, and he wished now he'd had time to show it to Danny. By the sounds of it, he would have been really excited to see it.

Danny hooted. 'No, JohnJoe, we do not got any castles in America. You don't listen in history class either, I guess, eh?'

JohnJoe gave a sheepish grin. Classes in the borstal were mostly about trying to avoid getting a hiding and much less about learning anything.

Danny went on. 'Christopher Columbus discovered America in 1492, and then it took hundreds of years for people to come from Europe and everywhere else, and they all together built up America. The Irish are big over there – they're gonna love you with your brogue and everything. Uncle Pat talks a bit like you, I guess. He's been in Boston for as long as I can remember, but he says he's Irish through and through. We stick together, y'know? You gotta understand that about America – you need to stick with your own kind. Don't go messing around with Jews or Italians or Russians – they got their own thing going, and we stay outta each other's way. Folks who know where they are, where they need to stay, they fare the best.'

JohnJoe had never in his whole life met anyone who wasn't Irish, so the idea of having connections to such exotic people as Italians or Russians was incredible to him. And the only time he'd ever heard of Jews was in the Bible.

Danny was fascinated by the castle, and to his apparent delight, the train slowed down for some reason and he was able to get a good look. 'What's that bit at the top, the bit of wall outside the main wall?' he wondered.

'It's a garderobe,' JohnJoe said, delighted to seem knowledgeable for once.

'A what?' Danny asked.

'Well, it was a toilet really. They would sit on the wall at the top and, well...' JohnJoe went red.

'Oh, gee...that's so amazing.' Danny was craning his neck to see inside.

'And inside the castle sometimes there was a murder hole, a place they could pour boiling oil or water or sometimes the contents of the chamber pots down on anyone they didn't like.'

'Ha, ha! We could use that back in Boston, any unwanted visitors getting a nice surprise!' Danny seemingly loved the idea.

JohnJoe was warming to his theme. His mammy had told him all about castles. There were many of them all around West Clare, and she and her sisters used to play in them all the time. 'The small narrow windows were because it was easy to fire arrows out and hard to get them in, and all staircases in castles went anticlockwise, because it meant the advantage was with the defender in a swordfight. Coming down an anticlockwise staircase, if you were right-handed like most people are, you would be dominant.'

'Go on.' Danny was hanging on his every word, and JohnJoe had never enjoyed such attention in his life.

'Well, that's why left-handed people were always considered strange or odd, sinister even. The Latin word for left is *sinistram*, and that's where we get the word sinister from. But they were kind of sought after as swordsmen because they were useful for attacking up a staircase.'

'No kiddin'?' Danny seemed intrigued. 'Uncle Pat's gonna love you, kid. He's all into the old Irish history and all of that, the kings and the druids and the chieftains. How comes you know so much? They teach ya that at school?'

JohnJoe shook his head. 'No, my mammy knew things like that. She told me and my sister. But is there no old buildings in America?' It was his turn to be fascinated.

Danny lit up another cigarette. He seemed to light one off the other, and he carried them in a beautiful case that looked like it was made of seashells, all smooth and greeny-grey. 'So no.' He exhaled a long plume of smoke. 'The castle-building stuff stayed back in the old countries. We got nice shiny new buildings, tall ones too. We got lots to see – the Bunker Hill Monument, South Station, Faneuil Hall, the Old North Church. And wait until you see the clock tower. It's beautiful, but new. Not like here.'

JohnJoe nodded.

'So your mom died, huh?' Danny asked kindly.

JohnJoe nodded, not trusting himself to speak.

'And you got two sisters? Where they at?' Danny asked.

JohnJoe shrugged. 'I don't know now. I asked my father, but he says he lost the address.'

Danny looked troubled. 'I dunno, but I bet if you asked Uncle Pat when we get to Boston, he might be able to find them. He wouldn't like the idea that your sisters, his nieces, were missing or something. And the aunt that took them, was it your mom's sister?'

JohnJoe nodded. 'Yes, my Auntie Bridget.'

Danny's brow furrowed. 'Yeah, I think Uncle Pat is in touch with his sister Bridget. You ask him, see if he don't do something.'

A glimmer of hope grew in JohnJoe's heart. Could this be true? Would Uncle Pat find Kitty and Jane? 'That would be so wonderful...' He longed for what Danny said to be true, but it seemed impossible.

Danny gave him a slow smile. 'He found you, didn't he? Look, what you'll come to realise about Uncle Pat is he gets what he wants, and he got influence, y'know?' Danny raised one eyebrow and JohnJoe nodded, though once again he had no inkling what the man meant.

'So if Uncle Pat wants something, he just gets it. It's how it is. So you tell him about your sisters – he'll help.' Danny seemed sure.

'He sounds really nice,' JohnJoe said, hoping he was right.

Danny chuckled. 'Oh, he's nice, all right, if you're on his side.' He winked and, as the train gathered speed again, stubbed out his cigarette with the heel of his boot, pulled his hat down over his eyes and went back to sleep.

JohnJoe sat happily, watching the land speed by. Travelling by train was so exhilarating, he wondered how Danny could sleep through it, but he supposed it wasn't his first trip on a train.

* * *

As the locomotive pulled into Cork station, Danny woke and stood up, stretching and yawning.

'OK, so this is Cork, but we gotta go to...' – he pulled out a sheet of paper from his pocket – 'to someplace called Queenstown. We're gonna stay tonight in a hotel, in the Queenstown place, and sail tomorrow back to Boston. Uncle Pat had my aunt arrange it all.' He pulled their bags off the luggage rack compartment. 'You ever stayed in a hotel before?'

JohnJoe stifled a giggle. Danny had no idea how outlandish his question was. Not only had JohnJoe never slept anywhere except his own house or at the borstal, he'd never even met anyone who had ever stayed in a hotel. 'Never,' he confirmed.

'Yeah, well, I guess the hotels in Ireland are a bit different from the ones we got back home, but hopefully they'll have hot water at least. I need a shower.' He shuddered as if suggesting that everything he might touch was dirty. He did take excellent care of his clothes, and he was neat as a new pin, as JohnJoe's mammy might say. 'So, kid, one more night here and then you ready for a new life in Boston?'

He pronounced Boston like 'Bah-ston', and JohnJoe wondered if he should do the same. He'd never heard anyone speak like Danny did. 'Danny?' he asked.

'What, kid?'

'Why does Uncle Pat want me? I mean what does he want me for?'

Danny sat back down, setting the suitcases on the floor of the carriage. 'I guess your old man didn't explain much, did he? That guy...' Danny shook his head. 'OK, kid, it's like this. Your Uncle Pat, well, he's a businessman, y'know? And him and his crew, all big Irish guys like you' – he grinned – 'well, they're busy, y'know? Doin' lots of different deals, stuff like that.' He raised his eyebrows in question, and JohnJoe nodded, getting accustomed to Danny's assumption that he had a clue what was happening.

'Well, it's best in our line of business to keep things in the family, y'know? People you can trust. Well, my Aunt Kathleen had some problems, health-wise, a few years back, and so she can't have kids, and Uncle Pat is crazy about her so he wasn't gonna get someone else or nothin', y'know?'

JohnJoe nodded again, trying to look knowledgeable, but this conversation was becoming more confusing by the second.

'He could have, easy. I seen plenty of broads over the years make a crack at him, but he's not interested. He badly wants a son, someone with his blood, but it wasn't gonna happen, and so he decided to ask your old man if you would like to come over, be adopted and, y'know, be part of the family. He talks about your mom all the time, little Sheila, and he was very fond of her. He don't got a blood relative of his own to train up in the business. He's got me, and everyone else is Irish and loyal to him, but it ain't the same – he wanted family.'

JohnJoe thought back to Danny giving his father money. 'Did my da sell me?' he asked quietly.

A shadow crossed Danny's normally open and cheerful face. 'What? No. Course he didn't. Uncle Pat just sent his brother-in-law a few bucks. Sell you? What are you, crazy, kid?' He ruffled JohnJoe's hair affectionately and chuckled, but JohnJoe knew he was lying.

'So he wants me to live with him, is that it? For a while or for ages or what?' JohnJoe asked.

Danny sighed. 'I told you, he's gonna adopt you, y'know, so you'll be his kid, his son. And one day, you'll take over the family business. It's gonna be great, and you and me's gonna be buddies.' He focused on JohnJoe, his eyes locking with his. 'Don't worry, kid, it's gonna be fine. We'll take good care of you. You're gonna be happy, I swear.'

This time JohnJoe knew he was telling the truth.

CHAPTER 14

*A*s the train pulled into the station at Queenstown, Sean O'Sullivan stood and took his bag down from the overhead shelf, his bulk filling the small compartment. Much to his relief, the young woman who had been wedged beside him had seemed engrossed in whatever she was reading, which suited him fine; he was glad of the time alone with his thoughts.

The woman stood and tried to reach her bag, but at less than five feet tall, she was struggling. He was eye level with the shelf, so he grasped the case by the handle and pulled it down, handing it to her.

'Thank you,' she said, blushing. Her hat was pulled down over her face.

'You're welcome,' he replied and went to leave.

The red-haired girl was behind him as they shuffled off the train. He was bad at chatting at the best of times, and today he just couldn't. Every mile took him further from Gwen, away from all he knew, but they'd agreed this was the only way.

His own parents had been mortified that he would even have the audacity to set his cap at Gwen Pearson. The Pearsons weren't their kind of people, and it was best, to their way of thinking, to never move outside of the box God had placed you in. His mother missed

Mass for the first Sunday of her life the weekend after she heard about Sean and Gwen's romance. She took to the bed, too ashamed to face the parish. If it weren't such a hullabaloo, it would have been funny.

Sean worked for old Major Pearson as his stable master. Sean had a way with horses, always had, and he took care of the stables at Oakwood, the Pearson place on the edge of town.

Gwen was the major's only child. Her mother wasn't there, so it was just her and the major. She was a wonderful horsewoman and they'd become friendly, and then that led to love. And it was true love; he was sure of it. Gwen was a wild child and cared nothing for the conventions of society. Her mother was in an asylum in England – she'd had a breakdown of some sort and was not of sound mind – so Gwen was raised by her father and a series of housekeepers. Major Pearson indulged her, up to a point, but marrying the stable lad was about ten furlongs beyond that point. He said no, straight out, that it wasn't right for either of them. And while he'd been nice to Sean in his dismissal of him, going on about his natural gift with horses and how he was a fine chap and all the rest of it, he was adamant that the match was a bad one.

Gwen had been confined to the house, and only because she was so brave and snuck out to see him had they hatched the plan.

He had cousins in America; they were making a fortune by all accounts. He and Gwen decided that Sean would join them, make his fortune – or at least enough that he wouldn't be going cap in hand to Major Pearson. He would make enough money to get them a place of their own and then send for her, and if their parents didn't like it, they could lump it. He tried to imagine his parents' reaction to having Gwen Pearson as a daughter-in-law and just couldn't.

Like everyone around Portarlington, Sean's father had worked the bog, cutting then drawing peat and loading it on the riverboats that brought it along the River Barrow all the way to Waterford, where it was either sold or exported. Every year it got harder to make money as a riverman. He had no land – his father before him had lost their tiny bit of a farm in a card game. Sean's two older brothers, Mick and Jimmy, had gone to England and nobody had heard from either of them for years. But Sean landed on his feet when Major Pearson saw him settle a wild filly the day of the hunt in the village and had offered him a job on the spot. He'd worked his way up from stable boy to running the yard. The major liked him, but not enough to let him marry his daughter.

Gwen had seen an advertisement for a guest house in Queenstown in the paper and had written to book him a room. When he'd admonished her for wasting her money when he could have stayed in a boarding house, she cited how she'd heard that one of the Brownes from out near Glenbarrow picked up conjunctivitis in the boarding house in Queenstown and was refused entry at Ellis Island. All manner of diseases and lice and filth were rife in those places, so she insisted on pawning her gold necklace to pay for it. The major had wisely cut off her allowance, fearing what stunt she might pull. There wasn't a boarding school in Europe that could keep Gwen Pearson incarcerated, so the major never underestimated his daughter's powers of escape.

Maybe she was right, Sean thought as he saw groups of people alight from the train, most of whom looked the worse for wear already, before they ever stepped on board a ship. Dressed up as best they could, they still looked what they were – poor people, leaving the only home they ever knew to seek a better life across the ocean.

His mother had tearily mended every stitch of clothes he had and had knit him two heavy jumpers and five pairs of socks. His shirts all had the collars and cuffs turned, and his good shoes and working boots had been sent to Tim Cassidy for soles and heels.

'Nobody will look down their nose at my son,' she'd said, then sniffed as he tried on the old overcoat she was repairing for him. 'You're the handsomest man in County Offaly, Sean O'Sullivan, and you'll be the handsomest on Aquidneck Island too. So mind those fast American women, don't they take a shine to you.'

As far as his parents and the major were concerned, the romance with Gwen was over and he was going to America to mend his broken heart. But it wasn't over. They were just biding their time.

He moved towards the ticket inspector, who was checking each ticket as people trudged up the platform and made their way towards the town. Was it true that in less than a week he would be in Rhode Island? It seemed impossible, and yet his ticket was in his pocket. He would board the *RMS Laconia* tomorrow, and five days later he would be in Boston.

His cousin Paddy had given him instructions on how to get to Aquidneck and assured him there was work there, and plenty of it, for a fella willing to graft, and he was. He would have rather done something with horses, but he had no contacts in that world in America so Aquidneck Island would have to do. The harder he worked, the more money he would make, and then he'd get a house and be able to send Gwen the fare and they'd begin their new life in the United States of America.

That image of himself standing on the quayside over there, watching the ship dock that held his darling Gwen, that was what would sustain him, keep him going. That was the only thought driving him on.

There was no future for them in Portarlington; people would never accept them. He'd always be seen as the stable boy who stole the daughter of the house, and Gwen was determined they would not be that. They would be just a young couple, like so many millions that went before, embarking on a new life together as equals. He wished he could write to her, but they decided it would be safest not to. If everyone thought it was over, then she wouldn't be under surveillance and the fuss would die down. But what if she genuinely lost interest? Maybe she would meet someone else. She was so lively and full of fun; she would be bored in that big old house all on her own with nobody but the old major for company. What if her father decided on someone else for her? The fears and doubts refused to leave him.

She was such a beauty, his girl, and so brave and ferocious when she had to be. He hated the idea of the major pushing some aristocratic military man on her, some chinless wonder from Bristol or Birmingham, someone he would deem to be more suitable than penniless Sean O'Sullivan. Sean saw the way men looked at her when she was out hunting, in her white breeches and velvet jacket, her jet-black hair tied back. She refused to ride side-saddle, though her father thought it unseemly to see a woman astride; she insisted she could ride faster and safer that way. She was home before all of the women and most of the men on every hunt, mud-spattered and sometimes having taken a tumble but always grinning. The British officers who came to dine with the major or to hunt or fish the Pearson lands couldn't help but admire Gwen. She was pale and fine-featured, with ruby-red lips and flashing green eyes. She came across as haughty, but Sean knew the warmth and passion of the woman underneath the glacial exterior. She was the one who made the first move on him, kissing him passionately in the stable. He'd never known a woman could feel like that about a man; he'd been brought up to believe that girls only endured the kissing and all of that because it was what wives did, not that they could be as enthusiastic as any man. But Gwen was. She took the initiative at the start, and feeling her hands on his skin, her lips on his body... He groaned almost audibly at the memory of their passionate times alone together. It was every kind of sin, he was sure of that, but he couldn't help himself. He was putty in her hands, and leaving her was physically gut-wrenching. She loved him, she swore, as she gazed into his face, her green eyes locked with his. She told him that she was his, that there was nobody else for her, that she would wait no matter how long it took. He had to keep reminding himself of that. She loved him and would stay true to him until he sent for her, no matter who the major dangled in front of her nose.

The likes of the major might not enjoy their position in Irish society for long more anyway. People were agitating for independence again; it wasn't right to be treated like a peasant in your own place by encroachers. His neighbours were getting involved politically, and there were rumblings of rebellion again, the hope being this time that another bid for Irish freedom would end better than all the previous attempts down through the years. Great as it might be to dream, he doubted it would ever happen. The British Empire straddled the globe, and a few Irish lads with pitchforks weren't going to send them packing no matter how committed they were. The thought of getting caught up in all of that was just another reason to get himself and Gwen out of this beautiful troubled land.

Outside the station he was surprised to see a man standing with a sign.

Mr Danny Coveney
Miss Molly O'Brien
Mr Sean O'Sullivan
Miss Eleanor Kind

Sean approached him, and as he did, he saw that in his carriage – a large affair with two rows of seats – already seated, was the heavy girl with the red hair who had been sitting beside him on the train.

'I'm Sean O'Sullivan.' He introduced himself to the man.

'Welcome, Mr O'Sullivan. My name is Matt Quinn. I'm operating a hackney service for the Cliff House, so if you'd like to take a seat, I'll just wait for the other guests. They were on the same train, I believe. And then we'll be off.'

Being cooped up beside the girl again wasn't anything he relished, as he would surely have to talk to her if he met her again, so he asked, 'Is it far? I could walk, I think. After the train it would be good to stretch the legs.'

'Well, 'tisn't far as such, but 'tis a climb.' Matt Quinn pointed to a large white house with red sandstone edging high above the town.

'Oh, that's grand. I'll walk so.' Sean decided to set off.

'How about you put your bag in at least?' Matt suggested.

Sean took a look at him. He looked like a decent type, not a man who would try to steal from him, so he agreed and placed his suitcase in the back of the carriage. He would have to take more care once he got to America – there were people there only looking to swindle a man fresh off the boat – but while he was in his own country, he knew who he could trust.

'You don't need to go on the road.' Matt pointed to an opening in the huge wall that held the cliff back from the railway station. 'There are steps there, and plenty of them.' He chuckled. 'About two thirds of the way up, you'll see a gate leading into the Cliff House garden. You can't miss it – it's the first one you come to. 'Tis about two hundred fine steep steps up, so you'll know all about it by the time you get there.'

Sean nodded his thanks, walked in the direction the man indicated and began climbing. It felt good to move again after the long journey. Halfway up the steps, his heart pounding and his back wet with sweat, he turned and gazed back over the harbour. It was a fine summer's day, and the water was busy with all manner of vessels. To his left, the huge cathedral watched over the town, and he thought he would go to Mass there before he sailed. His last Mass in Ireland. Would he ever return, he wondered? He doubted it.

* * *

ELEANOR STOPPED to pet the small, sleek, tan-coloured dog with one black patch around his eye and another on the tip of his tail that was sniffing around the tea stand in the station. He was some kind of a mongrel terrier, and the poor fellow was half-starved, his ribs showing through his skin.

Impulsively, she approached the woman running the stall. 'I'll take a chicken sandwich please,' she said.

The woman looked at her, her face a mask of disapproval. Eleanor didn't care. She knew her appearance meant women didn't trust her. All around the station, ladies wore cinch-waisted long skirts or dresses, high-necked blouses and elaborate hats. Even the poor women travelling third class followed the norm, albeit shabbier. But there was nothing normal about Eleanor Kind, never was and never would be.

She took the sandwich and paid the money over, trying not to smile at the woman's face as she almost recoiled at the sight of Eleanor's dirty fingernails. She unwrapped it and fed it to the dog, which wolfed it down in one huge bite.

'Good lad, there you are...' She saw the woman open her mouth to object to her food being fed to a dog, but one glance from Eleanor made her close it again.

Eleanor stood up, hitched her trousers up, tightened the bit of baling twine she'd used as a belt and threw her rucksack over her shoulder. The greatcoat had been her father's, bought in a pawn shop in Dublin one fair day when the bitter wind blew off the Liffey as he sold his cattle. It had served him well all his life and now it was hers, the dun-coloured woollen coat that skimmed Eleanor's ankles. It was a bit warm for it today, but wearing it was easier than carrying it.

A man was holding a sign with her name on it.

'I'm Eleanor Kind,' she said, thrusting her hand out for him to shake. He looked startled but took it.

She'd almost forgotten how her appearance unsettled people. The men she met at the fair and in the town of Ballinasloe were used to her now, and the women had learned to ignore her. Her straggly grey hair was unkempt and wild and hung to her shoulders. It had been longer but she'd taken a scissors to it herself before leaving. She didn't own a brush, so the result was patchy, and she couldn't be bothered tying it back demurely. The men's shirts and pullovers she wore didn't turn a hair in her own place, but down here, she had to admit she probably was a bit of an oddity. Not that she cared a jot; she didn't. The weight of other people's expectations wasn't something she usually bore, at least until now.

Nothing about this plan sat well with her. Her brother had more or less strong-armed her, using a combination of guilt and fear, into agreeing to this hare-brained scheme, and she'd regretted it the moment she said yes. She'd just lost her nerve after the fall, just for a moment, and he pounced on that weakness.

She was perfectly happy at Elmwood on her own. Her younger brother, Edward, had been in San Francisco so long now he had lost the ability to imagine any life other than his shiny brash American one. She could hear the pity and despair in every letter, genuinely foundering to understand how someone would choose a small windy farm in County Sligo over the delights of California. But Edward didn't get it; he never did. As the only boy, it was assumed he would inherit the land, but he'd never shown an iota of interest. Their father was disappointed, of course, but he knew things were in safe hands with Eleanor. She was eight years older than Edward, and from twelve or thirteen she was farming every day while Edward was mollycoddled in the kitchen by their mother. He got away as soon as he could. And she didn't begrudge him – farming was never for him – but why could he not accept that they were different people wanting very different things from life? She knew he'd pled with her from a place of kindness; that's what made resisting him for so long so difficult.

She was seventy-two years old. She knew that. He didn't need to point it out in every single communication. Besides, she was as well able to manage as she was when she was forty and their parents were still living. Since they died, Father twenty years ago, Mother only five, Edward had been plaguing her to sell up the home place and move over to San Francisco. He thought his vivid descriptions of orange trees and eternal sunshine would lure her, but he was wrong.

What he described as a tumbledown farmhouse with delusions of grandeur and a hilly stony farm were her home. And she loved it. Not alone that, but it was home to her animals, and to her they were everything.

The hackney driver who introduced himself as Matt Quinn helped her up into the carriage and threw her bag in the back. As he pulled away, his carriage and horses struggling against the steepness of the hill, she thought about poor Bonnie, her border collie. She and Bonnie were best friends; it wasn't too much of an exaggeration to say that. Most people didn't understand how a dog could be a person's best friend, but they didn't know Bonnie. She was so intelligent, she could almost talk to you. Eleanor had cried salty tears into her fur when she left her with the Harringtons. They would be kind – she couldn't have left her if she thought otherwise – but still it tore her heart out.

So many goodbyes. To Alf the carthorse, as old as the hills and not fit for much any more but strong and steadfast. She'd nuzzled into his neck, trying to preserve the sweet smell of him in her mind. Her goats, Billy and Milly, who were better than any guard dog. They'd run at any intruder and butt him so hard he'd be knocked into next week. Her hens, territorial and watchful, her one-eyed cat, Whiskey, her herd of milking cows, who each had her own friend and would not go

145

into the milking parlour until she was with her companion. Edward didn't understand anything about her life, how full it was, how busy, saying she was there all on her own, worrying about her. He couldn't grasp that she wasn't remotely alone. Her life was full of characters and friends – they just had four legs and not two.

She cursed for the fiftieth time that interfering old busybody Tom Sherrard. He had no right to stick his big beak into her business. She would have managed to get up eventually, but no. He had come by to collect her churns for the creamery and found her lying in the byre with a broken ankle. It was her own stupid fault, of course, climbing that rickety old ladder, but Sherrard had to go off and write to Edward, saying everyone was so worried about Miss Kind, fearful she'd do much worse damage next time, and she was all alone out at Elmwood. Edward believed him, of course, the stupid eejit, when Eleanor knew Tom Sherrard had been after her land for years. Men. They were such a trial. Thinking they knew best. So sure they had all the answers.

She'd never been tempted to marry. There were a few offers over the years, mostly fellas who had more interest in her land than her, but it didn't matter; she was never tempted. She had no need of a man following her around, thinking he knew best. She'd avoided that all of her life only to fall at the last fence. How maddening that at this last phase of her happy single life, Tom Sherrard and her brother were conspiring against her. Sherrard couldn't wait to get his hands on her long meadow. Owning it meant shortening his route driving his herd to and from the milking parlour every day, and any guff he gave Edward about being worried was a load of old nonsense. Only Edward was too dozy to see it. Anyway, it suited his argument.

Edward had mithered and begged; he'd even telegrammed the county hospital when she was laid up there, her leg in plaster – such unnecessary dramatics – begging her to come to America. She was his only family, he was worried, she was a danger to herself, what if she died...blah, blah, blah. She had no interest in America. She was sure Edward's wife, Linda, was a nice person – she sent totally ridiculous gifts of silk scarves and perfume at Christmas – and their children looked very healthy and well cared for in the photograph they'd had taken, in a studio no less, but she was happy on her own. Could they not understand that? No, apparently, and in a moment of weakness a week after she escaped the hospital, when the pain in her ankle was ferocious and the cows were bellowing for want of milking, she'd written and agreed. She wished with all her heart she hadn't, and she tried to back out but he was having none of it.

Their father had left the farm to both of them, with the knowledge that Edward would never come home and Eleanor would run it, and Edward went so far as to threaten to sell his half of it out from under her if she went back on her promise. He'd do it too. She knew he would. He'd bleat about it only because he cared, but she just wished he wouldn't.

Once she agreed, he was relentless and the wheels began turning with indecent haste. A passage was booked and people were contacted to come and take the animals. Poor old Alf had no idea what was happening when Charlie O'Gorman came to take him away. He said he'd use him for stud, but Eleanor and Charlie both knew the truth – Alf had no more interest in romance than she did. He was bound for the knacker's yard. Like she was. His was a glue factory, hers a garden with orange trees, but ultimately the same destination.

The cattle were sold at the fair, and she got a good price. She didn't care how much the farmer who bought them sniggered when she said it was critical that the bovine friends remain together, pointing out to him who liked who and which of her girls, as she called them, bore a grudge against another. He did buck up when she told him of their yield, though. A happy cow gives more milk; there was no denying the truth of that. And her girls were fine milkers so long as they were happy.

The hens had originally been bought by the Widow Desmond, but she had a flock already and there was near carnage that first day, with Eleanor's flock going on the full attack. Hens could be very jealous, so the widow had no choice but sell them on to the O'Connells, losing money on the deal. Katie Desmond tried to take it up with Eleanor one morning at the creamery gates, but the quirky Miss Kind was having none of it. Anyone who knew anything knew that hens were a law unto themselves, and no human person could be held accountable for their actions.

The goats she gave to young Joanie Mullen, who was good with animals and understood them like Eleanor could, and Whiskey naturally followed Billy and Milly, so at least Eleanor could be sure Joanie would care for them. But by far the hardest was Bonnie.

She'd had her since she was a pup, and they shared food, a bed, a life. Bonnie was such a faithful companion, an intelligent, compassionate soul, and Eleanor couldn't bear to sell her, though she was excellent at rounding up sheep. Many of the local farmers would have been delighted to get her, but Eleanor couldn't countenance the idea of her being worked to death, made to sleep in a cold barn, only fed meagre scraps. In the end she did the only thing she could do. She took her to Flick.

Felicity Harrington and Eleanor had been pals since childhood. Their lives had diverged when Flick was sent away to boarding school in Dublin; her mother had fierce notions of grandeur altogether. But their friendship survived. It survived Flick's year at a finishing school in Switzerland, her high-society wedding to Hugh, an investment banker and a crashing bore, and it had even survived as Flick became the toast of the county, beautiful and poised.

They made the oddest pair, she knew, but Flick was the only person who'd never tried to change her. She knew Eleanor didn't care for clothes or hairstyles, hats or finery. She knew her friend was different but didn't care. All through their twenties and then their thirties, Flick was the only one who never asked her why she wasn't married – she knew why. She never suggested she wear something else, or arrange her hair in a style rather than just letting it grow whatever way it liked. Flick liked Eleanor for who she was. And that was a rare thing in Eleanor's life.

She'd sobbed like a baby on Flick's front step at the prospect of leaving Bonnie, whose long pink tongue licked the tears from Eleanor's face.

'I'll mind her, El. You know I will.' Flick had bent down beside her and the dog, rubbing her back. 'She'll have a great life, I promise.'

Eleanor blinked back the tears, angrily wiping them on her sleeve. Luckily her fellow passengers in the carriage were gazing out on the town of Queenstown, the aquamarine sea, the white puffy clouds scudding across the sky, too busy thinking about their big adventure the next day, no doubt.

She would give anything just to get back on that train and go straight home, get her animals back, sleep in her own bed. But it was hopeless. She was alone. She had no husband, no children. Edward was all she had and maybe he was right. What would she do when she got even older, even less able? Edward had decided and she had no options. She had to go to America for the rest of her life.

CHAPTER 15

*R*ose was busy in the kitchen, putting the finishing touches to the evening meal, as Harp sat beside the range lost in *The Higher Education of Women* by Emily Davies.

On a whim, Rose had decided to offer dinner as well as breakfast to the guests, and to their astonishment, every one of the guests wanted to eat at the Cliff House.

'Will it be all right?' Rose asked, suddenly nervous that the simple food wouldn't be fancy enough.

Harp looked up and smiled at her. 'It will be lovely, Mammy. Sure what more would you want after a long day travelling and facing into the voyage tomorrow than a lovely bowl of home-made soup and a slice of fresh-baked soda bread, followed by bacon and cabbage, floury spuds and a lovely apple tart for dessert? It's a dinner fit for a king!' Harp announced with a flourish.

Rose laughed at the expansiveness of the compliment.

Mr Quinn had delivered the guests up from the station, and shortly afterwards Mr O'Sullivan appeared at the garden gate. He was only in his early twenties, Harp thought, and there was something sad about him. He reminded her of Heathcliff, all dark and brooding and melancholy. He had that look that was distinctively Irish; scholars said it came from the Phoenicians, an ancient people who traded with the Irish around the eighth century BC. He had dark, almost-black hair, cut short and oiled back from his high forehead, pale skin and sapphire-blue eyes. He was an intelligent-looking man; she instinctively knew he was a deep thinker. His clothes were old but well cared for.

They'd shown the guests to their rooms and they were all happy with their lodgings, so that was the first hurdle. Two of the bedrooms faced the sea and the other two were unfortunately at the back of the house, the cliff behind them, but Harp and her mother had filled window boxes with tumbling trailing flowers and hoped the bright, clean bedlinen and the extra candle they provided would do enough to dispel the gloom. They had considered charging less for those rooms but decided against it. It would be first come, first served with the front bedrooms. If someone was being very obstinate about wanting a sea view, they could use the rooms on the third floor if needs be.

They had put the two women in the front rooms overlooking the water and the men in the back, figuring men cared less about views.

The young American man in the very fancy suit, travelling with the boy, came looking for hot water. He thought there would be a shower available, and Rose had to tell him that there was just a bath and it was in the shared bathroom at the end of the hall, but he seemed fine about it. He'd winked at Harp. The boy with him, who looked about her age, was dressed like a young gentleman, but he didn't speak at all. He was Irish and about an inch shorter than her, and he seemed awestruck by everything. She was a little nervous speaking to them. She'd never met a real American before, and he seemed a very glamorous one. He even wore a gold ring on his finger.

The red-haired girl said she would not be dining that evening. As she was halfway up the stairs, Harp called, 'The hotel on the main street does a nice meal if you'd rather eat out?' Though in truth Harp had not the faintest idea what the hotel food was like, considering they could never afford to go there.

The large girl turned. 'No...no thank you.' Her eyes darted furtively this way and that. 'I'll be fine.'

Something about her made Harp more chatty than normal. Her mother was back in the kitchen and this girl looked like she needed something, though what Harp had no idea.

'But sure, you'll have to eat,' Harp pointed out. 'And believe me, eating a big breakfast ahead of a sea voyage isn't the best idea, if you know what I mean. Best to have a nice meal tonight and sleep soundly after it, and then a light breakfast. My mother is famous for her soup, and it's bacon and cabbage tonight with floury potatoes and loads of butter. And the dessert is really nice. And it's not too dear...' Harp wondered if perhaps the price was what was stopping the girl. Molly looked like a person who enjoyed her food.

'OH NO, it's not that, I just...' She seemed torn.

'Well, it's up to yourself, but I'll have to let my mother know, so you can have a think and decide.'

'Well, perhaps I should...'

'Well, George Bernard Shaw said that "there is no love sincerer than the love of food",' Harp said.

The girl laughed and Harp realised she had a lovely smile that lit up her entire face. 'All right, I'll be down for dinner then. You've convinced me.'

'Lovely. We serve at seven.' Harp impressed herself with how professional she sounded.

Miss Kind was at the front of the house but she had yet to appear. Her bag was in the hallway but she was outside, sitting on a bench watching the birds preen themselves at the birdbath. Mr Devereaux and Harp had kept a diary of all the different varieties of birds that appeared at the old lichen-covered stone bath.

Harp walked outside to ask her if she would like to be shown to her room.

'No thanks. I prefer to be outside. It's nice that you get garden birds and seabirds here. You're lucky,' the woman said without catching Harp's eye.

'Yes,' Harp agreed, 'though sometimes it's hard for the smaller birds to get the food. We have a lot of blue tits and robins in the garden as well as bullfinches and sandpipers, but they have to battle against razorbills and guillemots as well as the gulls, so it's a struggle not for the faint-hearted.'

'You know your birds,' the woman said, sounding impressed.

She looked like nobody Harp had ever encountered. Her iron-grey hair was wild and curly and hung down her back, and her face was lined and weather-beaten, making her look like someone who spent her life outdoors. She reminded Harp of nothing so much as the Rembrandt *Self-Portrait 1661*. Her clothing too was odd. She wore men's trousers and hobnailed boots, and on top she wore a man's shirt and a blue hand-knitted jumper full of holes. On the garden seat she'd thrown a huge brown overcoat.

'My father taught me.' Harp surprised herself. It was the first time she had said the words 'my father' aloud. She half expected alarms to ring, or Emmet Kelly to pop out of the bushes and laugh at her, but nothing happened.

'Is he a country man?' the woman asked.

Harp shook her head. 'He died, but no. He just knew everything.'

Miss Kind smiled. 'I'm sorry for your loss. Knew everything, did he? That's some achievement.'

'Well, maybe not every single thing, but he knew most things.'

'Was he a teacher?'

Harp shook her head. 'No, he...well, he just read a lot.'

'And he passed that love of learning on to you?' Ms Kind covered her eyes to shade them from the strong sunlight and looked at Harp.

Suddenly this was getting too close. She should never have said anything. Her parentage was a secret and her inheritance predicated on a lie, and here she was blurting it all out to this stranger. 'Um...yes, he did, but I'm not really supposed to talk about...' Harp felt foolish now.

'I understand. People need their privacy. Not enough people

understand that.' She smiled as a beautiful greeny-grey wood warbler sang from the branch of the oak tree in the garden.

'He's called a *ceolaire coille* in Irish,' Harp volunteered. 'The singer of the wood.'

'And a *Phylioscopus sibilatrix* in Latin,' Miss Kind added.

Harp found the woman's company restful but she had to remember her role. 'Is there anything I can get you?' she asked.

'No thank you,' Miss Kind replied. 'I think I'll stay out here and enjoy your lovely garden for a while. Would you care to join me?' She indicated the other recently repainted white wrought-iron seat.

'Thank you,' Harp said, sitting down.

'So what's your name?' the woman asked.

'My name is Harp D...Delaney, Miss Kind.' How she longed to say 'Devereaux'.

'Eleanor, please. I know children are supposed to refer to adults by Mr or Mrs, but I never felt grown up enough for that title, and now I'm too old to even try. Everyone calls me Eleanor. My brother, my only sibling, lives in America. His name's Edward. He couldn't say Eleanor when he was little, so he just called me El.'

'Is he who you are going to visit?' Harp asked.

Eleanor sighed heavily. 'Yes, but not just to visit, to stay. He lives in San Francisco.'

'On the West Coast,' Harp said quietly. 'That's a whole other journey even after getting to Boston. There was a huge earthquake and fire there six years ago on account of its position on the San Andreas Fault. How will you get there?'

'By train.' She sounded resigned and not at all enthusiastic.

'Aren't you excited?' Harp couldn't help asking. 'If I were going there, I think I would be.'

'About earthquakes and fires?' Eleanor chuckled. 'Is that what I can expect there?'

Harp reddened. She'd said the wrong thing again. Of course it was insensitive to bring up such perils to someone about to go there. 'Well, there is an earthquake most days, seismographs record them, but most people don't even feel them they are so slight. I just meant it would be a real adventure to go there, so different even from the East Coast. I often wonder if Boston and New York are like Ireland, as there are so many Irish people there.'

Eleanor smiled kindly. 'I'm sure for a young lady such as yourself it would be a very exhilarating adventure indeed, but for me it's complicated. I'm too old to go and too old to stay.' She shrugged. 'I'm of no use now, and so my brother says I must come to live with him where I'll be safe. Yes, safe and bored out of my mind.'

'Solon, the Greek philosopher, said that as he grew older, he learned more,' Harp said. 'You could use the time to read and learn.'

'True.' Eleanor nodded. 'A worthy pursuit, I suppose, but I'm not that into the books, not as much as you clearly are.'

'What is your passion?' Harp asked. 'If you know what that is, then where you are geographically in the world would be irrelevant.'

Eleanor cocked her head to one side and looked quizzically at Harp. 'You're a funny one, aren't you?'

Harp coloured, embarrassed that she'd sounded peculiar yet again. 'No... I'm sorry. I shouldn't have...'

'No,' Eleanor said, 'what were you going to say? I'm interested. Please.'

Harp swallowed. 'Just that happiness, according to Aristotle anyway, which is the highest of pursuits, is achieved through virtue. So to be virtuous – not in the social sense, but to live to your highest expectations of yourself, your best self – is the route to happiness. So if a person can find the best expression of themselves, then they will be happy.'

Eleanor nodded, seemingly thinking about what Harp had just said. Then she took the remains of a crust of bread from her pocket and placed the crumbs on the table.

Harp watched, fascinated, as the bird singing in the tree stopped and watched, then swooped down and snatched the crust. It stayed just a few feet away from them, pecking the bread, checking back with Eleanor every few seconds.

'How did you do that?' she asked, amazed. 'Birds eat what we put out, but they fly away the moment we arrive.'

'Animals, birds, anything non-human really, that's my passion. I have a way with them, even fish. They respond to me differently than to other people. I could tickle trout when I was knee-high to a grasshopper. Just because animals don't talk doesn't mean they can't communicate – they are better at it than most humans if you just know how to interpret them. I'd rather be with animals than humans, that's the truth.' There was no pride in her voice; it was just a statement of fact.

'Who taught you?' Harp asked.

Eleanor shrugged. 'Nobody really. My mother was never well so spent a lot of her life bedridden. My father was the farmer and he taught me a certain amount. But I just spent my days outside on the farm, wandering the land. I should have gone to school, I suppose, but nobody cared whether I did or not, so I chose not to. I found that I could connect with animals in a way I never could with people. Except my friend Flick. She was different, but most humans, no.'

'Even your brother?' Harp asked.

'Especially my brother,' Eleanor said darkly. 'He's younger than me but he left for America when he was seventeen, and I've not seen him since. He writes all the time and I reply occasionally, but he's never come back and I've never gone over there. He'd be sixty-four years old now, hard to believe. He was just a young buck when I last clapped eyes on him.' She sighed and picked a leaf from the bay tree growing beside the front door, cracking the aromatic plant between her fingers, then raising it to her nose, sniffing appreciatively. 'Great for a rash, this bay leaf, or for rheumatism either.' She nibbled on the side of the leaf. 'Edward thinks he knows what's best for me. He wants me to leave all I love. He's wanted it for years and I fought it off, but now I'm just too tired to go to war with him again, so I have no choice but to give in.' She sighed again.

'But you don't want to?' Harp asked quietly.

Eleanor shook her head. 'I don't, but as I say, there's no avoiding it now, it seems.'

'"While prudence will endeavour to avoid this issue of war, bravery will prepare to meet it."'

Eleanor smiled quizzically. 'Aristotle again?' she asked.

Harp laughed. 'No, Thomas Jefferson.'

'So you think I should stand up to him, be brave?' Eleanor asked.

Harp thought seriously for a moment. 'If it's what you truly want, if staying here in Ireland with your animals is your highest virtue, the thing that makes you happy, and you are positive about it, then yes, you probably should. Nobody should be dictated to by someone else, no matter what the reason. But I'm just a child so I don't know.'

'A wiser child than most adults, I'd wager.' Eleanor threw some more breadcrumbs for the garden birds.

'Not really. I don't really know a lot of things other children know, so I'm a bit odd.' Harp shrugged.

'Me too. Talking to dogs and horses all day long, no wonder people think I'm half daft.' She chuckled.

'That's wonderful knowledge to have, though.' Harp was impressed. 'The things I know are interesting but not that useful.'

Eleanor nodded. 'I suppose so. There isn't a vet for miles, so people round about home bring their sick or injured animals to me. But I don't suppose my skills will be much in need in San Francisco.' She sighed. 'Edward says I can't cope, and to a certain extent he's right, I suppose. My place is very far from the town, and it does take a lot of work to manage, and I'm not as young as I was.'

'But,' Harp said, 'and this is just a thought, what about if you sold your land and moved closer to the town? Into the town even. As you say, there's no vet for miles, so maybe you could set up a little clinic and people could bring their animals to you. It would be a way of making a living, and everyone knows how good you are with animals anyway, and you'd be part of a community, safer maybe?'

Eleanor's eyes filled with tears. 'That's a lovely idea, Harp, but it's all arranged now. And besides, Edward is waiting for me to come and without any other family, I'm vulnerable. When my parents were alive, it was different, but now…'

'I'm sorry about you losing your parents. That must have been hard when you had nobody else,' Harp said, changing the subject.

'I had my animals.' Eleanor shrugged. 'And I was grown up. But yes, losing a parent is hard, no matter what your age. You know yourself how hard it is.'

Harp nodded. 'My mammy is here, though, and she takes very good care of me.'

Eleanor smiled. 'You're lucky then.'

'There are animals in America too, you know, ones we don't have here, lots of them actually.' Harp listed what she'd memorised from the previous summer when she'd read a lot about the different continents and their individual features. 'Raccoons, weasels, otters, beavers, lizards, coyotes, skunks, snakes, cougars, black bears and even whales.'

'Maybe I'll make friends with a big old bear some day.' Eleanor smiled sadly.

'If you go, you might.' Harp smiled. 'I'd better go and help my mammy. I can show you to your room or I can tell you where it is and you can go in whenever you want?'

'I'll go in later,' Eleanor said, turning her face to the warm Irish sun, a gentle breeze rustling her hair.

'Oh, there's a dog there, I never saw it before.' Harp had spotted a small terrier lurking in the hedge.

'Ah.' Eleanor held out her hand and the dog trotted over to her fearlessly. 'I met him down at the station. Do you think someone around here owns him?'

Harp took a better look at the pup as he licked Eleanor's hand. 'I don't think so.'

'Well, he looks like a stray to me. I doubt anyone's been feeding him.' Eleanor smiled at the little dog and made some noises that Harp couldn't understand.

'Should I get some scraps for him?' she asked.

'If your mother wouldn't mind. I'm sure our little friend here would appreciate that.'

Harp skipped into the kitchen and returned in a few moments with some bacon fat and a bit of liver left over from their tea the previous night. She gave them to the little dog, who ate them hungrily.

'You have a kind heart, Harp,' Eleanor observed. 'I don't know if your mother will be happy about it, but you might just have adopted this little lad.'

'I don't think she would like that, Eleanor.' Harp shook her head. 'She's a stickler for cleanliness, especially now, and dog hair and droppings wouldn't really be part of her plan.'

'Well, we'll see.' The old woman winked.

Harp patted the little dog and handed Eleanor her key. 'Your room is the first door on the left as you go up the stairs. Dinner is at seven this evening and breakfast is in the morning between seven and nine.'

Eleanor took the key and put it in her trouser pocket. 'See you later, Harp,' she said as she stood observing the harbour with her hands in her pockets, the little dog resting on her foot.

CHAPTER 16

'*D*o you need any help, Mammy?' Harp asked as she entered the kitchen.

'No, I think everything is under control,' Rose said, smiling.

Harp was so relieved that the worried, anxious look her mother wore constantly in the weeks after Mr Devereaux's death was a thing of the past.

'Why don't you go and read a book for an hour before dinner?'

Harp nodded and walked upstairs. She would go to her room, choose something soothing. She had been given *Anne of Green Gables* as a gift by her mother for Christmas but had yet to read it; perhaps she would start that. It was a beautiful book, leather-bound and exquisitely illustrated. The books in Mr Devereaux's library were all to his taste, and though she loved them, she rarely read books written for girls her age, so she was very much looking forward to it.

She stalled on the landing outside Mr Devereaux's bedroom, thinking of the thousands of hours she'd spent in there with him, reading, talking, listening to music, examining a painting. She wished she could just go in, sit in her window seat and read her book while he read quietly by the fire. Now Miss O'Brien would sleep in there, having no idea of the man who had lived there for so long.

'Are you all right?'

The voice broke through her reverie and she was startled to see the boy who was travelling with the American man come out of the bathroom.

'Y...yes... I...I apologise, I was...' Harp was flustered and embarrassed to realise her cheeks were wet.

'But you're crying,' he said.

She swallowed. 'I'm fine, thank you... I'm sorry.' Feeling awkward around someone her own age, she turned to go, but he stopped her.

'I was going to walk down to the town. My cousin has gone to buy some tobacco, but he gave me some money to buy sweets for the voyage. Would you like to come? Show me the way?'

Something about the boy made Harp pause before refusing. She could see it had taken a lot for him to invite her, but she'd never been approached like this before, by someone of her own age wanting to spend time with her. She wasn't sure how to respond. Was he genuine? Was he trying to make a fool of her? Of course she should not go down to town with this boy, but he seemed as lost and as lonely as she was. She did have an hour to kill before dinner, and her mother had things ready. And all she was going to do was read anyway. It was a strange sensation for her, but just then she didn't want to be alone.

Alone had never meant lonely before, but seeing Mr Devereaux's study as the bedroom of strangers, the pleasant aromas of cooking food and beeswax polish were suddenly not comforting and welcoming; instead they felt alien, foreign, as if his memory was being erased. She hated the feeling.

'I'll just ask my mother if it would be all right,' she heard herself say. 'What's your name, by the way?'

'JohnJoe O'Dwyer. But Danny – that's my cousin, he's American – says nobody in America will know what I'm saying if I say that, so he advised I introduce myself as JJ.'

Harp felt a pang of compassion for the small freckled boy with the dark-green eyes and sticking-up hair. 'Which do you prefer?' she asked.

'I don't know. I was always just JohnJoe. My mammy's father was called Joseph and my father was Johnny, and so was his father before him. I was the only boy, so I was named for both of them. I remember both of my grandas well – they're dead now – and they were both really nice. My Granda Joe used to take me fishing, and he taught me how to draw birds and trees and things. It was the only thing I was ever any good at really, drawing. And my Granda Johnny was a great storyteller. He used to have us laughing when he'd be doing funny voices and everything. But I suppose JJ is all right. If people won't understand me, it might be for the best?' He seemed unsure.

Harp shrugged. 'I don't know. My name is Harp and some boys at school tease me about it, saying it's not a proper name, but whenever I get upset about it, my mammy says that it's irrelevant what people think of me. She asks me what do I think of me? What do I think of my name? And she says mine is the only opinion that matters.'

'I think Harp is a lovely name,' JohnJoe said, and Harp could tell he was being honest.

'Thanks. So do I. Now I'll probably spend my whole life explaining it, but it's who I am. And so maybe if your mother called you JohnJoe and you like it and it means something to you, then you should stick with it, force them to understand?'

He smiled and she saw his gap-toothed grin for the first time. 'Maybe you're right, Harp. I'll stick with JohnJoe. My mammy is dead and she named me, so it would be an insult to her memory if I changed it, wouldn't it?'

'Maybe it would,' Harp agreed.

'They might make me do it, though, but we'll see.' His brow furrowed.

'Who would make you?' Harp asked.

'My uncle in America. I'm going to live with him. He sent Danny to bring me over there. I...' His voice dropped to a whisper, and he looked around as if expecting someone to be spying on them. He swallowed and Harp waited.

'I...I was in borstal, and my father came and took me out and told me I was going to America because my uncle has no child and he wants one, so my father said I could go.'

Harp was fascinated. 'And what is this uncle like, is he nice?' she asked.

'Never clapped eyes on him in my life.' JohnJoe shrugged. 'But so far it's good. I've a new suit of clothes and loads of food, and I'm sleeping in a really fancy hotel.'

Harp smiled at the idea that their home was a fancy hotel. 'But won't you miss your father, your brothers and sisters?' she asked.

A shadow crossed his warm, open face. 'My father doesn't care about us. He drinks, and that's all he cares about. My sisters, Kitty and Jane, were sent to England, and I've not seen them since I was nine.'

Harp now knew why something in this boy sparked compassion. He was hurt and let down by life but still managed to stay as cheerful as he did.

'That's terrible,' was all she could add.

He nodded. 'It's how it is. I hope they're all right. I dream about them sometimes, and hope they were at least kept together. Danny says my uncle might be able to find them, and if he can, then when I'm older, I can come back and see them.'

'I really hope you do,' Harp said, meaning every word.

'So will we get some sweets?' he asked. 'My cousin said candy but I think he meant sweets. I haven't had anything like that since before my mammy died. She used to get us a Cadbury's chocolate bar for our birthdays.'

'Did you not get anything nice in the...' She was loathe to say the word 'borstal'. There was shame in it, as only bad boys were sent there, but she couldn't imagine JohnJoe being in trouble with the police.

He smiled and shook his head. 'Barely enough bread, let alone anything else.'

He walked beside Harp as she went downstairs and popped into the kitchen.

'Can I go down to Cronin's with JohnJoe? He wants to buy some

sweets for the voyage tomorrow, but he doesn't know where to go.'
Harp hoped her mother wouldn't say anything sharp; she could be a
bit too strict at times. Luckily the softening effect of her new friend
seemed to work on her mother as well. She eyed him up in a second
and seemingly deemed him to be unthreatening.

'All right, but straight there and straight back and no dilly-dally-
ing,' she said. 'Does your cousin know you're going out without him?'
she asked JohnJoe, albeit kindly.

'He's gone for tobacco and maybe to the pub, I don't know. He
gave me the money for sweets, though, so I think it's all right,' JohnJoe
answered honestly.

'Well then, I suppose it is.' To Harp's astonishment her mother then
went to her purse and gave Harp a half penny. 'You can buy yourself
something nice too. After all your work, you deserve it.'

'Thank you, Mammy,' Harp said with a grin.

It was turning into a lovely day. Mammy didn't like her to eat too
many sweets. Mr Devereaux used to have a box of chocolates sent
every month from Kavanagh's sweetshop in Dublin, and each afternoon he would offer her one. Deliberating over the card showing the
various different flavours and making a decision was one of their
many rituals and one she never mentioned to her mother. Mr
Devereaux always said he liked the coffee-flavoured ones or the
raspberry creams, which she wasn't partial to at all, but perhaps he
just picked those, leaving her favourites for her. She suspected that
was it.

As she led JohnJoe down the steps, she thought to herself how sad
it was that her first and only friend was leaving the country the next
evening. 'Are you really excited about going to America?' she asked. 'I
would be.'

He thought carefully about the answer. 'I am, I think. Up to a few
days ago, I was going to spend the rest of my childhood in borstal and
probably then get sent someplace when I got to sixteen that is just as
horrible, so anything is better than that. And then for Danny to turn
up and treat me so nice and that, well, it's not like it's real, you know?'

'I know.' And though she had no idea about going to America at a moment's notice, she understood perfectly how disconcerting it was to have your life suddenly change so much you barely recognised it.

'I'm scared too, though,' he admitted. 'Like what if Danny is really nice but my uncle isn't? My da is awful...'

He paused and she could see he was deliberating telling her something.

He made his decision and spoke up. 'I think he sold me to my mother's brother. Danny said he didn't, that he was just giving my da a few bob, which will go down his neck anyway, but I think it was a deal.'

Harp was shocked but knew she couldn't show it. 'Well, I'm sure he wouldn't do that, but either way, you get to have a better life in America, so does that really matter? As you said, the future looked kind of bleak before your cousin turned up, and well, it is the land of opportunity they say. And you're a clever boy, so even if it didn't work out with your uncle, you are somewhere new with all kinds of exciting prospects. And as you say, if you did well, you could come back and find your sisters.'

He smiled and his eyes twinkled. 'I'd love that.'

They chatted easily as they walked along, and JohnJoe marvelled at the beauty of the town in the summer sunshine. Harp had never before in her life had a conversation of this length with anyone her own age, and she was enjoying it. She felt pride in her home town. Queenstown looked like something from a painting, with the green grass in the town park and the boats bobbing about on the turquoise water in the harbour.

The footpaths were full of ladies in lovely dresses emerging from the Imperial Hotel on the promenade, their hemlines just short enough to avoid their skirts trailing in the mud, their hats works of art in themselves. Their husbands were immaculate in three-piece suits, and they puffed on cigars ahead of boarding the ship bound for Boston. The passengers emerging from O'Flaherty's boarding house would be much shabbier, but they were at the very end of the town, a place called the Holy Ground, and there were a few huckster shops down there to cater to their more modest needs.

Cronin's sweetshop was on the corner of the town square, right across from the park with its colourful bandstand and picnic benches recessed into the perimeter.

'It's so nice here. You're lucky to live somewhere so pretty,' JohnJoe remarked as they entered the shop.

The aroma of molten sugar and toffee that met them was delicious. There was a wide counter full of glass jars, each containing a different kind of sweet. Mr Cronin also had a cold box where he kept the ices, and as JohnJoe and Harp waited, a well-dressed man bought two ice creams for a pair of little girls in frilly pink dresses with matching parasols.

When it was their turn, they chose carefully, and Mr Cronin didn't rush them. He didn't mind if children chose one of this and one of that; he made each customer feel like they had all the time in the world, though the queue was building behind them. They each chose the same things – liquorice, peppermint creams, a lollipop, a sherbet lemon and a chocolate fudge – and emerged into the sunshine again.

Harp knew she should really go straight home, but the park looked so inviting. She and JohnJoe crossed over and sat on a vacant bench, looking out over the harbour, sucking their sweets and chatting amicably.

'Where is your home place?' she asked.

'Kilrush, County Clare. My mammy's people were from there and my father married into my Grandfather Joe's farm, but he was no farmer. Didn't like working, I think. Mammy was an only child. My granny and granda are dead now and so is Mammy, so my father lives there alone.'

Harp could hear the pain in his voice and identified with it. 'Is it nice?' she asked.

He shrugged and stuffed the bag of sweets into the pocket of his very fine trousers. 'It used to be. My granda was a great farmer, and he had cattle and sheep. My granny and then later my mam had a vegetable garden and kept ducks, geese and hens. They used to have a stall at the market, selling lovely fresh vegetables and eggs. But these days my father isn't much of…well, he's not much of anything, to be honest with you, Harp.'

'Well, it's all behind you now, JohnJoe, and I bet your granny and granda and your mammy would be so proud thinking of you going off to America…' As she spoke, she felt something hard hit the back of her head. She raised her hand to see what it was and discovered it was a big lump of wet mud. Just then another missile got her between her shoulder blades and she knew the back of her dress was ruined. She turned and saw Emmet Kelly walking outside the park railings, on his own this time, whistling nonchalantly.

'Did he just throw that muck at you?' JohnJoe asked incredulously.

'It's best to ignore him. He's only looking for attention,' Harp said calmly, standing up and trying to get the mud out of her hair.

JohnJoe took his handkerchief out of his pocket and started to wipe the back of her dress.

'Have you got yourself a boyfriend, Harp? He must be a quare hawk like your dear departed daddy,' Emmet called through the railings, then laughed. 'Stay away from that one, I'd advise you, boyo.' He pointed at Harp and her cheeks burned as people began to watch. A large crowd was gathered outside Dan Mac's pub on the corner, some men drinking bottles of stout in the sunshine. Dan Mac's had a reputation as being a rough kind of house, and the clientele were delighted with a bit of drama, even if it was just children.

'She's not right in the head, sure you're not, Harp?' Emmet pointed to his temple and twisted his finger.

Before Harp could register what was happening, JohnJoe sprinted out of the park and punched Emmet in the mouth, and then in fast succession dealt a series of blows to the abdomen, which caused Emmet to double over, howling. Harp watched in horror as Oliver Kelly, Emmet's father, who'd been drinking in Dan Mac's, appeared and pulled JohnJoe off Emmet. He was about to hit him when Danny sprinted across the road. He caught Oliver Kelly's fist mid-air and spun him around. Harp saw a glint of something in Danny's hand, and when he punched Mr Kelly, Mr Kelly's cheek burst open and blood spattered in all directions.

'Let's get outta here, kid.' Danny grabbed JohnJoe and ducked down a lane.

Harp heard the constable's whistle before she saw him and knew she needed to get JohnJoe and his cousin out of there quickly. She ran after them down the dead-end lane. 'Quickly, follow me,' she hissed as they encountered the base of the old town walls that dated back to medieval times, fifty feet high.

Harp opened the garden gate of the last house on the lane. Old Mrs Lynch lived there and was deaf as a post; she'd never notice them slipping through her garden and out onto the steps. Danny and JohnJoe followed her, and together they scrambled over Lynch's back wall and were soon on another narrow set of steps that linked to the main set that cut through the town. They scampered up the steps and into the Cliff House garden.

Danny took a metal contraption that Harp recognised as a knuckleduster from his fingers and was about to put it in his pocket. A villain in one of her detective books had an engraved gold knuckleduster. 'They're illegal here,' she murmured. 'Best get rid of it.'

Danny looked uncertain, but she took it from him and sank it into the large stone planter of newly dug soil positioned inside the garden gate. Her mother intended to set some petunias there the next day. She scattered the soil over the indentation and led them to the back of the house.

To her horror she saw Inspector Deane, the local constable, approach the front door. He was sweating profusely as he rested his bicycle against the wall.

Harp stopped and whispered urgently to both of them, 'You just punched him with your bare fist because he was about to hit your cousin, and JohnJoe was only defending me after Emmet threw mud all over me.'

Danny chuckled as he followed her inside. 'You got it, kid.'

They found Rose speaking to the policeman in the hallway, looking stern.

'I believe he is a guest here, Mrs Delaney, but I will need to speak to him immediately. Mr Kelly is in a very bad way, and the attack was entirely unprovoked it seems.'

Harp walked in. 'It wasn't at all an unprovoked attack, Inspector Deane.' She sounded more confident than she felt and she caught her mother's eye. 'Let me handle this,' her eyes said. She knew she needed to sound authoritative, so she did her best. 'Emmet Kelly, the son of the alleged victim, has been harassing me for several months and has been spreading rumours and malicious gossip about me and my mother around the town. Frankly we were to the point of reporting him to you. My mother has witnessed one such incident, but there are several. Today when I was showing a guest around the town, Emmet threw mud at me, as you can see.' Harp turned and hoped the back of her cream dress and her hair were sufficiently soiled as to make an impression.

Inspector Deane was not used to being spoken to in such a manner by a child, but something about Harp made him listen rather than dismiss her.

'JohnJoe here crossed the road to speak to him and ask him to desist, but it descended into fisticuffs.' She skimmed over the bit that it was JohnJoe who hit Emmet first. 'Then Oliver Kelly, a man we all know is prone to physical assault – had he not a conviction last year for actual bodily harm? – was about to attack JohnJoe, a boy considerably his junior. JohnJoe's cousin and guardian, Danny, happened to be walking on the other side of the street and then saw what was happening to his young cousin, so he dashed over to intervene. Yes, a fight did ensue, but it was started by both of the Kellys, so I suggest, Inspector Deane, if anyone has a charge to answer, it is them.'

The adults in the room were silent, probably struck by the sheer audacity of a girl speaking as such. Harp knew that it was not what one said that mattered but how one said it. She was a huge fan of Conan Doyle and Holmesian deduction and hoped she sounded a little like him.

Inspector Deane, a small-sized bald man who perspired at the slightest exertion, looked hesitant. He was an ineffectual law enforcer at best and was far more interested in his prize-winning greyhounds than entertaining petty squabbles. 'But Mr Kelly's face is badly injured and –'

Rose, taking her cue from Harp, intervened. 'Mr Kelly is a bully, Inspector, as is his son. My daughter is quite right – I was on the brink of making a complaint. Perhaps this encounter will teach both of them a lesson. It is up to you entirely, but I think it would be in everyone's best interest if this matter was left to lie. Otherwise we will have no option but to take it further. Slander and harassment are serious allegations to make, I know, but if you press this, I'm afraid we would have no option.'

Danny and JohnJoe read Harp's look correctly and remained silent.

Deane was a lazy man and the paperwork involved with taking statements and so on, not to mention having to deal with the unruly Kelly family, was not a prospect he relished. He thought for a moment, and Harp could see him weighing it all up and trying to find the least taxing option for himself.

Rose continued in her most imperious tone. 'You may tell Mr Kelly that if this matter goes no further, and he instructs his son to refrain from having any contact whatsoever with my daughter, we will, in the interests of peace and harmony, not proceed with a case. But should he wish to escalate this, then we will be only too happy to. The town authorities will not be best pleased with the newspapers reporting on perfectly respectable liner passengers being assaulted in Queenstown – it gives entirely the wrong message.' She glanced at Danny, who was failing at supressing a grin, and he put on a straight face.

'In addition, Mr Coveney here is a journalist with the *Boston Enquirer* and is writing a feature on Queenstown as a destination – we were just discussing it earlier. He was hoping to write a very positive piece about the place. I fear his experiences with one of the town's less desirable inhabitants won't improve our prospects.'

The town magistrate was none other than Mr Charles Bridges, the owner of the Imperial Hotel, and if he would be horrified at such a story reaching the Irish press, he'd have a heart attack if he thought it was going all the way to America. It was very much in his interest that the town be presented as a pleasant and idyllic location for the thousands that used the port every year.

Harp watched as the policeman thought quickly. The situation was rapidly getting out of hand, and his pores showed how harassed he was; he wiped the sweat from his brow.

'Yes, well, we're very sorry that you had to endure that, Mr...uh... Mr Coveney...' the policeman began.

Danny looked at him and held up a hand indicating he should forget the whole thing. 'Please, Inspector, think no more of it.' He took a small notebook from his pocket, removed the pencil in the spine and licked the lead before writing. 'Now, your name was Inspector Deane – is that with or without an "e"?'

Deane puffed up. 'I... That won't be necessary...' he began, growing more flustered by the second.

'Oh, but, sir, proper law enforcement is the cornerstone of any civilised society. I want our American readers to choose Queenstown, not just as a stop off on the way to England but as a destination in its own right. I really get a wonderful impression of your town, the occasional nincompoop notwithstanding.' He chuckled and Deane self-consciously joined in. 'If people feel they can come here and be looked after, then I'm sure everyone would appreciate the boost in business, and you would be the cause. There are so many Irish men and women in Boston who long to come home to the old country. Adding your name gives it the personal touch. I'll be sure to send some copies over once I file and it goes to print.'

'Well, when you put it like that, I suppose it would give any visitors a sense that they were safe...'

'Exactly!' Danny agreed. 'And in the light of all the negativity surrounding the tragedy that was *Titanic*, the town could use a boost, am I right?'

'Well, yes. It was a terrible loss, and while it had nothing to do with us here obviously, it still had a negative effect. And you say you could send some copies here so that people could read the article?'

'Of course.' Danny spread his hands expansively.

'Well, in that case it's Deane with an "e" – Inspector Albert Deane.'

He looked so pleased with himself that Harp couldn't look at her mother in case she giggled, and JohnJoe was watching the drama unfold with fascination.

Danny scribbled in his notebook as he asked a few more questions about how long Deane had been serving and so on. 'All right then, Inspector, I guess I got all I need. And thank you again for your time and your service to my cousin and me. We'll have such good things to say about Queenstown back in Boston, won't we, JJ?' Danny placed his arm around JohnJoe and gave him a squeeze.

'Oh yes, we will surely, sir,' JohnJoe said, and the inspector seemed pleased with the note of deference in his voice.

'Very well. I'll be off then.'

He departed on his bicycle, and the four gathered in the hallway watched as he freewheeled down the hill, united in their duplicity. Rose gave them a wry look as she returned to the kitchen, Danny went to retrieve his knuckleduster from the planter, and Harp and JohnJoe were alone.

'Thank you for sticking up for me,' Harp said shyly.

'Of course I would. And you were so confident talking to the policeman like that. I could never have done that. You're so brave, Harp.'

'Not really. Inspector Deane is a bit lazy and he's terrified of Mr Bridges, the magistrate, so I knew he wouldn't want to be drawing him on him.' She giggled. 'Will you write to me when you get to America?' she asked, blushing.

'I don't think...' JohnJoe said quietly.

'Oh...oh, all right. Maybe you won't have time, and anyway I'll be busy here...' She spoke quickly to cover her shame. She'd obviously read it wrong, thinking they were friends now. He didn't want to be friends with her, of course he didn't. She turned to go.

'No, Harp.' He grabbed her hand. 'I don't mean I don't want to – I do. I really, really do. It's just...'

She saw the brightness in his eyes and wondered if he was going to cry. 'What?' she asked.

'I can't,' he said miserably.

'Why can't you?' She was confused. 'I'm sure your uncle will let you have paper and stamps?'

He bowed his head and angrily wiped his eye with his sleeve. 'I can't read or write. I'm not able to. The brothers in the school and then the borstal tried to teach me, but I just can't do it, and they just beat me when I got it all wrong, so I never learned.'

'Oh, JohnJoe, I...' Harp was speechless. She had no idea what to say. Then she had an idea. 'I don't mind, send me a picture. I have some envelopes upstairs, so how about I write my name and address on them and you can take them with you and you can send me drawings? You said you like drawing and I bet you're great at it. And I'm sure your uncle will get someone to teach you, and once you learn, you can write to me and I'll write back.'

'Would you do that, write to me? Even if I can't write to you?' JohnJoe sounded choked.

'Of course I would. We're friends.' Harp smiled.

CHAPTER 17

$\mathcal{M}$olly O'Brien sat next to the window of her bedroom and watched the activity in the harbour. It reminded her of a scene from a picture book she'd loved as a child. She felt a pang. She'd never again see that book, or the small bookshelf her father built under the window of her bedroom, or that little room under the eaves, where she would sleep soundly no matter what the weather because her daddy and mammy were in the house and she was safe.

The thought of crossing the ocean filled her with dread. Not fear of drowning, though that was now on her mind as well, but fear of burning her bridges with her family forever. Round and round the thoughts went. Honour thy father and mother said one of the Ten Commandments, and she was flying in the face of it completely. Would her decision to enter a convent negate that mortal sin? Was she sinning by refusing to do as she was told? And poor Finbarr. He was a nice lad. He'd get such a hard time now because of her. And the land deal would fall through undoubtedly, which would mean there wouldn't be enough work for Kevin, Billy and Pius, so one or more of them would have to emigrate and break their parents' hearts. Again. They were good people, her parents; they didn't deserve that. And it was all her fault. Maybe she should just go up to the station now, go home and marry Finbarr. It would solve so many problems.

She stood up and paced the room. Dinner wasn't for another hour, so she decided to go to the cathedral, say a prayer and ask God for guidance, for peace, for protection.

She went downstairs and walked towards the gate in the wall, which led to the steps she'd been shown by Mr Quinn as they arrived. She encountered Harp again, kneeling in front of a flowerbed inside the wall, this time watering the plants now that the heat of the day was waning.

'Hello,' she greeted the funny little girl. She was like something from a fairy story, Molly thought, old-fashioned and quietly spoken, her grey eyes pale and deep, her red-blond hair tied neatly back from her small face. There was something otherworldly about her.

'Hello,' Harp replied.

'Your garden is lovely.'

'My mammy does it mostly, but I water the plants in the evenings.'

Molly admired the rows of flowers and hanging baskets. On the farm all available land was put to work; there wasn't space or time for the frivolity of flowers. 'What are those for?' she asked as Harp put down the can and began to pick some flowers from the bed and place them in a small basket.

'They're edible – violas and pansies. Mammy puts them in salads for colour,' Harp explained.

'You can eat them?' she asked, fascinated.

Harp nodded. 'The earth has more than 80,000 species of edible plants, but ninety percent of the foods we eat come from just thirty of them.'

'Really?' Molly smiled. Harp was so earnest, and though she was probably twelve or thirteen, she looked younger and sounded much older. It was an odd combination.

Harp nodded.

'I was going to go to the cathedral to say a prayer.'

'You can just cut down those steps there and then take the right-hand set up again, and it will bring you out opposite the cathedral,' Harp said, gathering her watering can in her free hand.

'It's so beautiful here,' Molly heard herself say. Suddenly she wanted company, and this quirky girl was a restful person to be around.

'It is,' Harp agreed, and together they stood in the garden. It should have been awkward, but for some reason it wasn't. They watched a tugboat pull a large trawler out to sea, gulls circling noisily overhead.

'Do you get to travel by boat much, living so close to the harbour?' Molly asked her.

'Never,' Harp replied. 'I thought that one day I would sail on *Titanic*, but now I won't.'

Molly suppressed a smile. Harp had a matter-of-fact way of speaking, and while she wasn't by any means impertinent or rude, she didn't sugar-coat anything.

'Indeed, that was so sad. I hope the *Laconia* is truly unsinkable,' Molly replied.

'No ship is unsinkable, but I suppose in life we need to take chances. The degree of danger is all we determine in each action.'

'What do you mean?' Molly asked, intrigued.

'Well, just that if we never did anything, stayed in bed all day, we would be safe but living an unfulfilled life, equally if we lived life on the edge all the time, taking huge risks. Like the Antarctic explorers or the men who fly test aeroplanes – that shows a spirit of adventure certainly but also somewhat of a disregard for life. Most of us do something in between. And we assess danger or risk every day, multiple times, and make decisions.'

'Which is better, do you think, to be braver and to take risks or to play it safe?' Molly asked.

'I think when I grow up, I'll take risks, calculated ones, though. Not reckless. But if we never try, never take a chance that we are making the wrong choice, then we'll never know our true potential, our destiny. So you have to push yourself, I think, make yourself do things that are frightening. The only way to create anything original is not be afraid to be wrong.'

'Is that what you want to do? Create something original?' Molly was fascinated; she'd never met anyone like Harp.

'Well, yes, I suppose, to leave my mark on the world. I'm not sure how yet, but I'd like to do something. What about you? What do you want to do with your life?' the girl asked.

Molly sighed. 'I want to be a nun.'

'Why?' Harp was candid.

Molly thought for a moment. Nobody had ever asked her that before. 'Because I want to serve God, I want to do good in the world, I want to help, I want to live among like-minded people.' She paused. 'I suppose that sounds awfully boring to someone who has such plans as you have?'

Harp shook her head. 'Not at all. I don't believe in religion and I'm not sure that God even exists, but the truth is nobody knows, not me, not you, not priests or even the Pope himself. They say they know but they don't, not really. They believe – that's a different thing. There's no evidence they are right. But if becoming a nun is what you are passionate about, then why not give it a try? If it's not right for you, then you can leave, do something else. You only get one life. *Carpe diem*.'

'What does that mean?' Molly asked.

'Seize the day. The Roman poet Horace, among others, said it. I think it means we should enjoy life while we can, do what we want to do, not worry too much about the future,' Harp explained.

'Even if what we want to do hurts others?' Molly asked. 'If it's selfish?'

Harp considered the question. 'In some instances, yes, that might be the case, but to be a nun, to dedicate your life to helping others, I don't think that's selfish. We all have only our own lives for which to take responsibility, I think. If someone is hurt by you doing what is in your heart, then surely that is their issue to resolve, not yours?' Harp turned to look up at her.

Molly blinked back a tear. 'My parents don't want me to go. They want me to stay at home and marry.' The words dropped like stones. 'They mean well, and they do love me, but I just can't do it.'

Harp remained silent for a moment. 'Have you read *The Jungle Book* by Rudyard Kipling?' she asked eventually.

'No,' Molly replied.

'Well, in it there is a boy called Mowgli and he is raised by wolves in the jungle. His best friend is a big bear called Baloo, and he is watched over by a panther called Bagheera. They need to keep him safe from a tiger called Shere Khan, who wants to kill him.'

'It sounds good. Maybe I should read it.'

'You should, but the point is that Baloo allows Mowgli to do whatever he wants, sometimes leading him into danger, while Bagheera is very cautious, trying to keep him safe from everything. Mowgli has to go his own way, though, he just has to, even confronting Shere Khan, and finally Bagheera realises that. You can't protect or control children forever. There comes a time when parents have to realise they created this person but the child has their own life path to pursue, and trying to stop them, even if it is to keep them safe, is a waste of time.'

'I know you're right, but I worry about my parents, all the people I've let down.'

'Well, it's either let them down or let yourself down,' Harp said, as if it were the most simple thing in the world.

'I don't know. They need to join two farms, you see. It would be much better for them if I married the neighbours' son.'

Harp stood and lifted her basket. 'Better for them, but not better for you?' she asked, mirroring Molly's own thoughts.

'I suppose that's it in a nutshell. I'll say a prayer for you too, even if you don't believe. It can't do any harm,' she said sadly as she opened the gate.

CHAPTER 18

*D*inner was served at the big table in the newly redecorated dining room. The room had, up until the previous week, been full of boxes of Mr Devereaux's correspondence, mostly unopened, bills, old newspapers and any amount of other rubbish. Rose and Harp had cleared it and held a large bonfire in the back courtyard. Then they sanded and polished the oak floorboards and painted the walls a lovely warm primrose yellow. They had arranged separate tables for breakfast for each guest, but for dinner they thought it might be nice for the group to dine together. The largest of the dining tables wasn't big enough to seat eight guests, so they improvised by adding half an old door and propping it up with the other half cut into two-inch-square posts. Without a tablecloth it looked very rough and ready, but once Rose dressed the table with a floor-length tablecloth of gold damask, a relic of the more opulent days of the past that Harp had found in the attic, and set it with the dinner service and crystal glasses, admittedly mismatched but not noticeably so, it looked much more sumptuous.

Though it was summertime and didn't get dark until almost eleven at night, Harp drew the gossamer silk curtains. They were repaired many times, as moths had got to them over the years, but like everything else in the house, they looked fine at first glance, so long as the guests didn't examine them too closely. The more subdued lighting meant they could find fewer faults with the room – the cracked window, the stain where the leaky roof created a dark patch on the ceiling, the broken floorboard. They promised themselves at each new decaying discovery that if the business was successful, they would return the Cliff House to the glory it deserved.

Harp rang the dinner gong. It had been in the cupboard under the stairs and covered with years of cobwebs and dirt, but she'd washed it and then polished the brass and was really happy with the results. It was a beautiful burnished colour now. The hammer to make it resonate was long since lost, but Mr Quinn donated an old mallet. It didn't sound as loud but perhaps that was a blessing. The gong itself hung from a brass frame by two steel chains and looked really lovely.

The guests began to move about upstairs. JohnJoe and Danny had thanked them profusely for their help in managing Inspector Deane, and though Danny seemed nice and so friendly and funny, Harp wondered if JohnJoe was in fact going into danger. The average person didn't carry a knuckleduster, at least not here. Perhaps it was necessary in Boston – how would she know? And as JohnJoe said, his new life could hardly be worse than borstal and being sold by an alcoholic father.

The tall, handsome young man with the sad eyes, Mr O'Sullivan, had not come out of his room since he arrived. Harp wondered what had happened to him to instil such melancholy.

She placed a phonograph record by Enrico Caruso on the gramophone. It was the last one Mr Devereaux bought before he died. It bore the name *His Master's Voice*, and she smiled at the image of the dog, his head to one side in fascination as he listened intently to the horn. She selected a needle from the box and inserted it carefully before placing it over the turning recording. Harp kept the gramophone doors closed all but for a crack so it was cheery without being intrusive, and the gentle music wafted around the room. The candles were lit, illuminating the table in a welcoming glow.

Molly was the first to arrive. Harp welcomed her. 'My mother is putting the finishing touches to the meal, but please, have a seat. May I get you a glass of water?'

Harp had read that offering guests a drink before dinner was customary, but she had no idea what would be usual, and besides they had no money for alcohol, so water was the best she could come up with.

'Thank you, Harp, that would be lovely,' the young woman answered.

Before the conversation went any further, Mr O'Sullivan appeared, freshly shaved and dressed just in a shirt and trousers.

'Good evening, Mr O'Sullivan,' Harp said. Her mother was cooking and so her job was to entertain and serve while Rose was left to it in the kitchen. Harp was sure they would get into a routine once they'd done it a few times, but for now it all felt a bit like they were in a play and each person had a part. Still, this venture had to work; her and her mother's future depended on it.

'Hello,' he said quietly.

'My name is Harp, and my mother and I run this place. Can I get you a glass of water?' she asked.

He gave a shadow of a smile. 'No thank you.' He looked like he felt out of place.

'Are you going to America for long?' she asked.

He gave her a cryptic smile. 'For good, I'd imagine, if things work out. I'm hoping to find work and set up a home there.'

Danny and JohnJoe next arrived, both laughing at something Danny said, and Harp was happy to see some of the anxiety of earlier when Inspector Deane was there gone from JohnJoe's face. He struck her as a worrier. She was sure borstal would instil a fear of uniforms in a person too.

Eleanor too had appeared and was chatting with Molly as they admired a portrait of Mr Devereaux and Ralph that hung over the large mahogany sideboard. The men were both in their late teens or early twenties when they sat for it, and they looked somewhat alike. They shared the same delicate features, but Ralph was dark where Henry was fair. Ralph looked more robust, though he was younger.

181

He was the more traditionally handsome of the two as well. Mr Devereaux rarely spoke of his brother but he did confide to her that on the days they had been forced to sit for the portrait, the artist much sought after in polite society, Ralph had designed a bottle and straw system, hidden up their sleeves, and both brothers sipped happily at the gin in their pockets during the entire sitting. By the time it was finished, he'd declared, both he and Ralph were pie-eyed and his mother livid because they wouldn't stop laughing. The painting gave her a lift every time she saw it.

She invited everyone to sit and made the introductions. The group made polite small talk as Harp went to the kitchen.

Rose was swirling fresh cream in the mushroom soup, the mushrooms having been picked early that morning by Harp. The butter was in pats and already on the table, so all that was left to do was slice the soda bread. Harp did that and brought it out on platters, one for each end of the table. Rose poured the fragrant soup into a large tureen that was decorated with some complicated-looking hunting scene and inserted the matching ladle.

'Can you lift it or shall I?' Rose asked, as Harp returned to the kitchen. 'It's heavy.'

'I can manage.' Harp sniffed appreciatively. 'It smells delicious, Mammy.'

'Let's hope they think so,' Rose said worriedly. 'It's very plain. I think I should have tried something more elaborate.'

'Of course they will. They are all happy, they are going on an exciting voyage tomorrow, and they are in a beautiful house, overlooking the most magnificent harbour on Earth. Your food is delicious, but even if it weren't, "the chief pleasure in eating does not consist in costly seasoning, or exquisite flavour, but in yourself".'

'Don't tell me.' Rose smiled, trying to guess this one. It was a game they played. She drummed her fingers on the table. 'Is it Horatio in *Hamlet?*'

'Close.' Harp smiled as she lifted the tureen. 'Horace.'

Harp carried the tureen through the door linking the kitchen to the dining room. Danny jumped up and took it from her, placing it in the centre of the table. She noticed how the atmosphere had turned so much more convivial in the few minutes she'd been gone.

Eleanor was telling a funny story about the time her goats took a set against her postman and refused to let him or his bike up the avenue. She was doing a hilarious impression of the man trying to do his duty while the evil genius goats plotted his downfall. Harp noticed with delight that Mr O'Sullivan was wiping his eyes with mirth. Eleanor had a wonderful way of telling a story.

They ate the meal, the chatter lively and punctuated by laughter, and everyone exclaimed at how delicious it all was. As they sat down to apple tart with light flaky pastry and their own Bramley apples flavoured with sugar and cloves, all smothered in thick, cold cream, they begged Harp to go to the kitchen and ask Rose to join them. When her mother entered the dining room, having removed her apron and fixed her hair, the group gave her a standing ovation.

Harp's heart filled with pride. They'd done it. The house was comfortable and welcoming, and the food was delicious. She caught Rose's eye and they shared a triumphant smile.

Harp thought her mother had never looked more elegant. Rose made most of her own and Harp's clothes, but they were always finished every bit as professionally as something you would buy in a fancy shop. Tonight her mother wore a chocolate-brown skirt, high waisted and fitted to her slim figure, and her blouse was long-sleeved and in a beautiful ivory satin, with a row of small buttons down the back. It had a round neck with pearl beading on the cuffs and collar, each one painstakingly sewn on by hand.

Indoors at home was the only time Rose Delaney would be seen without a hat, and she'd been telling Harp only last week how there were far too many grey hairs in her dark tresses for her liking, but Harp said, and meant it, that her mother was a beautiful lady. She was only thirty, but she had one of those ageless faces, like a sculpture or a painting. Everyone thought so, even if Rose herself never noticed. One only had to see how the normally taciturn butcher transformed into a Prince Charming the moment Rose went in the door for the week's meat. Or how Mr Quinn couldn't do enough for her.

'We won't be doing this every night,' Rose said with a smile. 'But many of you may have noticed already that you are our very first guests.' She walked to the sideboard and extracted a bottle of brandy. 'And I think we should all have a toast.'

'Hear, hear,' Eleanor said enthusiastically.

Harp got some glasses and Rose poured everyone except her and JohnJoe a small glass of brandy. They turned expectantly to the woman of the house and raised their glasses.

'Thank you all for staying at the Cliff House. It's been a nerve-racking few weeks, to say the least of it, but this house means the world to my daughter and to me, and it is our pleasure to share it with you.'

Seats were pulled to the table and the dishes removed, and soon the room was full of conversation as if everyone were old friends. Sean O'Sullivan talked about his plans to get work and find a home. He even told them about Gwen, explaining how wonderful she was but how nobody would accept them as a couple and how she pawned her necklace and insisted on using her savings to buy his ticket.

Danny immediately sought to reassure him. 'Well, nobody in the States is gonna care that she's the big guy's daughter. It's the land of opportunity, my friend. You work, you willin' to do what it takes, you could come back here and buy and sell her old man.'

Sean laughed. 'I doubt that, but I do want her to be able to hold her head up. Her father's not a bad sort really, he just wants better for her. I don't blame him, but I'm going to make something of myself. Prove it to him, to everyone. We'll get married, get a nice house – he might even visit once he calms down. Gwen loves him, and I don't want to be the reason they fall out.'

'I'm sure he'll come around, Sean,' Rose said. 'I think it's marvellous that you're so determined. Well done.'

'So long as some flashy British officer doesn't sweep her off her feet before I get a chance to set us up together.' Though Sean said it with a smile, everyone could see the vulnerability there. He looked suddenly very young and uncertain. He was clearly terrified to go, to lose her, but he had no choice.

'Well, if she's that kind of girl, you're better off without her, but it doesn't sound like she is,' Eleanor advised. 'She sounds sincere and decent. And she gave you her savings, didn't she, so she must trust you?'

'She does, and she can be sure of me,' Sean said sincerely. 'But I'm just worried it's all going to take so long and I won't be able to get the right place for her. She's used to a fine big house, with staff and everything.'

'I'm sure she's not expecting that. But be sure to ask a woman for her opinion before you buy a house,' Eleanor advised. 'Men see different things to a woman, so find the wife of a workmate or something and seek her opinion.'

Sean nodded. 'That's a good idea, Eleanor. I'd have no idea what would be the right thing.'

'You'd better learn, buddy,' Danny quipped. 'You'll find the States a very different experience from here, let me tell ya.'

'In what way?' Molly asked tentatively.

All eyes turned to Danny, the only one of the group with proper knowledge of America. He seemed to sense the need for reassurance and the nervous anticipation of his audience, and so he thought carefully before speaking. 'Well, it's big for a start. Like everything here is so tiny, so...I dunno, compact and old. But back home things are bigger, newer, I guess. America is the extremes, y'know? The best of everything and the worst. The whole world is there. Like everywhere I look here in Ireland, faces are the same. White, Irish-lookin', y'know?'

The gathering laughed.

Encouraged, Danny went on. 'But places like New York, or Boston, where we live, are cities of people from everywhere – Russians, Germans, Jews, Chinese, Italians, so many Italians, coloured folks, everyone. You hear so many languages just walking down the street. Different faces, different food, different clothes – it's a melting pot, y'know?'

'And do they all get along?' Eleanor asked.

Danny laughed. 'No way, they sure don't. Everyone is fightin' for his own space. Most immigrants come here – well, there, I mean – with nothin'. A lot of 'em can't even speak English. But they're determined to make it, and some do, more don't. It's not like here where people take care of each other. It's more cut-throat, and you need to stay on your toes.'

'Sounds tough,' Sean said, then sipped his brandy.

'It is, but best advice is to find your tribe, y'know?' Danny seemed anxious to reassure them. 'Find the Irish and stick with them, that's what people do. The Jews stick together, the Italians – every group has their own neighbourhoods, and if you stay within that, you'll be fine. People kinda make their own family. Everyone I know is Irish. Like it might be a few generations back, but that don't matter.'

Harp caught JohnJoe's eye. She could tell he was so proud of his cousin, being the authority on the excitement that was America.

'Have you ever been to San Francisco?' Eleanor asked.

Danny chuckled. 'San Francisco is as far from Boston as Ireland is from Russia. So no, I never have.' He smiled benignly. 'You got a helluva journey ahead of you, Eleanor. Getting to Boston is only the start.'

Eleanor nodded sadly. 'Unfortunately yes.'

'Don't you want to go, Miss Kind?' JohnJoe asked, speaking for the first time.

She shook her head. 'Is it that obvious? No, I don't want to go. My life is my home and my animals, but my brother says I'm getting too old to manage on my own and I might die there without anyone to care for me.'

JohnJoe's innocent open face was perturbed. 'But you'll die no matter where you live, won't you? I mean, we all will, so why not live and die where you want. And if you have your animals, you're not on your own, are you?'

Eleanor thought for a moment. 'I agree with you, JohnJoe, but I don't have any family there. Edward's all I have, and he's so insistent.'

Harp knew her mother probably wouldn't approve of her having had the audacity to advise an adult, and a guest, but she'd really enjoyed her talk with Eleanor earlier that day and felt there was something approachable about the woman. She didn't see people in terms of a pecking order, who was important and who wasn't. And animals got the same value as humans in her mind.

The evening outside was gloomy now, clouds obscuring the setting sun, and Harp drew the dark-green velvet drapes over the lighter silk ones and lit the oil lamps and the candles. The room was warm, and the candlelight softened the faces of everyone gathered around the table. It was almost 10 p.m. now, and the evening had turned into one of shared confidences and gentle laughter. Strangers, united only by the house and a common voyage the next day, chatted amicably.

Eleanor told them all about her animals, and she and Sean were kindred spirits when it came to horses. She explained to him how to use barberry bark for treating liver complaints in mares and foals. Molly described Christmas in Ballymichael to Danny, the thing she would miss most.

Harp and JohnJoe went to the kitchen to make another pot of tea, and everyone topped up their cups. JohnJoe told Harp more about his life before his mother died, and it sounded lovely.

As they were rising from the table to leave, there was a gentle knock on the door. Being summertime it was still bright, but nonetheless it was late to have a visitor. Rose stood and went to answer it, returning moments later with a stunning-looking dark-haired girl behind her. She was petite and curvaceous and reminded Harp of a painting she'd seen of a Spanish flamenco dancer by John Singer Sargent.

'Gwen!' Sean leapt up. 'Is everything all right? Are you all right?' he asked, sweeping her into his arms, not caring that everyone was watching. Together they made a striking pair.

The girl grinned and kissed him. 'I just couldn't bear for you to go without saying goodbye properly. We couldn't at home, so I came down to Queenstown to wave you off.'

Food was found and a place at the table laid. And Rose insisted she stay the night in the guest room as yet not used. The rest of the gathering retreated and allowed the young couple some privacy.

'That was nice for Mr O'Sullivan, his girl turning up like that, wasn't it?' Harp said as she and her mother prepared for bed.

'It was, and I think he'll feel less anxious about her now.'

'It went well, didn't it?' Harp asked.

'It really did.' Rose smiled and hugged her daughter. 'Now, another busy day tomorrow, so off to sleep, and no reading until all hours, do you hear me?'

Harp smiled sheepishly. Her mother had found her reading by candlelight at 3 a.m. the previous night, but she had been in a very good part of *Anne of Green Gables* and couldn't put it down. In the end, Rose confiscated the book until morning.

'I do. Goodnight, Mammy,' Harp said, going into her own room.

'Goodnight, Harp.'

An hour later, as Harp was drifting off to sleep, the stillness of the house was interrupted by the loud and persistent knocking of the brass ring on the front door. Harp checked the clock. It was two thirty in the morning.

She got up and watched as her mother drew her dressing gown around her and went downstairs, the moonlight lighting her way as she met Danny and Sean on the stairs.

'We thought we'd better come with you,' Sean said. 'I'm afraid it's the major looking for Gwen.'

Eleanor and Molly appeared out of their rooms, looking worried. But only Harp noticed Gwen emerge from Sean's room, as soon as all the adults went downstairs, looking furtive. Harp and JohnJoe positioned themselves on the stairs, far enough away but with a fine view of the doorway.

Rose opened the door to find two men, one heavyset and older, fifties maybe, the other in his twenties.

'We're looking for Molly O'Brien,' the older man said. He had thinning red hair and his face was like thunder. 'We know she's here.' He barged towards Rose.

CHAPTER 19

*R*ose stood her ground, glad of the two men behind her.
'Please wait here,' she said.

The men ignored her instruction and tried to move past her, but as
they did, Sean and Danny blocked their path.

'Get out of my way,' Seamus O'Brien said through gritted teeth,
shoving Sean, but the younger man was too large to be moved easily.
Sean and Danny moved closer together, both men realising they
would need to act quickly and as a team.

Molly recoiled, wrapping her woollen dressing gown around
herself more tightly. 'Daddy and...Finbarr!' she gasped.

'Get your things now! We're leaving!' Seamus shouted at his trembling daughter, who stood on the bottom step.

Finbarr had the grace to look somewhat abashed.

'I...I'm not going home, Daddy. I won't.' Molly's voice came out as
a sob.

Her father darted around Danny, crossed the hallway and grabbed
her by the arm, his grip vice-like. 'Now. Outside.' He began to frog-
march her out, Finbarr standing aside to allow him to pass.

Harp and JohnJoe crept down the stairs to the hallway.

'Let go of me! I won't!' She tried to get away from him but it was no use; his clutch was too strong.

'Molly' – Sean moved to stand between them and the door, his towering bulk blocking the older man's path – 'you don't have to go if you don't want to.'

By now the women were all in the hall too, including Gwen. Eleanor ushered Harp and JohnJoe behind her.

'Who the hell do you think you are?' Seamus bellowed. 'I don't know you, nor the sky above you, and I'll thank you to stay out of my business. This girl is my daughter and I say she's coming home. Where's your ticket?' he demanded of Molly. 'You'll not go to that heathen, godforsaken country, do you hear me? Where is it?' he repeated, shouting now, his face inches from hers.

Molly reached into the pocket of her dressing gown and handed the ticket to her father, who grabbed it, determined to rip it up.

'She's a grown woman, you jerk!' Danny stepped in and grabbed the ticket before Seamus could rip it, handing it back to Molly and placing a protective arm around her shoulder. 'She can go where she wants, and she wants to go to Boston.'

'Who the hell are you?' Finbarr demanded, a flash of temper flaring his nostrils and lighting his eyes. He shoved Danny roughly in the chest, pushing him backwards. Then he turned to Molly. 'If he's put a hand on you... Molly, I swear, it's not just about the land. I do like you, I promise, and we could be happy if only you'll let us.' Finbarr was pleading now, and Molly's tears ran down her cheeks.

Eleanor ushered Harp and JohnJoe away up the stairs to safety while Sean stood beside Seamus.

'Get outta here,' Danny ordered. 'Can't you see she don't want nothin' to do with either of you bozos?' He turned to Molly once more. 'You don't gotta do nothing you don't want to, sweetheart, don't worry.'

'Get out of my way, you big gob Yank.' Seamus turned and drew a punch on Danny, who ducked, his reflexes faster than the older, lumbering Seamus O'Brien. Danny laughed, goading Molly's father, then struck a combat pose, fists clenched, back bent, ready to duck again if needs be.

Seamus was incensed now and drove at Danny, who deftly jumped out of the way, sending him crashing into the hallstand. He knocked over the huge china urn that stood beside it, and it shattered into smithereens on top of Gwen, who was standing next to it. Sean rushed to her side, putting his arms around her to protect her as she shook shards of china from her clothes.

'Come on, old man, that all you got?' Danny cackled, clearly enjoying himself. Finbarr bore down on him as Molly screamed in warning, but a quick elbow from Danny sent him reeling, his nose pumping blood.

Finbarr was splayed out on his back, blood all over his face. Danny turned and landed another blow on Seamus, who was roaring like a bull now. As Seamus doubled over from a punch to the abdomen, Danny took full advantage and kicked him hard in the kidneys.

Finbarr lumbered to his feet, swaying unsteadily, and dived in once more, dragging Danny off Seamus. The two younger men rolled around on the floor, landing punches, as Molly begged them to stop, her face blotched from crying.

Danny was more than a match for Finbarr, who tried to get away from the young American. Danny ducked and dived and avoided the wild punches being thrown indiscriminately by Finbarr with no degree of skill whatsoever, only one in five efforts making connection.

Danny managed to stay upright and leaned on the bannister, dishevelled and nursing a burst lip. He seemed in good spirits. 'She don't want you, farm boy, don't you see that?' he teased Finbarr.

In a rage, the Irishman charged again at Danny. They tussled for a moment, then Danny lunged and fell forward, and a moment later, he rolled onto his back. Everyone watched in horror as they realised the knife Danny must have been carrying was now impaled in his abdomen. His blue and white pyjama jacket was rapidly turning crimson.

Sean released Gwen and rushed to Danny, kneeling to apply pressure to the wound, but the knife was still up to the hilt in Danny's belly. JohnJoe started to cry as he knelt beside his cousin on the other side. 'Danny, Danny... Please don't... Danny!' He was so distressed as to be almost incoherent.

Harp watched the scene unfold in horror.

As Rose returned with towels, she shouted, 'Harp, go and get Doctor Lane!'

Harp immediately sprang to action.

Finbarr sat on the bottom step, his head in his hands, but Molly's father stood and stared in horror at Danny, who was rapidly losing consciousness.

Harp dashed down the steps to the doctor's house, which was close by. Doctor Lane was in his pyjamas, but he pulled his overcoat on and grabbed his bag, calling to his wife to inform Inspector Deane and send him to the Cliff House immediately. Then, jumping into his car, they roared up to the Cliff House.

Entering the hallway, Harp saw her mother had put a pillow behind Danny's head and Sean was applying pressure to the wound with a blood-soaked towel. Eleanor was comforting JohnJoe, who was crying. Molly stood in pale-faced horror beside her father.

The doctor shooed them all out of the way and examined the wound. He took his bag and removed some liquid and dressings. 'Wet that with the antiseptic,' he instructed Rose, handing her some gauze strips. 'You did right in not trying to remove the knife. I'll take him to hospital in my car.' He bandaged the wound, securing the knife in place. 'He's lucky, it looks by the amount of blood that the knife is short, and I'm hoping it hasn't hit an organ. He'll need to go to hospital and have this properly seen to, but I'd be hopeful he'll be all right. I can fold the back seats down, and if you can find something to lie him on, a board or something, we could slide him in the back, keep him flat.'

Rose thought for a moment, then turned to Harp. 'The door from the attic – remember, it's leaning against the stable wall. It swelled and wouldn't fit so we took it off.'

'Right. Harp, can you show me?' Sean asked.

Inspector Deane arrived at that exact moment. Molly was still standing beside her father; Finbarr was still on the stairs.

As the inspector began to ask questions, Sean and Harp went in search of the door and Eleanor explained to the policeman what had happened.

'We were all asleep when two men forced their way in, past Mrs Delaney, the owner, and demanded that one of the guests, Molly O'Brien, leave with them. She didn't wish to go, and that man' – she nodded at Seamus O'Brien – 'and the other fellow got rough. Danny stood up for the young woman, and the other man and he got into a fight. The next thing we knew, Danny was covered in blood.'

'I never stabbed him, I didn't! It was his own knife, I swear. I would never carry a knife...' Finbarr was distraught.

Sean carried the door back single-handedly, and he and the doctor gently lifted a groaning Danny onto it. They placed him in the back of the car and Doctor Lane drove away.

'I want to go with him,' JohnJoe begged.

'You'd better wait here, JohnJoe, stay with us,' Rose said gently. 'They will do all they can for Danny and we don't want you up in the city all alone.'

'But what if he...' JohnJoe couldn't form the words. 'I've only known him a few days but he's the only family that...' The boy stood there, tears streaming down his cheeks.

Harp moved to stand beside him and took his hand. 'Doctor Lane is very competent, JohnJoe. He has a lot of experience, and I think Danny will be all right. He will take him to Cork to the hospital, and we will telegram for word later tomorrow.'

Rose and Sean were each giving statements as Harp drew the distraught JohnJoe away to sit on the stairs.

'I know it's silly, Harp,' JohnJoe said, 'but...but when my mammy died, my sisters and me, well, nobody cared about us. My da was all right when she was alive – well, we never really saw him, but he wasn't like he is now. But when Mammy was gone, he was drunk all the time and then the court took us and I was sent to borstal. And now if I lose Danny, I'll have to go back to my father, and he'll just put

193

me back in there again, and I can't...' His final words were incoherent as he was so distressed.

Harp placed her arm around his heaving shoulders, and he turned his face towards hers.

'JohnJoe, Doctor Lane said Danny had a really good chance of survival, and believe me, I know he's not a man for exaggeration. He had to stitch my head when I was little – I was playing and I landed on the fire surround and I was split over my eye. See?' She pointed to the faint silver scar from her eyebrow up under her hairline. 'And he said, "Harp, this is going to really hurt and you need to stay very still even though it's going to be painful, because I want to keep the stitches small and neat so you won't see the scar when you're older."'

'And was it very sore?' JohnJoe asked.

Harp nodded. 'Very, but I kept as still as I could and now you can hardly see it.'

JohnJoe nodded. 'I wouldn't have noticed it except that you said it.'

'I know. So the important thing to hold on to is that he tells the truth. And so if he says Danny has a good chance, then we should believe him. Besides, even if he died' – Harp tried to be delicate – 'it is your Uncle Pat who has sent for you, so you could still go to America, couldn't you?'

'On my own?' JohnJoe looked terrified. His small freckled face was pale and his hair was standing on end.

Harp shrugged. 'Well, it's just a matter of getting on the ship and someone meeting you on the other side. How difficult could it be?'

JohnJoe shook his head. 'I'm not brave or clever like you are, Harp. I could never go all the way there on my own.'

'Of course you could. Look how much you've survived already, and you lived to tell the tale.' She nudged him playfully and he gave her a watery smile.

He coloured at her praise. 'I suppose I could.' He considered it. 'But would there be reading to do, do you think?'

Harp considered the question. 'Maybe a little bit, but lots of people emigrate from all over the world who can't speak English, so I'm sure there are pictorial signs too. But if not I'd say if you had to travel alone, find some nice family and just do what they do.' She felt JohnJoe relax against her.

'I know I've only known you one day, but you're my best friend, Harp,' he said quietly.

'Well, I've never had a friend before, so I suppose that makes you mine too,' Harp said with a radiant smile.

JohnJoe leaned over and kissed her cheek. 'I think you are the best person I've ever met in my whole life, Harp Delaney – except my mammy, of course – and also the prettiest, and I'd be honoured to call you my friend.'

Harp blushed and smiled. Nobody apart from her mother had ever said she was pretty. 'Friends then,' she agreed.

'Forever,' he said solemnly.

'Can I give my father and Finbarr a cup of tea please, Mrs Delaney?' Molly asked, her face tear-stained. 'I know what they did was so wrong, barging in here, but they never meant to hurt anyone… and they're very shaken.'

'I think we could all do with a cup of tea,' Rose said wearily, and moved towards the kitchen.

Harp and JohnJoe helped, getting cups and jugs, while Eleanor led Seamus and Finbarr to the table. Sean and Gwen turned to leave when Molly called them back.

'Are you all right, Gwen?' she asked, looking horrified at the cut on the girl's face where a shard of china had nicked her.

'I'm grand, it's nothing,' Gwen reassured her. 'How about you? Are you all right?'

Molly nodded and exhaled. 'I've decided to go home. This is all my fault. I should never have caused such fuss, and maybe none of this would have happened and poor Danny would…' Her voice choked. She reached into her pocket. 'I won't be using this now, and it's not refundable, so if you would like it, Gwen, you could go with Sean tomorrow.'

The young couple looked incredulously at her, then at each other. 'But, Molly, are you sure? I mean, you don't have to go home if you don't want to...' Sean protested. 'Besides, we can't take that... It's too much...'

'I know I don't have to, but I...I want to. I'll marry Finbarr. He's a good man despite what you saw tonight, and my family need me to do this. I'll be fine. Honestly, if you don't use it, it will go to waste. It's second class, the same as Sean's, so you can work it out on board...' She handed Gwen her ticket.

Gwen took it and grasped Molly's hands, gazing sincerely into the taller girl's eyes. 'We'll pay you back, I promise we will. Thank you so much, Molly. It... I can't tell you what this means to us.'

Sean reached out and hugged Molly. 'Thank you. I can't... Words can't say what you've done for us. We'll never forget you for it, and as Gwen says, we'll pay you back just as soon as we're able to.'

Molly gave a weak smile. 'There's no need. I'll have no need of anything once I'm home and married. I wish you both all the best and all the happiness in the world.' She turned towards the dining room where her father and future husband waited.

CHAPTER 20

*A*n hour later, Molly sat at the table in her bedroom, looking at the stars twinkling over the harbour below. Her father and Finbarr had been given beds in the parlour. It was too late to try to get home now; they would take the first train in the morning. It was 4 a.m. The new moon hung incandescent in the sky.

After the night's events, everyone had eventually retired, but she couldn't sleep. The arrival of her father and Finbarr, the fight, poor Danny, who was only trying to stand up for her, the look first of disgust and then sheer horror on her father's face, the policeman – the whole scene unfolded frame by frame in her mind, an endless loop of shame, humiliation and remorse.

Such trouble she'd caused. Such embarrassment to her family. Her father in trouble with the police? Unheard of. There were probably not going to be any charges, as the knife was clearly Danny's own, but still. The O'Briens were respectable people with no history of ever causing offence to anyone, and now this. It was all her fault. It was right that she go back, try to make amends.

She sat, gazing out over the sea. She naturally settled her thoughts where they always went, in prayer.

She said formal prayers each day, but her inner monologue was –

she'd known all of her life – a conversation with God. She spoke to Him and she felt like He responded. Perhaps she was imagining it but didn't think so.

'What should I do?' she whispered.

Was she just running away from marriage rather than towards God and her vocation? Was she, as her mother said, afraid that no fat girl with flaming red hair and freckles would ever get a man so she'd put the obstacle of a religious life in the way to spare herself that humiliation? Round and round in her mind the questions went.

Perhaps if she'd been blessed with a slender figure, sleek dark hair and olive skin, the notion of spending her life in the habit would never have occurred to her. If she looked like Gwen or Mrs Delaney, then would the idea of being a nun ever have entered her mind?

She had a personal connection with God, she knew she did. She couldn't explain it. It wasn't like she heard a voice telling her to enter the convent or anything like that. She just knew that her soul was restless and that once she was within the walls of the convent, having dedicated her life to His service, she would feel peace. But that was a dream and it was over.

Another wave of misgivings followed that thought. Had she been doing it for selfish reasons? For her own peace of mind, not to serve? She thought of Sister Brid that day. The nun was so serene and radiated a peaceful happiness. As she spoke about teaching children from slums and tenements, fighting against child labour, bringing the word of God to the most needy, she lit up from inside, and Molly remembered how she couldn't wait to join her.

She undressed and got into bed, staring at the ceiling as the moonlight lit the room with its eerie silver glow. She tossed and turned, but it was no good – there was no way she could sleep, though the bed was comfortable and the house was finally quiet. Her alarm clock ticked loudly on the locker, clicking out each long second, inching slowly to the dawn and the day she would return to become Mrs Finbarr Casey. Some story would have to be concocted; Finbarr should not be humiliated like that, with everyone saying she was a runaway bride. She should be grateful, she knew. He was a good lad, and not bad-looking – better than she could have hoped to get anyway.

The seconds became minutes and eventually an hour passed and she was no nearer sleep. Sighing, she got dressed. She figured she might as well forget about sleeping now.

She knelt by her bed and prayed. She begged God to make Danny all right. She felt responsible for him. She prayed for JohnJoe, that the life that awaited him in America was better than the one he'd left behind. She prayed that Rose and Harp would make a go of their guest house, and that Harp would get to live out her dreams of travel and an education. And she asked St Francis of Assisi, who had a special affinity with animals, to take care of Eleanor, whatever path she chose. Finally she asked him to watch over Sean and Gwen. She quelled the surge of envy that it would be the beautiful Gwen who would start her new life in America. She didn't begrudge her it but just wished it could have been her, and she shed a tear for her lost dream.

She crept downstairs as the dawn broke and the buttery yellows and pinks of a summer morning flooded across the sky. She let herself out into the garden, admiring the ancient mossy and lichened wall. It surrounded the lawn in front of the house and enclosed the house except for the entrance gate behind that led from the road and the small gate onto the steps, linking the Cliff House to the town. Molly would never forget this place, a house of such beauty, such history, mainly because it was the place where her heart broke.

Dotted around the grounds there were various stone seats, placed there by a generation of wealthy people who had nothing to do and all day to do it. Outside the drawing room bay window was a wooden bench, slightly rotten but recently painted a cheery yellow and surrounded by ancient pots overflowing with flowers, and Molly sat down, observing the harbour. She studied the star-shaped Fort Mitchell on Spike Island, a prison, then a British military base, a place of dread and fear. She wondered if the men incarcerated there looked back towards Queenstown from their small dank cells and felt as trapped as she did right now. Marriage to Finbarr wouldn't have bars or jailers, but it was a prison nonetheless.

She remembered her grandmother telling her how her brothers were imprisoned there during the famine on totally spurious charges because they were agitating for change, for respite for the starving women and children. Nana O'Brien remembered the days of hunger, when shiploads of food were sent daily by the British from the port below as the people of Ireland starved.

It was hard to believe such an idyllic place could be the source of such deprivation. Those men, her grand-uncles, were transported to Australia in chains for their efforts, never to be heard from again. For so many, this location was their last glimpse of home; it very nearly was hers.

She heard the crunch of feet on gravel and looked up towards the driveway, surprised to see Eleanor walking towards the house, looking chirpy. Behind her were two dogs, thin and malnourished.

'Good morning, Eleanor,' Molly said.

'Good morning, Molly. Did you manage to sleep?' she asked kindly.

Molly smiled sadly and shook her head.

'So you'll go back with them, will you?' Eleanor asked. 'I saw you gave Gwen your ticket – that was kind.'

Molly shrugged. 'I've no need of it now. I've caused enough upset. I need to try to put it right.' She looked at the two dogs. 'You've made some friends here?'

Eleanor laughed. 'I found this one yesterday. He's skin and bone but he's a character, look...' She dug into her pocket and produced a piece of bacon that Molly remembered her pocketing after the dinner last night. The little dog bounced up on his two back legs, doing a little dance, as she dropped the tasty morsel in his mouth. He had an adorable face, with a black patch around one eye. He wolfed it down and then nuzzled Eleanor with his silky head.

Beside him a larger black dog, something between a Labrador and a retriever, stood, looking despondent.

'I found this one this morning. She needs worming, poor thing. I'll get some caraway seeds from Rose and add them to this – I've robbed some-one's herb garden.' She extracted a bunch of leaves from her pocket. 'See? Parsley, chervil and dill. Mix them in with the caraway and she'll soon feel much better, won't you, darling?' She went down on her hunkers to be eye level with the dog, who gave her a feeble lick on the face.

'You know a lot about animals, don't you?' Molly asked. 'Did you study animal welfare or something?'

Eleanor smiled, still stroking the big black dog while the smaller one wound in around her legs. 'Not formally, but over the years, trial and error. I learned a lot from the old people where I'm from, and from the travellers too.' She took another bit of bacon from her pocket and fed a piece to each dog. 'When I was a girl, they would come and camp on our land, in time for the fair. They would go into the town then, fixing pots and pans, and the women would sell paper flowers and things like that. But they knew about animals, cures, use of herbs and bark and seaweed that grew around the locality. They taught me how to make a poultice for an injured horse using milk and bread, or to make a mixture of wild garlic, salt and water if a cow ate ragwort and was poisoned. Using that trick, I saved a sea eagle that had eaten meat deliberately poisoned by a land owner. Things like that.'

'That's wonderful knowledge to have.' Molly was impressed.

Eleanor nodded and sighed.

'So you're going and you don't want to, and I'm staying and I wish I didn't have to,' Molly observed calmly.

The intimacy of the dinner they'd enjoyed together the previous night, followed by the dramatic events afterwards, had bonded them somehow, and the normal formality that would be expected between strangers had dissipated.

'It will be fine, I'm sure. I have nieces and nephews and a sister-in-law to meet, and the sun shines there all the time apparently. So nothing at all like County Sligo.' Eleanor's eyes filled with tears.

Neither woman speaking, the intense despair hanging between

them, Eleanor and Molly gazed out to sea. The tan little dog sat on Eleanor's foot, the black one right beside her leg.

'I hope it all works out for you, Eleanor. I'll pray for you,' Molly said, standing up and giving the black dog a rub. 'I bet that one is called Patch,' she said, and patted the little brown dog before walking inside.

Eleanor smiled as the tan dog with the black patch on his eye jumped up on his hind legs again, dancing for another scrap of meat.

CHAPTER 21

*H*arp woke as her mother came in and opened the bedroom curtains. The bright sunlight filled the small room, and Harp sat up, rubbing her eyes sleepily. 'Am I late to help with breakfast?' she asked.

'Well, I should think so – it's after ten. Everyone is up and has eaten already, but you looked so tired after everything last night that I let you rest on. You needed it.' Her mother sat on the edge of her bed.

'Did you manage on your own all right?' Harp asked, and Rose smiled and tucked a strand of hair that had come loose from Harp's plait behind her ear.

'Which of us is the adult?' Rose gazed into her daughter's eyes but there was something else, and instantly Harp knew she had something on her mind.

'What is it?' she asked.

'You're uncanny. You know that, don't you? An old soul, my granny used to say.'

Harp smiled. 'I must be, but I don't know. Maybe that's why other children find me so odd.' She shrugged. 'Either way it's who I am and I can't change it, so I'd best get on with it.'

'JohnJoe doesn't find you odd,' Rose reminded her.

'It's true, he doesn't. It's nice to have someone my own age to talk to.' Then she remembered. 'Oh...any news of Danny?'

'Dr Lane called earlier. He brought Danny to the hospital last night and they sent word this morning that he was stable. He's still weak and will take some time to recover, but he's going to be all right, I think.'

'Oh, that's wonderful news. I'm so happy for JohnJoe – he was so worried.'

'Indeed.' Rose paused. 'I wonder what is best to do now? I feel like I should contact someone, just to tell them that he's with us and he'll be taken care of. But from what he told us, his father is less than responsible and the uncle in America, well, he's never even met the child, so I'm not sure.'

'We can let him stay here until Danny gets out of hospital?' Harp was delighted, liking the idea of her new friend staying around for a bit longer. 'Not in a guest room obviously, they're all booked up, but in the other room at the end of this landing. It's small but he'd be fine and cosy in there.'

'I suppose that's best, until we can speak to Danny anyway. I wondered if I should send him on the ship with Eleanor, Sean and Gwen. They could take care of him on the voyage and perhaps the uncle would have someone meet him, but that would mean him leaving Danny here to recuperate. But I hardly know the boy, and we have no way of knowing if anyone would be there to meet him. And if not, Sean has an arrangement to go directly to a job, so he couldn't be responsible for him, and Eleanor is taking a train west right away, so that wouldn't be suitable either.'

'And Molly's not going now, but even if she was, I don't think she could take him to a convent?' Harp said with a wicked grin. 'Her story would have been complicated enough without bringing a lone fourteen-year-old boy into it.'

Rose chuckled. 'You have Henry's wicked sense of humour. The absurd and the ridiculous you both find hilarious.'

Harp felt the familiar stab of pain. It happened within a few minutes of waking up every day, that sickening realisation that it had happened, that Mr Devereaux had died, that she and her mother were alone. For such a quiet man, he'd taken up so much of their lives, and her mother was right, he could be very funny sometimes. She was learning that grief was like that; it had phases but it wasn't linear. It wasn't as if one moved seamlessly from shock to anger to desolation and eventually to acceptance. No, it was something different. At first, it was all-consuming, an almost unbearable pain, a physical and emotional heartache. But then she'd feel lonely and bereft, and then she would forget and laugh and smile. But a smell, a word, a book, a sound – anything could trigger it, the ice wave of realisation. It was real; he was gone and he wasn't coming back.

'I miss him so much,' Harp whispered.

Her mother drew her in for a hug. 'I know, darling. I miss him too. But he'd be proud of us, wouldn't he? All we've achieved.'

Harp nodded. 'And he would have been fascinated by the high dramatics of last night.'

Rose released her and nodded, adding in a whisper, 'Or horrified that we filled the house with mad strangers?'

'There's a book in this, isn't there?' Harp said. 'All the comings and goings of a house like this.'

'There certainly could be.'

Harp considered it. 'I was thinking I would record somehow the stories of the people who stayed. Of course none would ever be as explosive as last night's crowd.' She laughed. 'But it would be a nice way to remember, wouldn't it? The people who slept here, before leaving for a new life in another world, this was their last night sleeping on their native soil.'

'I think it would be a wonderful book, and you have the right pen and everything,' Rose said, lifting the navy-blue box from Harp's bedside locker and opening it. Harp hadn't touched the box since the day she brought it to school; it was too hard to look and see the initials they shared engraved there.

Rose opened the velvet box, offering it to Harp. It was just as it was on the day Henry gave it to her, the pale-blue silk lining, pleated to give it a luxurious effect, the navy velvet swivel clasp ensuring the pen stayed snugly in the moulded groove, created for that exact piece. The elegance of it and the symbolism of their shared words, written words. Books and the love of them united her and Mr Devereaux, and they always would. She realised that though he was physically gone and his loss was a source of deep grief, while she lived, while they stayed in the Cliff House, while she had his books, he wasn't gone, not really. She could remember him, hear his voice, see his writing in the margins. He was there, and she would never be alone ever again.

She took the box and with her thumb slid the clasp out of the way so she could lift the pen out. It felt heavy between her thumb and finger, and the silver barrel was polished so it glinted in the morning sunlight. She removed the cap, and the gold nib shone. Then she ran the pad of her thumb over the engraving. *H. D.*

'I'll write the story of this house, all the people who come and go, with this pen. Maybe it will become a book, maybe it will never see the light of day. But he loved this house and he loved me, and so that's the best way to honour his legacy, I think.' Her voice cracked on the words. 'I think he'd like the idea of it.'

'He would,' Rose agreed. 'This is your house now, your home. You were born here and you own it, so you should write its story.'

Harp was intrigued; it was the first time she'd ever heard her mother speak about her birth. 'Which room was I born in?' she asked.

'The small room off the kitchen. But not long after you were born, I told Mrs Lenihan, the old housekeeper, I would be fine. It was the early hours of the morning by that stage, and the doctor and the midwife had gone home, confident that all was well with us both. You were sleeping peacefully in the crib, and I was tired and sore but relieved that you were here and all was well.

'I just looked at you, your blond hair...and your eyes were blue then, not grey yet, but still an unusual shade, and you were so beautiful. I didn't care that I was a mother without a husband. The worries I had about people talking, or the scandal, even though everyone seemed to accept the dead husband story, it all disappeared in an instant. It was as if the hard judgemental world outside these four walls didn't exist.'

Rose sighed. 'You whimpered a little, and I lifted you out of the crib. I just gazed at you – I hadn't even named you yet – and you gazed back, and then I placed my finger near your tiny hand and you curled your fist around it and I...'

To Harp's astonishment, tears welled in her mother's eyes.

'I named you Harp then, and that night we eventually slept, snuggled up together.'

'Why did you pick such an unusual name?' Harp asked, her personal story fascinating to her.

'I was down in the town one day, and there was an American woman there – oh my word, she was so pretty – and she was dressed in grey and silver silk. She was having a debate with her husband, a distinguished-looking fellow, and he was pleading with her to be reasonable. I heard him say, "Oh, Harp darling, you know I'd give you the moon if I could, but please, just listen to me..."

'She could have made that man do anything, such was the adoration in his eyes for this remarkable-looking woman. She was poised and confident and she was playing with him really, but there was something about her, something unusual, that was entrancing. She seemed to have the world at her feet. They were boarding a huge liner and clearly had a lot of money, and I thought if I ever had a daughter, I would name her Harp. It was such an unusual name.'

Harp was enjoying hearing this; the subject had been taboo for so long.

Her mother went on. 'Then you were born, and though I was a poor single servant girl, I just knew deep down you would be destined for something much better. I knew you were going to be different to everyone else in the whole world, so you couldn't be called Mary or Jane or Kate. I remember old Mrs Devereaux was appalled when she heard your name. Though she never acknowledged she was your grandmother, so she got no say. But she thought, like everyone, that I had notions above my station. She was probably right.' Rose chuckled wryly.

'Whenever I think of her, Mrs Devereaux, I think of Catherine of

Medici and how horrible she was to her daughter-in-law, Mary, Queen of Scots,' Harp said.

Rose smiled and ruffled her daughter's hair. 'You are a unique child, Harp Delaney, that much is true, with a wild and romantic heart and a brain that will be the envy of the most learned of men. But I was nothing like a young queen, and she never saw me as a daughter-in-law or anything but a servant who had led her precious son astray. To her I was nothing more than the worthless daughter of poor people who would want nothing to do with a girl in trouble as I was.' She patted the bed. 'Now best get up. We have new guests arriving today and last night's ones will be leaving for the embarkation station shortly. You get dressed, and I'll speak to JohnJoe and see what he would like to do. I'll offer that he could remain here until Danny improves.'

Harp threw back the covers and began to wash in the water in her basin. Her mother was hovering, as if there were something else.

Harp looked up questioningly. 'Is everything else all right, Mammy? Did Inspector Deane come back?'

Rose shook her head. 'No – well, yes, he did. But nothing more will happen after last night. Danny doesn't want to press charges, as the knife was his. And now that he's going to be all right, it's all going to be forgotten, I think.'

'"All's well that ends well",' Harp quoted.

'A poem?' her mother asked. Though she liked to read, she never pretended to be as well read as her child.

'No.' Harp grinned. 'A ridiculous play by Shakespeare, where a very smart woman, Helen, a healer actually, cures the king of France of an illness, and in return he gives her the hand in marriage of a man she is in love with but who has no interest in her because of her low station. She spends the whole play trying to get him to want her.'

'Did it work?' her mother asked with a smile.

Harp shrugged. 'She got him in the end, by pretending to be someone else and getting into his bed. She became pregnant with his child and so he finally agrees to marry her. So yes, Helen gets

Bertram, but I think she was foolish to waste her mind on such a man, or any man. I'll never marry. I'll be my own boss.'

'Ah, my dear girl, one day you may think differently,' Rose said as she went out the door.

* * *

ROSE LEFT THE BEDROOM, the letter still in the pocket of her cardigan. She'd decided she should not burden Harp with this worry no matter how grown up the girl had been of late. The thought of seeing Ralph Devereaux again made her stomach churn. Part of her, a small part, was excited, and she hated herself for it. She'd been such a foolish girl thirteen years ago, star-struck by the handsome young man who used her shamelessly and cast her aside. She should have had more respect for herself then, and certainly she should not be mooning over him now. She knew what she should feel was fear, and she did. He was coming back, the time of his arrival was looming ever closer, and what would happen then? A legal battle? Would he contest Henry's will? Wouldn't the people of Queenstown love to see that juicy story played out before their eyes? The thought made her sick.

She would have to be strong, stoic and full of resolve. She would do it for Harp, for Henry. Besides, hadn't Mr Smythe said the will was robust? And that when combined with two affidavits confirming Harp's paternity, it would be a difficult thing to challenge legally?

Still, she was sick with worry. It could sound so sordid, so terrible, though Rose decided she would rather people thought Henry was Harp's father instead of Ralph. Ralph was a reprobate and a cad, whereas Henry was a decent, lovely man. But still, the thoughts went round and round of the speculation and hearsay being passed from the butcher counter to the church gate, from the shoemaker's to the draper's, a juicy titbit of gossip about a woman who always came across so high and mighty, too uppity to lean on a shop counter and trade scandal with the ordinary people. And her peculiar child with such notions of upperosity. There were enough rumours going around; she didn't want to add fuel to the fire, and the arrival in Queenstown of Ralph Devereaux would most certainly do that.

Still, she thought, squaring her shoulders, there was little point in trying to anticipate what might happen. He said he was coming but didn't say when, so they would work hard at establishing their business and let the future hold what it may.

She considered writing back, saying…saying what? That she was looking forward to seeing him? That his niece would be happy to receive him, in his own house, the one that should rightfully be his? That she, a girl from a two-roomed cottage in the country, would sit in the drawing room of this fine house, acting the lady of the manor, and take tea with the true heir?

Stop it, she admonished herself. This was silly and pointless. She would not write. Let him come.

CHAPTER 22

*H*arp was playing a particularly difficult piece in the corner of the drawing room after her breakfast as the sunshine flooded in, dust motes dancing on the warm rays. It was by O'Carolan and called 'Lord Inchiquin', and she closed her eyes, hearing Mr Devereaux's gentle voice. 'Just don't think too much, Harp. Feel the music – let it come from your soul to your hands. Hear the tune in your head and just relax.'

She allowed the harp to rest on her shoulder and flexed her fingers once more, breathing into the tips and feeling the music. Her hands danced over the strings, and to her delight, she had it. It was one of Mr Devereaux's favourites, and just for a fleeting second, she could feel his presence at a particular phrase in the piece. It was so fleeting it was almost imperceptible, but she remembered how his face would reflect his rapture as she played it. At that exact turn of the melody, he would smile, and it felt like that smile could light up the whole world.

The creak of the floorboard stopped her.

'I'm sorry, I shouldn't have disturbed...' JohnJoe went to back out of the room.

'It's all right, come in.' She turned. His eyes were red; he'd been crying obviously. No wonder. What a frightening position to be in.

However woebegone she felt at the loss of Mr Devereaux, she had her mother and her home. Poor JohnJoe had been cast adrift. Her heart went out to him. 'Did you meet my mother?' she asked gently.

He shook his head.

'She was looking for you. She was wondering what you wanted to do now?'

JohnJoe looked like a dazzled rabbit. 'I should go. I don't have any money to stay here another night...' He was trying to sound confident, but the quiver in his voice gave him away.

'You can stay here with us, for free of course, until Danny gets better, or else you could go on the boat today and hopefully someone would meet you? Eleanor and Sean will be travelling too, so you wouldn't be alone.'

'But what if nobody comes to meet me? They all have their own plans, and they'd need to get on with whatever they're doing. I... maybe I should go back to my father...' The dread at that prospect was written all over his face. 'What do you think, Harp?' He clearly trusted her, though he was two years older.

'I would stay here, at least for now. JohnJoe, let's try to be logical about this and look at the facts. Your uncle wants you to come so badly he sent Danny to fetch you and paid for you both and put you up here and got you fancy clothes and everything, so he must be wealthy. He can afford to buy new tickets or exchange those ones or something. If you go back to your father, he'll return you to that awful place you were before, so that's a terrible idea. And Danny is going to get better, but it might take a bit of time, so waiting here for him to recover is the best option, isn't it?'

'Well, it would be...' JohnJoe said slowly, 'but I can't just stay here, with no money or anything. Like you and your mother are running a business, not a charity.' He sounded unsure.

'All right, how about this?' Harp had an idea. 'We did the best we could with the house, but the grounds are still in a bit of a state. You said your mother was a good gardener and you used to help her, so why don't you help us to get the outside – the gardens and the sheds and stables – tidied up while you stay here in exchange for bed and board?'

JohnJoe's eyes lit up. 'And your mother would be happy with that?' he asked.

'I think she'd be very relieved. Are you afraid of rats? We think there's one in the shed.'

He laughed. 'If you'd seen where I've spent my life, between the farm and the borstal, a lad would have no business being afraid of a rat, I can tell you.'

Harp smiled, glad to see her new friend cheered up. 'That's settled then,' she said with satisfaction. 'Now another thing, how would you feel about me teaching you how to read and write properly?'

'Could you, Harp?' He looked doubtful. 'I don't think I'm able to do it. The brothers tried over and over, and I just couldn't get it through my thick head.'

'I can, I'm sure of it. You were just too frightened of them to learn. We can't take in anything if we are scared or hungry or tired. But if you're happy and relaxed, it can be done, trust me.' She smiled.

'I do,' he said sincerely. 'But don't you need to check with your mother about me staying and everything?' he asked doubtfully.

Harp shook her head. 'No, we discussed it this morning. She'll be happy, I promise.'

'You are wonderful at playing that.' He nodded at the harp.

'Thank you. Though a girl called Harp who plays the harp is a bit ridiculous, I know.' She gave a rueful grin.

'I think your name is perfect, and I don't know how you can play that – it looks so complicated. I mean, how can you even see which string to pluck?' He walked around the oak harp, fascinated.

She shrugged. 'I kind of just feel it. It's not a mental thing. Mr Devereaux used to say you play straight from the heart to the fingers, don't involve the head, and he was right.'

'Can you play me something?' JohnJoe asked tentatively.

'I can try,' she said, settling the harp back on her shoulder again.

'My mammy loved that song "I Dreamt I Dwelt in Marble Halls". Do you know it?'

Harp nodded. 'I've never tried to play it before but I do know it. It's from the Balfe opera *The Bohemian Girl*. Give me a moment.' She closed her eyes and recalled the tune, humming it quietly, then plucked out the melody slowly on the harp. 'Yes, I think I can play it.'

'Don't you need the music on a sheet or something?' JohnJoe asked.

'No. I can do it, but I'm slow at reading music – it's easier this way. It may take a few goes.' She laid her hands on the strings and began to pluck. She hit a couple of wrong strings, but within a few moments, she had it.

She began to play, and as she did, JohnJoe opened his mouth and sang, his voice sweet and clear.

'I dreamt I dwelt in marble halls, with vassals and serfs at my side, and of all who assembled within those walls that I was the hope and the pride. I had riches all too great to count and a high ancestral name. But I also dreamt which pleased me most that you loved me still the same. That you loved me, you loved me still the same. That you loved me, you loved me still the same.

'I dreamt that suitors sought my hand, that knights upon bended knee, and with vows no maidens heart could withstand, they pledged their faith to me. And I dreamt that one of that noble host came forth my hand to claim. But I also dreamt which charmed me most that you loved me still the same. That you loved me, you loved me still the same. That you loved me, you loved me still the same.'

Harp accompanied him, plucking the strings as his voice soared in a clear tenor, and it wasn't until she opened her eyes that she realised their music had drawn her mother, Eleanor, Sean and Gwen. Of Molly and her father and fiancée there was no sign. They stood and listened as JohnJoe sang, word-perfect, and Harp played. When they finished, their audience burst into enthusiastic applause. JohnJoe blushed to the roots of his spiky hair and Harp giggled.

They were all ready in their travelling clothes; it was time to go. The guests who were booked in for that night would be picked up that afternoon from the train by Mr Quinn, and Harp and her mother would have to have the rooms serviced for them. The accounts were settled, and the song seemed to round off the experience.

'My mother loved that song,' Eleanor said. She choked on the words.

'So did mine.' JohnJoe smiled.

'The hospital telegrammed, JohnJoe,' Rose said. 'Danny is feeling much better and is awake and talking.'

JohnJoe's face lit up. 'Will he be able to come back soon?'

'Oh, I would think they'll need to keep him there to recuperate, but in the meantime would you like to stay here with Harp and me?' Rose crossed the room to where the boy stood beside Harp.

'I invited him, Mammy, and he said he would stay but only if he can work, so he's going to do some gardening and clear out the old stables for us,' Harp explained.

'Well, that sounds like a wonderful arrangement. Now, is everyone ready?' Rose turned to where Sean, Gwen and Eleanor stood.

They nodded.

'Thank you so much for such a nice last night, Mrs Delaney,' Sean began. 'And for letting Gwen stay too – that was very kind of you.'

'Rose, please. I think we've been through too much together to be so formal.' She smiled and shook his hand. 'I wish you both all the success in the world.'

'Rose,' he said. His handsome face looked so much more relaxed and less forlorn than it had the previous day.

Molly appeared and crossed the room to stand in front of JohnJoe. Seamus and Finbarr lurked behind, seemingly afraid to let her out of their sight. 'I heard you and Harp upstairs. What a talented pair you make. It was beautiful, thank you.' She smiled but it wasn't the radiant smile of yesterday; there was deep sadness in her eyes. 'I'm so sorry for what happened to Danny, I truly am. I'm so relieved to hear he will be all right. I wanted you to have this.' She reached into her pocket and pulled out a medal on a gold chain. 'It's a St Christopher medal, the patron saint of travellers, to keep you safe. I bought it the day I bought my ticket to go to America because I was so unsure of what the future held and where it would take me. But I now know where I'm going and what I'm doing, so I want you to have it.'

JohnJoe held the medal in his hand and looked at the words

inscribed around the edge. Harp leaned over his shoulder and read aloud. 'St Christopher. May you go in safety.' In intricate relief was a depiction of a man with a crook.

JohnJoe smiled at Harp, relieved she'd spared him embarrassment, and then turned to Molly. 'Are you sure? It looks gold.'

'It is gold. And yes, I am sure. I won't need it, but I would like to think it was keeping you safe, JohnJoe.'

'Thank you,' he whispered, and allowed her to fasten it around his neck. He tucked it inside his pullover.

Molly then turned to face the group. 'I'm so sorry to you all for the upset caused last night.' She looked exhausted, her eyes red-rimmed from crying. She was dressed in a floor-length navy dress and a three-quarter-length black coat, buttoned over her large frame. Her simple hat was unadorned, and only a slight wisp of her red hair was visible beneath it. 'It was the last thing any of you needed as you were trying to prepare for your adventures. I truly am. I wish you all well in the future. Mrs Delaney and Harp, how kind you've been to us all, and I hope everything works out wonderfully for you both. Sean and Gwen, the best of luck. I doubt you'll need it, though, as you are made for each other.'

Sean smiled, his arm around Gwen's shoulder as she leaned into him.

'And Eleanor, I hope you find lots of animals to love in San Francisco. The creatures of the West Coast will be delighted to have someone who can care for them as tenderly as you can.'

'Well, since everyone else is making speeches...' Eleanor smiled. 'Thank you, Rose and Harp, for your hospitality, and I apologise for any stray hairs you might find in the room I slept in – I had two visitors in the night. I don't know how they got in or found my room, but I woke up to find those two at my bedside.' She pointed to the two dogs that had been following her since the previous day, now waiting expectantly on the gravel outside. 'So everyone, I wish you all the best of luck.'

'Molly?' Gwen asked. 'Since you were so kind and gave me your ticket, would you come to wave us off? We'd love to see a friendly face on the quayside as we pull away.'

'I... Well, we should really get going.' Molly glanced at her father.

'The train is in an hour and a half, but we should go now to be sure,' he said gruffly.

Finbarr glanced at them both. 'Look, Mr O'Brien, why don't I take Molly down to wave her friends off. We might get an ice cream or something before the train home.' He smiled hopefully at Molly, who managed a weak smile in return.

Seamus O'Brien exhaled. 'Well, she'll soon be your wife and your problem, so if you want to do that, then do, but be sure you're both back in plenty of time for the train.'

'Come on, Mol, let's go down and see the sights of Queenstown.' Finbarr offered Molly his arm, which she took.

Harp had an idea. 'Could you all write? Once you are settled?'

Rose interrupted. 'I'm sure everyone will be far too busy...'

'I will,' Molly answered instantly.

'And so will we,' Sean added.

'I don't know what I'll have to say, but I'll certainly let you know how I'm getting on if you would like me to, Harp.' Eleanor smiled.

'Mr Devereaux, who owned this house, gave me a beautiful pen. I'd like to compile a book, the stories of the people who spent their last night here with us, where they went and what became of them. Also, if you ever needed to keep in touch with each other, we would have addresses for everyone, so if you wanted to hear how the others were getting on...' Harp coloured as she realised everyone was looking at her. Perhaps it was a silly idea. They were just guests at a hotel – why would they want to do that?

'That's a wonderful idea,' Molly exclaimed. 'For so many, this house will be where they will spend their last ever night on Irish soil. It is a clever idea to keep a record of it all. I think that's a book people might like to read years from now.'

'She's right, Harp.' Eleanor winked mischievously. 'Based on just last night alone, it could be a bestseller.'

Harp immediately responded. 'Of course I wouldn't say anything about...' She looked at Molly, who flushed.

Finbarr picked up Molly's leather travelling bag, and Molly hung her plain black leather handbag over her shoulder. 'We'll see you on the platform in an hour, Daddy,' she said quietly.

Seamus nodded and turned to leave. Sean, Gwen and Eleanor did the same, and with another flurry of goodbyes and promises to write, they were gone out the garden gate, onto the steps and away to the New World.

'Right, my dears.' Rose looked at Harp and JohnJoe. 'Let's get to work.'

CHAPTER 23

$\mathcal{T}$he bustle on the pavement outside the Cunard ticket office was noisy, with people pushing, babies crying and people embracing and saying goodbye. Sean and Gwen hugged Eleanor and Molly before walking down the gangway to the tender, their tickets clasped in their hands.

The overall mood was more jubilant than Eleanor would have imagined after the tragedy of *Titanic* only last month. Cunard were at pains to point out that there were enough lifeboats for everyone on the *Laconia*, something that was notably absent from the allegedly unsinkable *Titanic*. There was disgusted astonishment at the discovery that Bruce Ismay, the chairman of the White Star Line, had actually got into a lifeboat, leaving women and children to their watery fate. The press on both sides of the Atlantic were scathing in their reporting of how Ismay demanded the number of lifeboats aboard *Titanic* be reduced from forty-eight to just sixteen because he didn't like how the boats cluttered up the handsome deck.

There were calls for the white star in the company's flag to be changed to a yellow liver, and though there were a few people defending him, most saw Ismay for what he was, a cowardly selfish man of privilege saving his own skin at the expense of others.

Eleanor stood and watched Finbarr and Molly gazing up at the ship at anchor at the mouth of the harbour, not a word passing between them.

She knew she should get on board. Edward was right about one thing – she couldn't manage that farm alone. It was too big and the land was being neglected as it was. She had no problem with that – it was returning to nature, providing a habitat for so many species of wildlife and birds – but her neighbour didn't like it. The seeds from the weeds blew onto his land, foxes took his chickens, badgers brought disease – or so he thought. She'd tried to explain that badgers are wonderful creatures and that he should watch them going about their business at night, building their long setts and clearing the farm of rats and mice, but he was not keen on her laissez-faire attitude to land management. She sighed, thinking of Sherrard, her neighbour. He'd be delighted when he saw it up for sale. She had put off selling until she left, telling Ignatius O'Hare, the local auctioneer, to hold off. He was practically salivating at the prospect of ninety acres of goodish land, but she could not bring herself to say the words, 'Sell it.' Her father had worked that land and his father before that.

Foolish, she supposed. Now it was going to be more drawn out what with her being in America, and what did she want with the money anyway?

Poor Edward was most anxious for her to know that the money from the farm was hers and hers alone. He was a dentist and did very well by all accounts, and his desire for her to sell up was in no way related to his wanting to liquidate his half share of the land. She believed him. He was a good man at heart, her little brother, if a little high-handed and full of self-righteousness. But she knew that his motivation was simply her welfare, not greed. Besides, she couldn't live forever and he was her only heir, so he'd have it all eventually anyway.

All around her people pushed and shoved and called to each other. The foghorns blared. The men loading mail and other supplies had formed a human chain, tossing bags from one to the other until they landed unceremoniously on the floor of the tender.

The ship looked nice, a huge white liner silhouetted against the clear blue sky. It was the first liner to be fitted with anti-roll tanks, Danny had explained before Molly's father turned up last night. Apparently they were fitted to counteract the rolling of the sea and made the crossing less turbulent and passengers less prone to seasickness. Not that it would matter to her, she decided.

She waited until Finbarr and Molly were both looking up at the ship. He was pointing something out to her, and she was trying to look interested. Eleanor led the two dogs that had been her constant companions since yesterday to the railings of the embarkation area, tying them up with a bit of string from her pocket.

'Now you two just wait here. It's all going to be fine, I promise,' she whispered as the two dogs nuzzled her. Patch danced on his back legs, and she gave them each a sausage she had liberated from the breakfast table. Their trusting liquid-brown eyes reminded her so much of her lovely Bonnie, that unconditional love. Dogs didn't care if her house was tidy or if she wore nice clothes or brushed her hair. A dog just loved its person and wanted to be with them. They never got themselves tied up in emotional knots like humans did. That was all there was to it. Giving each of them a pat, she wound her way back to the quayside just as the purser opened up the gangway for the next tender.

The crowds surged forward, pressing her almost against Molly and Finbarr.

'Finbarr! Finbarr!' Eleanor cried. 'Please, you have to help!'

The brawny lad turned around. Molly was clearly alarmed to see the normally serene Eleanor so upset.

'Please, there's a group of boys up there by the bandstand. They're kicking that little dog that was following me, the one with the patch on his eye. Please, I dare not intervene – they look nasty – but I can't go knowing the poor little creature is being hurt. Can you go rescue him, please?'

'Of course we will,' Molly answered. 'You go and we'll take care of the dog. I promise, Eleanor.'

'Which way?' Finbarr asked, glad to be back in the ladies' good graces again.

'Over there. By the bandstand.' Eleanor pointed. There was a throng of several hundred people between them and the brightly painted bandstand in the middle of the park.

'Let's go,' Molly said, but before Eleanor could say anything, Finbarr stopped her.

'No. You wait here, Molly. I'll see to it. I don't want you around people like that. You just say goodbye to Eleanor here, and I'll be back. Don't worry, the little fellow will be waving up at you. You just get aboard. The best of luck to you, Miss Kind,' Finbarr said chivalrously.

'Thank you, Finbarr, thank you so much,' Eleanor said, fishing her ticket out of her bag. 'I just couldn't...'

'Of course, don't worry,' Finbarr called as he pushed his way through the throng, going in the opposite direction to all the passengers.

'Right.' Eleanor turned to Molly. 'Take this and get on that boat. Here's your bag, everything you need.' She held out her ticket.

'I can't do that...' Molly replied, shocked. 'I told my family that...'

'*Carpe diem*, Molly. Harp told me that and she was right – either you let them down or you let yourself down. You don't want to marry that lad, nice as he is, and your parents will get over it. But you never will if you make the wrong decision now. Take your chance, girl, live the life you want, not the one chosen for you by people who've had their own chances. Go...take it.'

'But...but what about you?' Molly asked.

'I'm going home. As JohnJoe says, you have to die somewhere, and 'tisn't like I'd have eternal life in America either. I want it to be at home, surrounded by my animals. I've thought about what you said, and I'm going to take your advice, move into town, start a little clinic. And Edward will just have to enjoy his oranges without me.' She chuckled. 'Now go, they're closing the gangway.'

The last stragglers were saying teary goodbyes, and the pursers were calling for the last remaining passengers to board the ship.

Molly gripped her bag with one hand, slung her handbag over her shoulder with the other, seized the ticket and nodded at Eleanor, unable to speak.

'Go…for God's sake, before he comes back.' Eleanor laughed.

Molly showed her ticket and climbed the gangway, the last passenger aboard *RMS Laconia*. The dockers pulled the gangway onto quayside, and the embarkation door of the tender was sealed for sailing.

Eleanor stood and watched as the ropes were cast and the boat bore the last of the passengers away from the quayside, out to the *Laconia* and a new life. She smiled to herself. Sure as she was that the sun set in the west over Benbulbin, she knew she would never go to America.

She turned and walked back to the railing, and there they were, as she knew they would be, waiting patiently for her. 'What shall we call you then?' she asked, untying the pieces of twine as the dogs licked her hands delightedly. 'Good idea, Poppy,' she answered, as if the dog had spoken. 'Patch and Poppy it is. I wonder what Bonnie will make of you two? She's an old lady now, like me, so mind you two young-sters treat her with respect, do you hear me?'

She set off in the direction of the station. Mr Quinn was there with his sign, just like yesterday, four new names written on it, collecting a new group of people, all destined to sleep at the Cliff House.

'Ah, Mr Quinn.' She walked up to him with a smile. 'Would you pass a message to Mrs Delaney and Harp for me please?'

'Certainly, Miss Kind, what is it?' he asked with a smile, taking in the two dogs gazing adoringly at her.

'Could you tell them that I went home?'

'Home to Sligo?' he asked, incredulous.

'Yes, home to Sligo. A pair of very wise young people showed me the error of my ways and told me I have to die somewhere. It might as well be where I want.' She grinned and hoisted her bag on her shoulder.

He grinned. 'The bright lights of Broadway not for you then?'

She shook her head. 'No indeed, and I had to come to the brink of Ireland to discover that.'

CHAPTER 24

*O*lly tried to get used to dry land, but it still felt like everything was moving. The voyage had been arduous. She was sick the entire time despite Danny's information about the new anti-roll bars or whatever they were supposed to be. Her cabin shared a bathroom with the cabin next door, and whoever was in there had locked the door permanently from their side – they must have wedged a heavy suitcase against it or something – resulting in her having to find a bucket to throw up into.

One girl in her cabin said she could no longer stand the stench of vomit, so she left to sleep in the dining area, forbidden apparently, but she had been free with her favours with the steward and was allowed to stay there. The fourth bunk was unoccupied, and the one opposite was taken by a girl from Dublin called Meg, who was joining her brother and sister in Pennsylvania. She assured Molly that she worked on a pig farm in Dublin so her sense of smell was long gone. She advised to remain lying down. Her sister had been very seasick also when she went over and had told Meg to lie down and stay that way until they docked. She kindly brought Molly water and dry bread, all she could stomach.

Molly thought of Sean and Gwen on the same ship, the only

people she knew, but they could do nothing for her, and besides, she couldn't make conversation. In her more lucid moments, she tried to compose a letter to her parents, and another to poor Finbarr, but she couldn't. Though she felt awful for slipping away as she had – lying and treachery were not in her nature – her heart sang at the thought of finally reaching the convent.

Arrival at the port had been long and exhausting. They were checked into the arrivals hall, and there were endless tests, medical assessments, questions and forms. She was weak and her head was pounding, but Meg advised her to buck up or they might put her in quarantine, or worse, turn her back. The name on her ticket was Miss E Kind, but thankfully no further paperwork was required, so she just answered to that name.

She drank a nip of brandy Meg had in her bag for medicinal purposes and ate a sweet bun and did feel marginally better. Thankfully she got through all the checks and found herself eventually in the terminal building. She had no American money but there was a change office, so she took the remaining money she had from the housekeeping jar at home and exchanged it for American dollars. It seemed a paltry sum, and she just hoped it was enough to get her to Somerville. She remembered Sister Brid saying it was not far from the city and that the sisters worked in the poorer areas of South Boston, where a lot of Irish immigrants had settled, so it couldn't be too far. She could walk if she didn't have enough money for the bus.

A uniformed man who could have been a ticket inspector was standing on the kerbside, and she decided to approach him. She'd dressed in a clean dress and tried to brush her teeth in the large communal washroom near the dining room on board the ship, but she suspected she smelled as awful as she felt.

'Excuse me, sir, could you tell me how to get to Somerville please?' she asked.

The answer was given so quickly and seemed to be made almost entirely of the 'ah' sound. She thought he said something like 'streetcar' and another word like 'haavaah', but she had no idea what that might be. His arm pointed to the right, so she walked in that direction.

As she rounded a corner, a narrow-gauge railway snaked on the ground beneath her feet. She saw several small railway carriages and saw 'Harvard' written on the front of one. Was that the word the man was saying?

'Excuse me?' she asked a foreign-looking woman standing beside the railway car, a child in each hand. She had brown skin and was dressed in the most colourful robes Molly had ever seen. Each arm was adorned in gold bangles, and in the middle of her forehead was a red dot. The little children in her arms had the biggest brown eyes Molly had ever seen.

'Yes?' she answered, her English accented.

'Is this the way to get to Somerville?'

'Somerville?' she repeated. Her brow furrowed. 'Yes, Harvard, near, yes.'

Hoping Somerville was near this Harvard place, whatever that might be, Molly stepped aboard. The driver, a dark-skinned man, then appeared and she thought she might get a chance to ask him, but he jumped into the seat and was moving before she had time to sit down. The streetcar left the port with a 'ding, ding, ding'. People walking on the track jumped out of the way to safety. It was like nowhere she'd ever been.

She settled her large frame into the small streetcar seat and gazed out the window. This was Boston. She could hardly believe it. She'd done it; she'd seized the day.

* * *

SEAN O'SULLIVAN STOOD tall and to attention as the inspection agent eyed him up and down. He had his eyelids pulled back by the dreaded buttonhook, the crude method of checking for trachoma Paddy warned about in his letters. Gwen was fifty feet away in the women's queue, which the Americans called 'a line'.

The inspection only lasted seconds, and he was waved on to the next station. His hair was checked for lice; his teeth and ears were also examined. The inspection officers didn't see him as a person; he was just another unit to be processed.

He allowed his bag to go into the pile of luggage to be checked, but in his inside pocket he kept his money.

He'd asked the purser on their first day at sea if the ship's captain would marry him and Gwen but was told that it was a service for first-class passengers only. They'd resigned themselves to having to wait until they got to America, but one evening he and Gwen were walking the deck and overheard one of the officers tell another that a horse had made itself lame by kicking out the box. The animal was valuable, having been bred in Ireland, and was being transported to Kentucky for racing.

Sean offered to help, explaining he knew a thing or two about horses, and was taken down to the stables in the bowels of the ship. There was a terrified stallion, eyes rolling. He'd kicked and reared up on anyone who tried to go near him. The rolling of the ship was distressing the poor animal. Sean urged the rest of the crew to stand back and risked entering the stable. The animal kicked and reared, but Sean remained calm and after two hours managed to soothe the animal enough that the vet could sedate him and treat his injury. Sean visited every few hours after that and was the only person the stallion would allow near the box.

On the last day of the voyage, having visited the stallion after breakfast, he and Gwen were taking the air on the third-class deck, discussing what they might do once they landed, when a purser came to find him.

'Mr O'Sullivan? The captain would like a word, sir,' he said respectfully.

Sean looked at Gwen nervously. Would Major Pearson have connections that could stop them in their tracks? He followed the man to the bridge, where the captain was enjoying a cup of tea, his navy uniform, with its gold braid and hat, looking resplendent. He was a slight man with a white beard and twinkling eyes.

'Ah, Mr O'Sullivan, I believe?' he boomed as Sean entered.

'Yes, sir,' Sean replied, trying to gauge what was going on.

'I owe you a debt, I believe. Mr Hodges, the veterinarian, tells me we would have surely lost that stallion had you not been able to use some kind of sorcery to calm the beast down in order that Hodges could look at the injuries the animal sustained.'

Sean heaved a sigh of relief. 'Well, he was never at sea before, sir. He was terrified,' Sean said. 'The horse I mean, not the vet,' he added, feeling foolish.

'Indeed.' The captain chuckled. 'Terrified and terrifying if the accounts of my officers are to be believed. But nonetheless you were able to save the day, so I just wanted to thank you. Now, I believe you are travelling with your fiancée? Would you both like to dine at my table tonight? As my guests? I'm quite sure the owner of the horse, who will be there, would be delighted to hear your theories on management of the animal in the future. He paid rather a lot of money for him, I believe, so will be anxious to get the best out of him.'

'I… Well, yes, we'd love to, but I'm afraid we don't have the right clothes, sir…' Sean said.

'Oh, don't worry about that, my dear chap. We'll sort you and your lady out in that regard easily enough. Do you two plan to marry in Boston?' the captain asked, checking some dials on the bridge and murmuring an instruction to his first officer.

'Well…' Sean paused. 'It was our hope to marry on the ship, but we were refused since we're not first-class passengers…'

'Oh! Well, my dear boy, if I can do the honours, I'd be more than happy to. Believe me, our equine friend was causing quite a headache and your intervention is worth at least that small favour. How about the pursers sort yourself and your fiancée out with something smart to wear and we'll perform the ceremony before dinner?'

Sean beamed. 'Thank you, sir. That would be smashing.'

'Jolly good.' He turned back to his bridge.

The next few hours were a whirl of activity. Sean was kitted out in evening attire and Gwen in a stunning scarlet dress. They even found a ladies' maid to do her hair and make-up. She looked divine.

The marriage was performed on the first-class deck as the sun set over the Atlantic. The glints of gold on the azure ocean created the most romantic backdrop, and once the first-class passengers heard of the magical horseman, many of them turned out to witness the wedding, clapping as Captain Ellingsworth proclaimed them man and wife. Sean kissed Gwen as the ship's band played, and he felt his heart might burst with joy.

There followed a lovely evening of fine food and music, and Sean and Gwen were surprised with the news that the Kentucky horse owner had paid for them to have a first-class cabin for their wedding night. They made love for hours and afterwards stayed awake all night talking about the amazing job offer for Sean at Dora Creek, a large racing yard on the outskirts of Lexington, Kentucky. Their future looked very bright indeed.

Most of their fellow passengers were heading to South Boston, where so many people from Ireland had gone before. There was work there, and in what seemed to be a predominately Irish enclave of the vast country, the men and women they travelled with were hoping to find a welcome, a job and a home.

He would write to Paddy once he was settled in Kentucky. Paddy and his brothers had a fine set-up in Rhode Island, and it would have been ideal had this better opportunity not arisen. Paddy had not married – he was a confirmed bachelor – and neither had two of his brothers. His third brother had married an American girl but she died in childbirth, so he sent the child home to Ireland to be raised by his sister and mother and he lived in a house with his brothers.

Sean remembered that the Nestor household was rough and ready in Carlow, and that was under the care of his Aunt Maggie, Paddy's mother, so he dreaded to think what sort of lodgings would have awaited him and Gwen in a place run by four Irish bachelors. He was glad to be spared that.

He was determined to work day and night if he could. The job came with living quarters and everything. And when they'd told Mr Masterson, the owner of the stallion, that Gwen was a champion hunter, he was very interested. He said he'd surely find something for her to do too. He had a racing school for up-and-coming young people who showed promise, training flat and jump jockeys, and

Gwen could perhaps teach there. They'd barely been able to contain their excitement that America had more opportunities for women. In the early hours of the morning, she fell asleep, her body curled around his.

He watched her face in repose and wondered if he was dreaming. This amazing woman was always on his side, always positive, and now she was his wife. He could hardly believe it. He loved sleeping with her soft curves curled into him, he loved the smell of her hair, the peal of her infectious laugh, the touch of her hand. She was beautiful, and with her by his side, he could do anything.

'Name?' the clerk behind the counter barked as he approached the final booth.

'Sean O'Sullivan,' he said loudly and clearly.

A series of stamps, and the bored-looking young man slid his papers under the glass at him. Five minutes later, ten booths down, Gwen came through. She grasped her stamped cards in her hand and ran to him. He scooped her up in his arms, swinging her around. They were in; they'd made it.

CHAPTER 25

*J*ohnJoe must have checked the clock in the kitchen fifty times as they ate their breakfast.

'He'll be on the one o'clock train, JohnJoe,' Harp said gently, spooning honey on her porridge.

Danny had been in hospital for three weeks and was by all accounts well on the road to recovery. A letter from America awaited him on the hallstand, and Harp and JohnJoe had examined it closely. The writing was scrawly but not uneducated, and the name and address were written correctly.

'We could steam it open?' Harp suggested one day after it had sat there for almost a week. 'We could use the kettle to melt the gum on the envelope and then reseal it?'

'But it's so wrong...' JohnJoe said.

But Harp knew he longed to know the contents. His entire future was contained therein. 'Yes, technically it is, but if it was me, I would open it. You're being shoved around like a pawn on a chessboard, JohnJoe, nobody telling you anything about what's going to happen to you, and that's not right, is it?' she asked. She knew her mother would be horrified at them opening a letter addressed to someone else, but in this case she believed the ends justified the means.

Since Danny's injury, JohnJoe and she had become very close friends. They had cleared the stables out in just a few days and had been astounded at the treasures they found. Boxes of books certainly, but lots of china, crystal, even some paintings that had been placed in timber boxes and survived the years reasonably well. Harp suggested her mother have them valued, and a man came from the auction house in Cork and estimated they were worth quite a bit. He explained that at various times in Irish history, houses such as theirs came under attack as symbols of British occupation of Ireland, so it was not uncommon for families such as the Devereauxes to hide treasures in obscure places.

'Did Mr Devereaux know about these things, do you think?' Harp asked her mother one evening as JohnJoe was whitewashing the stables. They were admiring a painting of a field the man told them was a Constable.

'I don't think so. He would surely have said it in the letter if he did.'

'So what will we do? Should we give them to Ralph?' Harp's brow was furrowed.

'Indeed we will not!' Rose exclaimed. 'This house and its contents were left to you, so we should keep them. Besides, the roof is leaking and the windows at the back badly need to be replaced, and there are so many other jobs need doing. I think we should sell them and use the money to repair the house.'

Harp smiled. ' I suppose. Besides, we haven't heard from Ralph since he got the letter from the solicitors informing him of the will, so we can safely assume he has no interest in us or the Cliff House, so –'

'He wrote.' Her mother's words were quiet.

'What? Who wrote?'

'Ralph Devereaux. He wrote to say he was coming.'

'When?' Harp tried to quell the panic.

'I don't know. He didn't say. Look, Harp, you know what Mr Smythe said – the will would be difficult to challenge, and with the affidavits confirming you as heir, it should all be fine…'

Harp heard the uncertainty in her mother's voice. She was terrified, as was Harp herself now.

They'd had no more conversation on the matter. Her mother just said they would meet him and see what he had to say and that speculation based on no information whatsoever was pointless. Harp knew she was right, but it was still hard not to worry.

'All right, let's do it.' JohnJoe had put the envelope in his pocket and gone to the kitchen. Rose was down in the town ordering provisions for delivery. They were full most nights, as their reputation grew and people came on holidays as well as those sailing, so food was being ordered daily now and business was booming. JohnJoe was a great help. The kitchen garden he'd planted would give great yield once it got established; he'd set every fruit and vegetable they might need. He also served at the table and carried guests' bags to their rooms. Harp and Rose wondered how they would ever manage without him.

Harp lifted the heavy kettle onto the range, and together they waited for it to boil. It seemed to take hours, though in reality it was just a few minutes. Carefully, Harp held the seal of the envelope over the steam, trying not to soak the paper. Several times she tried to pull the flap open, but at points the gum seemed stuck hard and they didn't dare risk tearing it. Eventually the gum melted, though the paper was by now rather soggy.

'We can dry it out in the sun. It will be fine,' Harp assured a worried-looking JohnJoe. 'This letter has come all the way from America – it is bound to be a bit battered.'

Together they carefully peeled back the flap and extracted the two folded pages. They went upstairs to the nook on the turn of the stairs, used at one stage for servants to hide from the Devereaux family if they happened to pass by. It wouldn't do for someone as high and mighty as a Devereaux to lay their eyes on a servant. Those lesser mortals were meant to be neither seen nor heard. Now it was where they stored cleaning things, saving dragging everything upstairs every day.

Harp handed it to JohnJoe, who shook his head. 'You read it – you're better at reading.'

'No, JohnJoe. You've been getting so much better, and in such a short space of time too. Read it yourself.'

He took it and read it aloud, slowly but correctly. 'Danny, what the hell you doing? I sent you over there to get the kid, and now you tell me some guy put you in the hospital. You never saw him coming? I thought you were faster than that, Dannyboy.

'OK, look, just get yourself and the kid back here pronto – I need you here. Stuff is going down and I'm having to take care of things myself. Our neighbours need management and I got Jimmy and Dodo on it, but you know how that works. Subtle they are not. On top of that, our friend uptown is getting too uppity to get his hands dirty, so he'll need a reminder too.

'So get on a ship as soon as you can. Bring the kid. I'm looking forward to meeting him. Kathy is getting a room ready for him – books, clothes, a bicycle, the whole nine yards. I told her he's fourteen, not a baby, but you know how she gets. Should have thought of this years ago, when my sister died.

'Good that you say he's smart and a nice kid, not a total knuckle-head like his old man. I guess you met him, huh? He's a piece of work. What Sheila was thinking there, I'll never know. Johnny O'Dwyer was behind the door when they gave out the brains.

'I'll wire some more dough to the account we usually use. Pat.'

Harp and JohnJoe gazed at each other.

'What do you think that's all about?' JohnJoe said breathily.

'I've no idea,' Harp answered truthfully. 'But it sounds like they're looking forward to meeting you. Kathy must be your aunt and she's getting things ready for you, so that sounds nice, doesn't it?'

JohnJoe nodded uncertainly. 'It does, but...what does the rest of it mean?'

'Look, it's addressed to Danny and he said he worked for your uncle, so I suppose it's to do with the business or something?'

'I suppose so,' JohnJoe said. 'Books and clothes sound nice, and do you think they really got me a bicycle?' His eyes shone with the prospect.

'It sounds like it.' Harp grinned. She knew the day was coming when they would leave and she hated the thought of losing her only friend, but this new life he had ahead of him did sound wonderful. And Danny was very nice, so the uncle probably was too.

'You will write now, won't you?' she asked, feeling suddenly very lonely. 'Though you can send me drawings too, of course.' She had a whole scrapbook of drawings of birds he'd seen in the garden. She'd labelled them, and they were remarkably good. It had been her mammy's birthday last week, and JohnJoe had given Rose a lovely drawing of Harp as a gift, framed and everything. Rose loved it.

'Of course. Every day if they let me.' JohnJoe smiled. 'Though my writing and reading won't ever be as good as yours. You can do it like an adult. But now I can go over there with my head up and not feel so stupid. You should be a teacher, Harp. You managed to get me reading and writing in just a few weeks when the brothers couldn't do it over years and years.'

'You're clever, JohnJoe. They were teaching you badly. I liked it. I never had a friend before,' Harp admitted sadly. 'I'm happy for you, but I'll miss you too.'

JohnJoe took her hand. 'I never had a friend either, Harp, and I'll miss you too. Maybe when we're grown up we can visit each other? I could come back here or you could come to America?'

'I'd love that.' She smiled.

CHAPTER 26

*R*ose and Harp stood on the quayside, waving. They didn't normally come down to wave anyone off as they were too busy preparing for the next guests, but Danny was recovered enough to travel and it was time for him and JohnJoe to go.

The man and boy hung over the railings of the liner, which was small enough to be berthed by the quayside, dressed in their finest, and Danny looked none the worse for his ordeal, smiling and laughing as Harp tried hard not to cry. It was still summer holidays, but in a few weeks she would return to school. Her mother had taken on a local woman to help in the kitchen and with the laundry. In one sense she was looking forward to formal lessons again, but in another she dreaded it, especially seeing Emmet Kelly every day. Even Brian Quinn was now finished with school and going off to study at the university in Cork, so she would have nobody at all.

Her home life had changed so much in the last few months, what with losing Mr Devereaux and then setting up the guest house, but school would remain unchanged. The thought of sitting in there day after day, listening to Kelly and the rest of them haltingly reading and making a mockery of the teacher, was a horrid prospect, but she told herself it was a means to an end. She loved the guest house, but it wasn't her future.

The guests were from all walks of life, and sometimes they got to know some of them a little bit. They came by train from all over Ireland and spent their last night at the Cliff House, and then it was time to go – to New York, Boston, some to Quebec or Montreal, and even a few to Sydney, Australia. Their sense of adventure was infectious; if they could go, so too could she. She wanted more than a lifetime of cooking and laundry. She wanted to get away, to see the world.

Before they left, JohnJoe and Danny had gone into the town and they'd brought her and her mother back beautiful gifts.

'From Uncle Pat.' Danny smiled and handed Rose the beautifully wrapped package. 'He wants you to know how grateful he is, you takin' care of JJ like you did. I hope you like it. And he said to tell you, if you ever need anything, you just call on him, that he owes you one.'

It was a silk scarf that had been made in Italy, a beautiful thing in shades of peach and pink that glided through her hands. It must have cost a fortune.

'Oh, Danny, there was no need. JohnJoe was such a help. I don't know what we'll do without him.' Rose ruffled the boy's hair and he blushed pink.

Then JohnJoe handed Harp her present shyly. She opened the brown paper wrapping and was delighted. It was an exquisite leather-bound notebook, with her initials engraved on the front. Inside he'd written an inscription in his childish hand.

August 1912

To Harp,

My first and dearest friend. I got you this because you said you wanted to write the stories of the interesting people who came to stay at your lovely house. The engraving matches your pen. Thank you for all you did for me. I will never forget you.

Love,

JohnJoe

'I'll treasure it,' Harp said, and hugged him.

The foghorn sounded and the ship began to pull away from the quayside. The passengers could hear the brass band playing a merry tune in the park to send them on their way. Rose and Harp waved until they could no longer see Danny and JohnJoe, then they turned for home.

The cheque for the auction of the paintings had been lodged that morning, and for the first time in their lives, they were in a solid financial position. Mr Quinn was helping them find a reliable building firm to take on the renovations, but not until the end of the season.

'The house will seem so empty without him, won't it, Mammy?' Harp asked as they turned up the stone staircase between the green-grocer's and the shoemaker's.

'It seems strange to say that, considering how many people sleep under our roof every night, but yes, it will. I hope life is kind to him.'

'So do I,' Harp said, taking her mother's hand. She was a bit big for hand-holding these days, but today she felt young and sad and lonely and needed the comfort of her mother's touch.

They climbed up the steps, stopping halfway for a breather and to admire the ship now under full steam ahead out of the harbour, the ship that would carry JohnJoe O'Dwyer off to his new life, whatever that might be.

As they came to their gate, they paused.

'Will we go up?' Harp asked. They had not been to the grave together since the day she ran away from school, but she knew her mother went there alone, often very early in the morning.

Rose nodded and kept on climbing. She shoved the gate of the churchyard hard, and it opened.

The Protestant graveyard was a riot of blood-red and royal-purple fuchsia and flame-orange montbretia. Some gravestones, listing names of dead gentry, leaned to one side, some had fallen over completely with time, and others were perfectly upright.

'So do you think he can see us, Mammy?' Harp asked as they wound their way around the small narrow path between the graves.

'I don't know, Harp, truly I don't. Henry didn't believe any of it,

239

you know that, but he wasn't right about everything.' Rose smiled and ran her hand lovingly across the words newly engraved on the black stone: Henry Devereaux, 1860–1912.

'He was right about most things, though,' Harp replied.

'True.'

'I sense him. When I play his favourite music, or when I open a book to find a note he's made in the text. But he would say it's just memory.'

'Maybe, but maybe not.' Rose smiled again. 'Nobody ever came back, so how can anyone be sure? It's a lovely grave, though, isn't it, with the angel protecting them and everything. Someone back along in the Devereaux family must have been fanciful to put up something so nice.' She touched the foot of the life-size angel that stood guard over the dead generations of Devereaux.

'It's the nicest one in the whole churchyard,' Harp said. 'I like the ones that have inscriptions, though, not just names.'

'I do too,' Rose agreed. 'I remember a grave beside our parish church at home where I grew up. My mother used to take us past it when we went for a walk, and she always remarked how she wished she could afford it on her grave. "May God grant you always a sunbeam to warm you, a moonbeam to charm you, a sheltering angel so nothing can harm you, laughter to cheer you, faithful friends near you, and whenever you pray, for heaven to hear you."'

'That's lovely, Mammy. She must have been nice if she wished that on people.' There was a note of hope in Harp's voice. She knew her mother felt that she could never go back to where she came from, but Harp knew only one relative in the whole world, her mother, and she would like at least the chance to meet her grandparents. She could never raise it, not wishing to hurt her mother, but she wondered often what they were like.

'She had her moments,' Rose said cryptically.

'You never talk about them, your parents,' Harp said as she sat on the edge of the grave and pulled at a few stray weeds. Sometimes Harp wondered if she really was only twelve years old; she often felt like an old person. People had told her in her life that she was an old soul, and she felt it. She knew she was. It was what allowed her to relate to her mother as another person, not just as a parent.

Rose sighed. 'I suppose I don't. They were nice, good, decent people, but they were appalled at the idea of me having a child out of wedlock, let alone with a member of the Protestant gentry. They were like everyone, very religious, very poor, and on top of that, my father was political, my brothers too. They believed in a free Ireland and hated the English and everything they stood for. So when I went back, expecting the child of what he saw as the enemy, they threw me out.'

'And what did you do?' Harp asked.

'The only thing I could do. I came back to the Cliff House, and Mrs Devereaux let me stay, knowing you were Ralph's child. But I had to promise not to ever tell anyone in return for our bed and board.'

'And did your parents ever make contact again?' Harp heard the note of hope in her voice.

Rose shook her head sadly.

'So they don't know whatever became of you?' Harp was shocked at their cruelty. 'Surely they would want to know you were all right, even if they couldn't support you?'

Rose shook her head. 'I doubt it. They were not demonstrative people. They worked hard, believed in God and the absolute power of the Church and the rules and thought of little beyond that.'

'But your mother – I mean, you were her daughter. Imagine if I came back like you, would you throw me out?' Harp asked.

Rose looked shocked at the prospect. 'That would never happen because you know that no matter what happens, you can come to me. I would never turn my back on you.' Rose's eyes burned with intensity, and Harp knew her mother was telling the truth.

'Do you think my grandparents ever wonder about me?' Harp heard the words come out of her mouth before she'd decided to voice them.

Rose gave her a look that was hard to read.

'Say it,' Harp said.

'They...' Rose exhaled, trying to find the right words. 'Don't romanticise them in your head, Harp, just because you've never met them, imagining some lovely family reunion, because it just wouldn't be like that. They would never accept you, being Ralph's child, and us never married, and I won't ever put you in a position where they could reject you. So I know you feel like an adult, and in so many ways you've had to become one, but trust me on this – it would not end well.'

'So it's just you and me then,' Harp said, leaning back against the plinth that held the angel, shielding her eyes from the sun.

'Yes, just you and me.'

'Are you very worried about Ralph?'

'No. Well, yes and no. I trust Mr Smythe despite his foppish demeanour.' They'd often joked about how Algernon Smythe was better dressed than any woman in Queenstown. 'But I'd be lying if I said I didn't have some sleepless nights. If we have to take him on legally, a single woman and a child against someone of his class with powerful connections, I wouldn't like to bet on our chances.'

Harp sat on the kerb, rested her head on the headstone and allowed the sun to warm her face. Her blue serge dress would probably be creased and even soiled from sitting there, but she didn't care. Her mother sat on the other side, doing the same.

'I think it will be all right,' Harp declared. 'We'll keep the money from the paintings we found, and if we need to spend that money engaging Mr Smythe to fight for us to keep the house, then we can. The roof can wait. We've lived with the leaks this long. Another while won't kill us.'

Rose laughed affectionately, a sound Harp would never grow tired of. 'It was a lucky day the day you came to me, Harp Delaney. Henry was absolutely right – you are one of a kind.'

'I suppose I am.' Harp smiled.

'And no matter what the future holds for us, Harp, I don't want you to worry. We can weather it together.' Rose reached over and took her daughter's hand.

Harp squeezed her mother's hand in return and smiled without opening her eyes. '"It is not in the stars to hold our destiny but in ourselves",' she quoted.

Rose smiled. 'Sherlock Holmes?'

'No, William Shakespeare.' Harp chuckled.

They sat in silence for a minute, enjoying the silent companion-ship and the warm sun, but they both opened their eyes as a shadow crossed their faces. Rose swallowed.

He was older certainly, and bit heavier around the middle. His dark hair was grey now at the temples, and his skin was burnished with a dark tan from years of the Indian sun no doubt. But it was him for sure. He was dressed in an expensive-looking cream silk suit more suited to the tropics than Ireland, and on his waistcoat a gold pocket watch glinted. Harp could smell his floral cologne. He was still good-looking, but there was something intimidating about him.

'Well, isn't this the touching scene. The family grieving at the graveside,' Ralph said pleasantly. 'Rose, you're looking well, and this must be the famous Harp.'

Rose scrambled to her feet, dusting down her skirt, clearly wrong-footed. 'Ralph, I...I wasn't expecting you,' she managed.

Harp noticed her normally confident mother pale beneath his cool gaze. 'Yes, I'm Harp,' she said.

'Hmm.' He turned his eyes from her mother to her and eyed her up and down. Then he turned his attention back to her mother. 'Well, Rose, I must say, you've lost none of your allure in the intervening years. No wonder my poor hapless brother was smitten. I can certainly see why.' Ralph's voice dripped like honey.

Rose moved beside Harp, placing her hand on her shoulder.

Ralph stood foursquare before them, his hands in his pockets, seemingly perfectly relaxed. 'Well, Harp, you do look like him.' He paused and examined her more closely. 'You're not what I expected, though. I'd rather hoped you'd take after your mother, but then I daresay, so do you. And you now own the Devereaux family home, do you?'

Harp drew herself up and replied, her voice showing no indication of the inner turmoil she felt. 'I do look like him, and he was not poor or hapless. He was a wonderful, intelligent man, and I'm very proud to call him my father. And yes, the Cliff House is mine.'

Ralph smiled, but it never reached his cold grey eyes.

The End

I REALLY HOPE you enjoyed this book, I certainly loved writing it. I live quite close to the port of Cobh and so I was lucky enough to spend a lot of time there researching and getting a feel for the place. It really is a special place with a strong sense of history.

If you would like to read on and discover the next part of the story, Book 2, The West's Awake is available here: https://geni.us/ TheWestsAwake

If you would like to hear about my books or to download a free novel please go to www.jeangrainger.com and join my readers club. It's 100% free and always will be.

HERE'S a sneak preview of the next book!

Chapter 1

QUEENSTOWN, County Cork. July 1916

'IS THAT ALL, MISS DEVEREAUX?' Cissy Devlin asked, wrapping the ham she'd just cut from the large joint in greaseproof paper. Almost everyone in Queenstown called Harp 'Miss Devereaux' now, ever since Henry had named her as his daughter in his will.

Harp smiled and checked her list. 'Em...a tin of mustard powder and some Epsom salts too please.' If she arrived back to Cliff House without all the items she'd been sent for, her mother would not be happy.

It was mid-July and they were full every night in the guest house, which meant she was constantly having to run out for one essential or another. The Devlins' shop was the best grocer in the town; it was immaculately clean, the produce arranged neatly and held mostly behind the counter. The more discerning housewives preferred it to the cheaper huckster shops, where rats and mice were hard to keep out and everything always smelled a bit off.

'And what about you, Mr Quinn?' Cissy smiled over Harp's shoulder. 'What can we delight you with today?'

Harp turned in pleased surprise to find Brian Quinn behind her. *He must be home from Dublin for the holidays*, she thought. The undertaker's son was universally liked and instantly recognisable, tall and thin with freckles peppered across his pale skin and a shock of red curls that he tried to tame with hair oil with limited success.

'Nothing, Miss Devlin, thanks. I'm a penniless student. I just popped in to say hello.'

Brian smiled warmly at Harp, and she suspected he had spotted her on her way into the shop and was there to see her as well.

Cissy arched an eyebrow at them both. 'I suppose the two of ye have gone too big and sophisticated altogether for a few pear drops?'

'Never.' Brian chuckled as she poured a few of the boiled sweets into two paper cones and handed them to him and Harp. 'I might look grown up, but you know my weakness, Miss Devlin.'

'I do well. Didn't I serve you enough of them over the years? Now tell me, how are the studies above in Dublin going? I'd say medicine is very hard all the same.'

Cissy was a great one for talk, whereas Liz, who was quietly stacking tins on the shelves behind her sister, was much more reserved. Neither woman had ever married, but they seemed very contented living together. They looked alike, both small and wiry with dark hair set in respectable waves. They wore housecoats, one pink, one blue, and only took them off for Mass. Liz had thick glasses and Cissy was the friendlier of the two, but when they weren't wearing the different coloured housecoats, people often confused one for the other.

'Medical college is fine and hard, I can tell you, Miss Devlin. I don't know if I'll make it at all some days,' Brian said ruefully. ''Tis Harp here should be doing the complicated books of anatomy and physiology – she's the brains of the town.'

Harp glanced at him with a shy smile. She'd always thought he'd make a good doctor; he had the sort of open face and gentle manner that people trusted.

'We'll be losing Miss Devereaux to the halls of the university soon enough, I'd say. You'll be the first girl from here I ever heard of to do it, fair play to you. I suppose 'tis to Cork you'll go, is it? What will you be studying?' Cissy asked as Harp popped a pear drop into her mouth.

At sixteen she probably shouldn't be accepting free sweets like a child, but the Devlin sisters had been so nice and kind to her all her life, from when she was a tiny little scrap of an oddball. 'Well, I have to matriculate next year, but I think it will be all right if I work hard enough. And then I'm still not sure – it will depend on lots of things, I suppose.' She reddened as she spoke but was still pleased at how confident she sounded. What a difference four short years had made to her. Having the whole town know her as the daughter of Mr Devereaux had changed her. She looked even more like him now as she grew older, her strawberry-blond hair the exact shade of his. She loved it when people remarked upon it.

Cissy nodded. 'Well, you've all the time in the world – sure you're only a child still. Are ye busy above? The place is teeming with people all the week.'

'We are busy,' agreed Harp. 'There are two ships going this week, one to Boston, the other to Canada.'

After Henry had left her the Cliff House in his will, she and her mother had converted it into a successful guest house. They catered mostly to the second-class passengers, as the first-class passengers stayed at the Queen's Hotel and the third class were consigned to Mrs O'Flaherty's boarding house in the part of Queenstown known as the Holy Ground, an area best avoided if possible.

The guest house had gained quite the reputation as a lovely place to stay, without the hefty price tag of the hotel, so the Cliff House was becoming increasingly popular with well-to-do Irish who could afford a holiday by the sea, or British officers and their wives and families enjoying some leave. It meant they were no longer dependent on sea passengers alone, which was just as well, because with the war raging in Europe, passenger travel wasn't what it was. The deliberate sinking of the *Lusitania* last May had really rattled people. The Germans had given an undertaking to allow civilian traffic across the ocean, but people were still nervous. The sinking of *Titanic* in 1912 had shaken Queenstown to its foundations, and though the *Lusitania* was sunk off Kinsale, on the other side of the harbour, the rescue mission was launched from Queenstown.

Harp remembered the pathetic sight of the notice board up in the hotel, people seeking information about family and friends who were aboard. She and her mother had watched in horror as the ship went down, nine miles off the Old Head of Kinsale. They had a view from the top window of the Cliff House. It sank in eleven minutes, with the loss of 1198 lives. The British said it wasn't carrying munitions, but it would be hard to imagine how it would have sunk so fast if it weren't.

'And another one next week,' added Cissy. 'Though just to England. There seems to be an awful exodus altogether on.'

'I suppose the carry on above in Dublin at Easter means there's plenty need to get out of sight of the authorities,' said Brian darkly. 'Idiots. You should see the state of the city in Dublin after them and their shenanigans. Hotheads and romantic fools is all they were, and what have we to show for it? A needless waste of lives and a city in ruins.'

'It wasn't a "needless waste of lives",' Harp protested indignantly. 'It was an armed insurrection demanding independence from our oppressors. And you shouldn't speak about the rebels so disrespectfully, when their leaders were slaughtered so coldly and callously.' She had liked Brian ever since he stuck up for her as a tiny terrified child in the schoolyard, but he was a person who saw the world very differently to her and she wondered if they would ever agree on anything.

Clearly, he considered the Easter Rising a reckless adventure, but Harp had felt a thrill of excitement and patriotism. She'd followed the progress of the rebels carefully and felt the pain of the Cork men and women who were not given the opportunity to participate due to a series of misinformed messages that said the Rising was off.

'Populist claptrap.' Brian dismissed her objections. 'If the rebels were so wonderful, how come they allowed women to fight? Big brave men they were for sure, sending girls no older than yourself out to die.'

'Why shouldn't women fight? I think they were marvellous. Why should we not have a voice? We are part of this country too, and we suffer at the hands of the British even more than the men sometimes. If you listened – and I mean actually listened – rather than scoffed at what Countess Markievicz had to say about women's suffrage and the links between the equality of the sexes and the ideas of sovereignty, you might learn something.'

The Devlin sisters shot each other a look, and Harp blushed once more. She knew she shouldn't argue in public, but honestly, Brian Quinn was infuriating sometimes.

The undertaker's son smiled at the sisters. 'I'm sorry, Misses Devlin, for our outbursts. Harp and I have a lot of debates. She's a young lady who knows her own mind, I'm afraid.' He nudged Harp affectionately, but she didn't respond. He was typical of so many men and boys, thinking women were there to have babies and keep houses.

'What are you afraid of, Brian?' Cissy asked, her blue eyes innocent.

'Oh, I'm not afraid of anything, Miss Devlin. I just don't want my young impressionable friend here falling under the spell of glory-hunting hotheads.'

Liz stopped putting tins on the shelves and turned to face him. 'Oh, I don't think Miss Devereaux is in any danger of being impressionable. She's clever enough to know her own mind.'

'Thank you, Misses Devlin.' Harp was pleasantly surprised, first at Cissy's question and then at Liz's intervention. Smiling, she placed the groceries in her basket and turned to leave.

'Good day to you both,' called Cissy as Brian followed Harp out and another customer entered. 'And, Harp, please make sure to come again soon.'

Chapter 2

'Ah, Harp, you were ages!' Rose Delaney exclaimed as Harp entered the Cliff House by the back door. 'I thought I'd have to send out a search party.'

'Sorry, Mammy. I met Brian. He insisted on carrying my shopping, and we argued all the way here about the Rising.' Harp placed the basket on the large table in the centre of the kitchen, then glanced up at her mother, who looked beautiful in a pale-green dress. Harp envied her mother's beauty. Her dark hair and eyes, her alabaster skin and her slim figure made people stop and admire her wherever she went. *Unlike me*, thought Harp. *I still have the scrawny figure of a child.*

Rose looked concerned. 'Matt and Brian are coming to supper tonight – is that all right?'

'Of course. Why wouldn't it be?'

'I just thought if you and Brian had fallen out...' Rose turned back to the pot on the range, and Harp wondered what had got into her mother; she was normally never flustered by little things.

'Oh, that. Don't worry about that. I like Brian, but it's just he's so infuriating when he's losing. He makes it personal, trying to make me feel like a silly little girl when he's such a worldly man according to himself. Just because he's studying medicine up in Dublin. Cicero was right – he said that when you have no basis for an argument, abuse the plaintiff.'

'Harp...' Her mother stopped stirring and gave Harp her full attention. 'I think Brian Quinn might have an eye for you, and maybe that's why he teases you. You really are a lovely looking girl, so no wonder he does, but it doesn't do to lead boys on, thinking there might be something going to happen if there isn't. Do you know what I mean?'

Harp was astonished. It was the first time her mother had made such a suggestion. If anything, she treated Harp like she was younger than her sixteen years, and so her raising the possibility of Harp having a boyfriend or anything like it was astounding. 'Brian Quinn has no more interest in me than the man in the moon, Mammy, I can assure you. He thinks I'm an annoying little twerp with ideas above my station, so you need have no worries about that.'

'I'm not so sure.' Rose clearly wasn't convinced. 'He rushes to see you the moment he's back from college, and Matt says he talks about you a lot. He says you're fascinating, which of course you are, but I just want you to be on your guard, you know?'

'He doesn't find me fascinating – that's just Matt being nice. I'd say it's more like giving out about me, no doubt.' Harp was sure her mother was worrying unnecessarily.

'All right, but just be careful. You are growing into a very pretty woman, Harp. Men will notice you, and you need to be careful, for lots of reasons, not just having them think something that isn't there, but...well...other things too. Even walking alone with him might set tongues wagging.'

'Don't worry, Mammy. I'm no Fanny Hill.' Harp chuckled.

'Harp! How do you even know about that book? It's banned, isn't it?'

Rose was extremely proper. She had been only seventeen when Henry's brother, Ralph, had seduced her with false promises; later, Henry had told the world in his will that Harp was his child and a Devereaux. As a result of being known as an unmarried mother, Rose was very anxious never to give anyone the impression she was a woman of loose morals. Since becoming lady of the house, she had started to wear brighter clothes, but she kept her slim figure covered up completely.

'Don't tell me Henry had a copy in the library.' Rose rolled her eyes and sighed. 'That man.'

'He did. He didn't believe in banning books. But he made me promise to wait until I was sixteen to read it, so I did.'

'Harp, that's not suitable reading for a girl of any age. It's...well, it's...' Rose flushed, struggling to explain what was so objectionable. Everyone knew the book *Fanny Hill: Memoirs of a Woman of Pleasure*, but nobody admitted to reading it.

'Mammy, this is all part of the problem, making women feel less important than men. Why shouldn't a woman appreciate her body? Why shouldn't she get pleasure from it? What's so wrong with that? Men's pleasure is all that seems to matter, with women just helpless objects to be used. Either the men are gentlemen and want to marry a nice chaste girl, or they are cads seeking wanton seduction. It's all so demeaning to us. We're expected to take their names, have their children, run their houses and bend to their wills. I'll tell you what I think – I won't ever do that. I mean it, Mammy. I'll never marry. Who on earth would sign up for that life of drudgery, at a man's beck and call?'

Rose laughed despite herself. 'Henry said you were unique, Harp, and he was right – you really are. And I suppose you've got a point. I'm hardly in a position to judge anyway, but maybe you'll fall in love, and what will you do then?' Rose placed the apple pie in the oven and washed her hands.

'I won't, simple as that.' Harp was certain. 'I know my own mind. Socrates said to know yourself, for once you know yourself, then you can begin to care for yourself. I'm paraphrasing, mind you.'

'Yes, well, Socrates had no opinion on peeling potatoes, I take it?' Rose replied, nodding at the pile of dirty potatoes in the sink.

'Not that I know of.' Harp grinned and began peeling.

Still fired up by the argument with Brian, her young mind was not on love but on the Rising. The treatment of the Irish by the British was never good, but it was getting worse. The police were taking on a much more military stance nowadays, swaggering about like they were cock of the walk and sending officers over from England all the time, who treated the local people with disdain. She glanced at her mother. 'You know Liam O'Halloran?'

'The Liam in your class at school?'

'Yes, that one. Well, Lieutenant Groves and about ten RIC men barged into his family's house one evening last week when the little ones were in bed and started shouting and demanding that Mrs O'Halloran tell them where Liam's father was. They suspect him of being involved with the Volunteers. They got very rough with Mrs O'Halloran, so Liam stepped in to defend his mother, and when he arrived to school, he had a big bruise on his chin and a split lip. Groves himself hit him, and Liam is not big, as you know.'

Rose stirred the gravy to go with the lamb, a shadow of concern on her face. 'Harp, it's best if we stay out of things. Since the Rising, everyone is jumpy, and it's best to keep a low profile. I know you feel strongly about it, and I don't blame you, but we are a single woman and a girl and we don't need to be drawing the likes of Groves on us, do you hear me? So please keep your opinions on that matter inside these four walls, do you promise me?'

Harp gave a derisory snort, and Rose shot her a warning glance. Her mother preferred her as a docile little girl, but Harp had been awakened by the plays performed in the newly founded Abbey Theatre and by the performances and writings of Maud Gonne and Yeats and Countess Markiewicz. She'd only been able to read the plays, of course, but one day she would go to Dublin and see them on stage for herself. She'd read all she could get her hands on, especially about the women of the freedom movement, and she rejected the claims made by many that the Irish women's movement was subservient to the male revolutionaries. She knew her heroines didn't see it that way, and neither did she.

She thought of how Henry Devereaux would have understood her growing interest in the equality of the sexes. He'd pointed her in the direction of Karl Marx, Millicent Fawcett and Emmeline Pankhurst. She felt a pang of loneliness; she missed him still, his gentle presence, his love for her. He had written her a letter to be given to her after his death, explaining how he cared for her and how proud he was of her. The truth was, he was not her biological father despite him claiming her as such in order to make her his heir. But she saw him as her father in every way that mattered.

'Has everyone checked in?' she asked her mother, changing the subject away from the thorny matter of politics.

'Yes. There's a couple in the blue room that seem a bit strange – I don't know why. They are older than the usual couple that emigrate, easily in their fifties, and I don't know, they seem kind of furtive or something.' Rose was chopping the carrots and parsnips. 'And there are the three brothers – they're joining Sean O'Sullivan on his ranch in Kentucky, would you believe? They are cousins of his mother's.'

'Sean O'Sullivan! Imagine! He left here with Gwen, having no idea what the future held. They wouldn't even have been going together if Molly O'Brien didn't give Gwen her ticket. And now look at him. In his last letter, he told me he owns his own ranch in America, breeding winning racehorses. Life is so strange, isn't it?' Harp put the peeled potatoes into the large saucepan to boil.

'I'm so glad things worked out for him,' Rose agreed. 'That's another one for your book, isn't it?'

Since the guest house opened, Harp had been keeping a record of all their guests and their adventures.

'And talking of letters,' Rose added, 'there are three for you on the hallstand, and one is from JohnJoe, judging by the clever little drawing on the envelope.'

'Oh, really?' Harp was delighted. 'I haven't heard from him for weeks and weeks. I hope he's all right.'

Rose shot her a curious glance. 'Why wouldn't he be all right?'

'Oh, no reason. I just like to hear from him, that's all.' Harp reddened; she was a terrible liar and her mother could see right through her.

'Hmm.' Rose's gaze locked with Harp's. 'Would I be correct in thinking that your feelings for JohnJoe might extend beyond a child-hood friendship?'

'No! Of course not! We're just friends –'

A deep, smooth voice interrupted her. 'Fall in love or not, my charming niece, one day soon you'll have to be married…'

In mutual shock, Harp and her mother turned towards the garden doorway. There stood Ralph Devereaux, Henry's younger brother, clearly back from India for the second time that year. Tall and muscular, he had suspiciously dark wavy hair for a man his age, and his skin was tanned from years under the Indian sun. He always dressed fashionably and smelled of a woody cologne; he was said to be attractive to women, and he could be charming at times. Yet whenever she looked at him, Harp was reminded of the words of Cicero: 'Ut imago *est animi voltus'* – the face is a picture of the mind. That was true in the case of most people, but not her uncle. She never knew what was going on behind those eyes. It felt like a malevolent force.

Of course, to be fair, there were things that Ralph Devereaux didn't know about Harp either, for instance that he wasn't her uncle – he was her biological father. And therefore that his brother, Henry, had not the right to leave the crumbling family home to Harp when he'd named her as his own daughter in his will.

Rose tried to put a good face on the sudden appearance of her one-time seducer. 'Ralph! When did you arrive?'

He lounged in the doorway, preening. 'Got here on the one o'clock train. Might stay for a month or even more this time. The house looks well. You've done a lot more work on it. I assume I can have my usual room?'

'Of course.'

Harp's mother always gave the best bedroom to Ralph. Harp knew that part of Rose felt guilty; Cliff House was, after all, his ancestral home. Six generations of Devereauxes had lived there, and to have his inheritance snatched from under his nose by the former maid and her daughter must have been hard to take. So whenever he arrived, she treated him as an honoured guest, with room service, meals and drink – and never once did he put his hand in his pocket to pay for any of it.

'Then I'll go on up. No need for dinner. I'll be going out later. That excellent fellow Groves is staying at the Queen's Hotel, and he wants to stand me a drink. You should join us, Rose.'

Rose kept her head down. 'I have other dinners to cook…'

'What a shame. You shouldn't work so hard. Yet even with all the skivvying, you're as beautiful as ever. And, Harp, you're looking very grown up. Very pretty as well, in your own little way.'

Harp emptied the potato peels into the bucket for the hens without answering. She hated the way Ralph's eyes rolled over her and her mother as he spoke, as if they were cows at the mart. And it disgusted her that her biological father would drink with Lieutenant Groves, or any British officer.

When he had left for his room, she blurted, 'Urgh. What's he doing back here so soon? He's only been gone a few months. And he says he might stay for more than a month! That's not acceptable. Honestly, who does he think he is? I can't bear him, Mammy, I really can't.'

'I know, Harp, but what choice have we?' Rose said gently. 'He's here, and I can hardly ask him to go. Look, we'll just endure it, try to stay out of his way, and hopefully it won't be for as long as he says.'

To READ on just click here:https://geni.us/TheWestsAwake

AFTERWORD

This is a story about a mother and a daughter.

A friend once told me that it struck her as strange how all the songs and films and novels were about the relationships between men and women. To her mind, and I'm inclined to agree with her, those are fairly straightforward and didn't warrant the level of introspection they are afforded in popular culture. Men love women, women love men, or desire them, or endure them or loathe them, whatever they feel it's usually fairly simple.

According to my friend, the most complicated relationships on earth are between mothers and daughters. Here, she and I diverge.

I do not have a complicated relationship with my mother. She loves me and I love her. She is my accountant, my advisor, my loudest cheerleader and biggest fan. Since embarking on this rollercoaster life as an author she has been my business manager, but long before that, since the day I was born in fact, she has been the rock, the strength, the shoulder that my siblings and I have needed. Always.

This is my twenty second novel. And I write about families, relationships, and complications. The inspiration for the mothers in my books, Isabella, Elizabeth, Anastasia, Carmel, Rose, Solange, Mrs

Kearns, Ariella, Mrs Tobin, all come from Hilda. They are all versions of my own mother. I can create these wonderful women because of the mother I have. I am very lucky.

Cork, Ireland February 2021.

ABOUT THE AUTHOR

Jean Grainger is a USA Today bestselling Irish author. She writes historical and contemporary Irish fiction and her work has very flatteringly been compared to the late great Maeve Binchy.

She lives in a stone cottage in Cork with her husband Diarmuid and the youngest two of her four children. The older two show up occasionally with laundry and to raid the fridge. There are a variety of animals there too, all led by two cute but clueless micro-dogs called Scrappy and Scoobi.

Last Port of Call is her twenty second novel.

ALSO BY JEAN GRAINGER

To get a free novel and to join my readers club (100% free and always will be)

Go to www.jeangrainger.com

The Tour Series

The Tour

Safe at the Edge of the World

The Story of Grenville King

The Homecoming of Bubbles O'Leary

Finding Billie Romano

Kayla's Trick

The Carmel Sheehan Story

Letters of Freedom

The Future's Not Ours To See

What Will Be

The Robinswood Story

What Once Was True

Return To Robinswood

Trials and Tribulations

The Star and the Shamrock Series

The Star and the Shamrock

The Emerald Horizon

The Hard Way Home

The World Starts Anew

The Queenstown Series

Last Port of Call

The West's Awake

The Harp and the Rose

Roaring Liberty

Standalone Books

So Much Owed

Shadow of a Century

Under Heaven's Shining Stars

Catriona's War

Sisters of the Southern Cross